A HABIT OF DYING

D.J. WISEMAN

Matador
5 Weir Road
Kibworth Beauchamp
Leicester LE8 0LQ, UK
Tel: (+44) 116 279 2299
Fax: (+44) 116 279 2277
Email: books@troubador.co.uk
Web: www.troubador.co.uk/matador

ISBN 978 1848765 436

British Library Cataloguing in Publication Data.
A catalogue record for this book is available from the British Library.

Typeset in 11pt Aldine by Troubador Publishing Ltd, Leicester, UK

Matador is an imprint of Troubador Publishing Ltd

Printed in Great Britain by the MPG Books Group, Bodmin and King's Lynn

with my best wishes

David Wiseman

July 2011

DJ Wiseman has lived and worked in Oxfordshire since 1973. Lifelong interests include travel, maps, reading and photography. For the last 20 years he has had a passionate interest in genealogy, discovering branches of his family scattered round the globe. Despite a lifetime of writing, A Habit Of Dying is his first published full length novel. www.djwiseman.co.uk

A HABIT OF DYING

Much of this story is true, the rest is probably true.

1

Lydia splashed a little milk that was probably past its best over her bowl of cereal and hurried back to her bedroom, acutely aware that she was running late. Not so late as to matter but later than she intended to be. It was only a twenty-minute drive to the auction rooms but she had planned to leave earlier to give herself another chance to inspect the lots that she was interested in. Now she was in a rush, grabbing mouthfuls of her breakfast as she slipped out of her dressing gown and pulled on her familiar jeans and baggy sweater. It was her usual, one-outfit-suits-all-occasions, way of dressing. She squeezed into her jeans and pretended that it was less of a squeeze than it really was, then slipped the sweater over the frayed shirt that would be good for just one more day. Briefly, she contemplated her reflection in the mirror as she passed a brush vigorously through her hair. For a few moments she considered the satisfactorily shapeless person who stared back at her. As with a dress which when first bought seems so right, so bright, so absolutely it, then one day quite suddenly is dated and a little faded, a little tired, so Lydia saw herself. She let the thought weigh a moment or two and then took a last spoonful from her bowl before grabbing her keys, her bag and setting off.

The Saturday morning traffic was light as she steered her little Nissan out of Osney and along the Botley Road on her way to Eynsham. It was the same route as she had taken the previous night when she had been to view the two lots for which she was planning to bid. The place had been busy with the usual eclectic selection of people poking through the equally varied boxes of china, well-thumbed books and bric-a-brac. It was the staple fare of the house clearance world, mainly worthless junk to anyone but the cheap collector or the car-boot sale enthusiast. But amongst it all there were a few good looking pieces of jewellery, a few real antiques of value and her own particular targets. The first was a box containing two service medals from the First World War. If she were successful in her bidding, Lydia planned to research them and then attempt to re-unite them with a relative of their recipient. It was something that she had done before, not with medals, but first with a family bible that she found at a market stall and months later with a photograph album she had picked up from the St. Frideswide's church jumble sale.

For many years Lydia had enjoyed researching her own family history but more recently she had grown weary of the subject, for it seemed there were so few pieces of the jigsaw left to put in place. Those that she had found lately concerned only the most distant of relatives, and the more distant the cousin, the less the discoveries enthused her. But the whole business of researching and assembling the results to form a picture, sometimes from the most obscure of places and with only the tiniest of clues, that element still gave her great satisfaction. The idea of finding a living relative of the family who had dutifully filled out their details in the Victorian family bible had come to her the instant she had seen it. And that Californian woman - where else, Lydia had thought rather uncharitably - had been more than happy to have the heavy volume air-freighted at considerable cost to her home in Sacramento. Lydia had asked no more than the cost of the bible itself and the freight cost, but Ms Tammy Mills had insisted on adding fifty dollars to the payment.

The second re-uniting had taken a good deal less effort. The photo-album had looked as if it dated to the late nineteenth century and Lydia was not surprised to see that she recognised parts of Oxford in a few of the photographs. She loved the musty smell of the paper and enjoyed staring at the images, immersing herself in the sepia world they portrayed. As her Oxford was right there on her doorstep, she once took the album out with her to compare a scene in Jericho with one of the pictures. Best of all was a photograph of an old couple standing in front of their house on Osney Island itself, just a few streets away from Lydia's own. Most likely a family who might still have a local presence she had thought, and so it had proved. Since the great boom in family history it has been said that today there is at least one researcher for every family on the 1851 census. It had taken Lydia no more than a few weeks of careful investigation and some judicious web postings to find a great-great grandchild to whom the album was very special indeed. Of course, the task would have been almost impossible without at least one of the photographs having a name attached to it.

Today it was her intention to buy another such album, part of a job lot in a battered cardboard box, but under some of the pictures were names and places, neatly written in what Lydia had taken to be a young female Edwardian hand. The two medals were a different matter, not least because she had no idea of what price they might command or what interest there might be. She could afford whatever they might fetch for they were not special in any way, simply examples of the medals given to hundreds of thousands of servicemen for their part in the so-called Great War. From all she had read and learned there was precious little that was great about it apart from the number of savage deaths. But Lydia was not inclined to spend much of her money on a whim or what she still considered to be the luxury of her little hobby. Month on month she saw a small increase in her accounts and it had become an easy habit to fall into. If she could get the medals without endangering that monthly gain then she would, but if they went beyond her limit then she would let them go. It was all too easy to be a little carried away at an auction, each bid being just a few pounds more. If you were going to spend a hundred then why not a hundred and five, and if that then why not a hundred and ten?

It took a few minutes to find a parking space on the little industrial estate behind Eynsham where the auctioneers had their rooms. It amused Lydia that despite being no more than a scruffy little industrial unit sandwiched between a roofing contractor and an electrician, the auctioneers still liked to call it their 'rooms'. There was a better crowd than usual, which did not bode well. The hot snacks van parked outside was doing a good trade in bacon rolls and the inevitable dripping burgers. The sickly waft of hot fat and onions made her grimace and wonder, as it always did, how it was that she could have been so attracted by it as a teenager. Distant days now.

Pushing through the knot of people at the entrance, Lydia made her way past the rows of cheap furniture, up the metal staircase to the upper floor where the sale would be held and where the crowded racks of smaller items were displayed. First, she checked that the little box with the medals was still in its glass display cabinet. A moment of anxiety as she couldn't see it, but even as she looked closer an attendant placed it back on its shelf. She became aware of another interested party, a man, in a threadbare black coat far too long and too thick for the clement weather. Unkempt grey hair, shiny and curling, hung over his collar. In another place he might have warranted no more than a glance, dismissed as a down and out, but the glint of heavy gold on podgy fingers said otherwise. Lydia thought she might have seen him at a previous sale and marked him down as a dealer, someone with more money than she had and with profit the only motive for purchase. But the medals were there, they had not been withdrawn at the last moment. She turned away, unwilling to show any further interest, and looked to the back of the room where the crowd was beginning to thicken. A few steps back and she could just see the cardboard box with the albums, tucked away under a table where she had carefully placed it the previous night. No point in making it too easy for a casual browser to find.

Positioning herself where she might have a good view of the room and still be able to see if anyone rummaged in the box, Lydia spent a few moments observing the potential opposition. She had noticed in coming to these sales a few times that the less experienced would stand close to the item in which they were most interested, while the regulars would take a seat on the random selection of chairs set out in rows facing the podium. A lot of dealers were in, she thought, and realised that she had barely looked at the rest of the catalogue, so intent had she been on her own two prizes. She fumbled in her copious bag for the crumpled sheets. Big blue crosses marked her two lots, numbers thirty and eighty-nine. The medals were the first of these. About an hour and a half might see a result one way or the other.

Lots one to twenty-eight came and went in fewer minutes then, on twenty-nine, a hiatus as the lot could not be found. Nervous laughter all round as the item, a gold wedding ring from the glass cabinet, was located on a lower shelf. An unremarkable piece that attracted little interest. And yet, like nearly every item in the sale, it had a history and a story to tell, had once been a treasured possession, only to now be reduced to anonymous insignificance. Lydia prepared herself to follow the bidding for the medals. The auctioneer invited a start at a hundred, Lydia's limit, but for the moment she was unperturbed. It was quite normal for no one to join on the opening offer. It started at fifty and leapt past a hundred in three bids. She watched in amazement as several bidders took the price to two-fifty. She could see one bidder sat close to her but the other was more camouflaged. The unseen buyer won the day at three hundred and twenty five. Lydia was astonished. She was sure that the medals were completely standard issue, unique only by the name engraved on them. She could not believe that such things would command so high a price without there being some other story behind them. In thinking that, she immediately resolved to research the person to whom they had been issued, regardless of the fact that their medals now belonged to someone else.

Judging there to be at least thirty minutes before she needed to be in her place, Lydia took herself back down the stairs and out of the building. She wanted a cup of tea and regretted leaving home so hurriedly, for she had planned to bring a flask. Instead she was reduced to buying a cup from the burger van. It did not meet her needs, too hot to sip at once and too unpleasant when it had cooled sufficiently. But she was in the fresh air and took the opportunity to people watch, a favourite pastime. She would imagine whole lives based on a moment's observations. The clothes, the age, the smile or lack of it, the hands, the walk - she fancied that they told her everything and there was never anyone to tell her differently. She checked her watch. Time to go back and see how the sale was going, see if there was any life in the room.

There was not. Lot seventy-one, a pair of binoculars, well used, went for five pounds, seventy-six, a box of assorted ephemera for two. Eighty-four was a selection of Second World War books and magazines that she had looked at carefully. They were interesting but not unusual and she had a copy of one of the books that her father had collected. Eighty-nine – A Quantity of Assorted Albums. This was her. Opening offer is twenty with no takers. Lydia keeps quiet and waits. Who'll start at ten then? No takers. Come on, a fiver. Lydia waves her catalogue. Five, we have five do I see ten? Thank you, ten. Do I see fifteen? Lydia's catalogue flutters again. Yes, fifteen. Twenty anywhere? Thank you, twenty. He looks at Lydia. Against you madam. Twenty-five? She nods. Twenty-five. Back to you sir, I'll take two. Twenty-seven? Somewhere behind Lydia a man shakes his head. And he is probably right, thinks the successful bidder, twenty pounds should have been the top. To her surprise Lydia's heart is thumping and, she mocks herself, all over twenty-five pounds plus commission for a box of old photo albums.

⋆

Placing the box on the table next to her desk, Lydia contemplated its dusty contents. It was tempting to immediately open them up and pore over them but she resisted. It was not her way. First, she preferred to savour the prospect, rehearsing the method and the rewards to be gained in the next few weeks, perhaps even months. Now the cost of her purchase seemed more than justified, a paltry sum for the hours of investigative pleasure that would ensue as she followed each hint and clue until she'd unearthed all that could be discovered of the people fixed in the sepia pictures. Four photograph albums, one postcard album with most of the postcards missing and a couple of old ledgers. Of these seven remnants of forgotten lives, she had looked at only one volume during her flying visit of the day before. That alone contained the whole basis of her purchase, a photograph of a group of people in a garden, crucially dated as 1911. Vitally, right there beneath the print were written the names of the group. This she had taken to be the key to unlocking the door of discovery.

For the rest of the afternoon Lydia held the prospect and possibilities of the photos in her head, the project enlivening her before she had even begun. Finally, when the domestic routines of her day were complete, she settled at her desk and began the first stage. Each of the volumes would be inspected in turn, no notes taken, no bookmarks placed at interesting points, just a slow turning of the pages, an absorption of their contents, their feel, their texture. Even then Lydia would not turn first to the album that contained her presumed key, but rather she would take each from the box in turn and let herself sink into their contents. She had called it her immersion therapy before discovering that the phrase meant the exact opposite to what she understood by it. Nonetheless, it remained as the way that she described it to herself.

The first album she took from the box was not an album at all but a ledger, completely devoid of any entries. An account book without accounts, every page still waiting for its first debit or credit to be entered in the proper boxes between the green feint denoting the columns. Its emptiness in some peculiar way saddened her. She guessed that it could have been printed at any time before around 1970. It was the spreadsheet of its day and its day had ruled for hundreds of years in one form or another. It had certainly ruled more elegantly, if rather less efficiently. Lydia put it aside, thinking that if nothing else she might one day find a use for it.

The next album that came to her hand was in a sorry state, its cheap paper-and-card covers splitting, the black pages barely held in place by the thin cord binding. But of the photographs it once contained, there was not one remaining. It had been used, it had been well used, its twenty or so pages had once held the faces of friends and family, often turned through and, in Lydia's imagination at least, turned through with love and affection. All that remained of this gallery were the carefully written captions beneath the spaces that once contained their subjects. A woman's hand, Lydia supposed, in white ink on the black card, reminding the viewer of the dates and the places. Ethel, Violet, Rose and Albert; Tooting, Clapham and Chelsea; first birthday, VE Day, Christmas 1938, August 52. The life of a family in snapshot captions. There was little to inspire beyond a certain sadness, a certain nostalgia for people and places unknown. The white writing on black pages brought to mind her own family and her mother's little collection of photo albums. A parent's own childhood, forever alien and obscure to the child, forever other-worldly, forever showing a different person than the mother or father that the child knows. Lydia allowed herself a few moments on each page, seeing the words rather than reading them, sensing the thoughts of the author rather than struggling to find perfect meaning where none would be found.

Still she deferred the album that she had quickly flicked through, the album with names and places and photographs to match, the album she supposed to be the key to the ultimate satisfaction that awaited her. Preferring to savour that prospect, she chose instead a slimmer one, one she thought might be a little more modern, a little nearer her own time. Her guess proved correct. This third selection was indeed closer to her own childhood, a family album of smiling faces, of holidays and ice creams, of round faced children in plimsolls and airtex tops. There were a handful of colour pictures scattered on the last few pages. but mainly they were of a muddy black and white that spoke of cheap processing and Box Brownie imaging under an inexpert hand. A few had captions that gave a name or a year. Lydia let herself drift into the scenes, taste the ice cream that cost three pence when a threepenny bit was a single twelve-sided coin. She looked at the man posing proudly beside the shiny car, all chrome bumpers and white-walled tyres and wondered if his wife took the same pride in it. Their first car? Certainly the finest car that they had ever owned, something to mark them out from their friends and neighbours. And where to go in their new found affluence? Why, to Hastings and to Margate to make sand-castles across the promenade from the Beach Hotel, sea-view rooms a little extra. Lydia spent maybe half an hour slowly absorbing the scenes and the family, touching their lives, sharing their moments, becoming familiar with Fred and Archie, with Susan and Paul and the enigmatic 'self'. At length she put them all aside, knowing that they would be revisited and examined as clinically as she was able.

Choosing the second of the two ledgers next, at first glance it also appeared unused, but in fact it was neither empty nor a ledger. Whatever its original purpose, the pages had once been separated by very thin sheets of something which to Lydia seemed akin to the grease-proof paper that her mother might have used for cooking. These sheets were all that remained, since the pages that they separated had all been removed. So it was a book not only void of writing but also of pages and she was about to discard it when a final flick through took her to the last few sheets. It was not void of writing at all. In fact it had a lot writing in different styles and inks, covering perhaps twenty of the translucent pages. It was not what she expected or thought might be valuable in her original purpose, but true to her curiosity she began to read the last and most legible entry.

It has taken forever to get these first words out of my head onto this page in this old copy book. I have struggled so long and now they are written but none of the words are about what I need to write about. They are written now like this because a woman who I see once a week, an old woman, a volunteer at our local centre, has listened to me breaking into pieces over the last few weeks and the idea of writing out my demons has come up again today.

Lydia stopped, suddenly shocked and embarrassed that she found herself reading these private words. This was not for her eyes, this was nothing to do with her. It immediately and vividly reminded her of finding letters from her grandfather to her grandmother amongst her mother's things. They had been written from Tokyo bay in the days after the end of the war in the Pacific. Eventually, she had screwed up the courage to read them and found them so personal, full of love and yearning to be home, full of disgust for the scenes of war still fresh in his mind. Even though it was several years after her mother's death and more since her grandparents', she still saw herself as a thief, a peeping Tom. Now these raw words gave her that same sensation. She closed the book and put it back in the box.

As if needing an antidote to the unexpected intrusion into her own sensitivities, Lydia seized the prize from her collection, lay it squarely on her desk in front of her, hesitated a second to catch the last frisson of anticipation, then opened the collection of Edwardian photographs that had first attracted her. Unseeing faces from long ago looked out at her from the pages, fixed in aspic, forever sepia. Men and women caught at an instant in lives that had long been led, with all the superiority of age, the unknowing freshness of youth. Lydia turned the first leaf and let her eye settle to the photograph that had brought her to this point. A group of fifteen, casually arranged in the time-honoured way, adults seated with younger folk standing behind them, children on the ground. A family, certainly, most likely with grandparents seated in the middle with their children around them, their grandchildren at their feet. Lydia let her gaze fall slowly on each in turn, looking into the eyes, reaching out for the warmth of the summer day, listening for the sounds of an Edwardian summer. And beneath the photo, arranged in three lines to correspond to the three rows of faces, were written the names *Mr Melville, Self, Alice, James, Henry* and below *Beatrice, Isabella, Papa, Mama, Albert, Joseph* and finally the youngest *Phoebe, Albert M, Albert, Harriet*. In the same hand beneath the names was written *Longlands 1911*. Priceless stuff, thought Lydia, already letting her mind take her to a moment at some point in the future when a great great grandchild of Papa and Mama would be joyfully united with these Alberts and Phoebes and Josephs.

For maybe half an hour or more Lydia leafed through the album, soaking up the people, studying faces, noting the change in dress, the uniforms towards the end of the album, the same names repeated, children maturing through adolescence. Just as important were the absences of some as time passed. But this was detail that would be noted and catalogued later, for now the only purpose was to get a feel for this family, slip under the skins of these people. For all her looking, for all her breathing in of the faces and lives, it came as a shock to realise suddenly that 'self' and Alice must surely be twins. At this stage of her process she did not trouble herself with detail, with noting each name. Lydia looked through again to see if there was a photograph of just the two of them together, but there was not. The 1911 tableau was the only one in the album where they appeared together, stood side by side behind Papa and Mama. At length Lydia put the album aside, content with her progress. She guessed that it covered perhaps the ten years to 1920.

Two volumes remained in her cardboard box. One she knew already to be a postcard album, but someone had been there before her and stripped out all but a few. Lydia looked at those that were left, carefully removing them from their mounts to check for the message they had contained. All were blank, collected presumably for the sake of the scenes they depicted. A church in Whitehaven, the High Street in Braintree Essex, Christ Church, Oxford, which Lydia recognised with surprise. Random images? Any possible connection remained elusive.

The last album was more productive. Another family album, most likely from the 1930's she supposed, with perhaps thirty or forty crisp snapshots, all carefully mounted in the pre-cut slots of the brown card pages. Some with names like Bertie and Henry and Verity. Bertie in an RAF uniform, Verity as a bridesmaid, Henry and Kathleen, smart on town hall steps. Distant lives, distant times. Lydia searched for a key that would move her closer to these people, but found none. Perhaps she was too tired, still thinking perhaps of Papa and Mama in 1911, seeing them as her best way in. She put Bertie and Verity aside, closed her eyes and considered the way forward. She knew what she would do but still rehearsed the process. The first question to consider was whether or not this little job lot of other people's lives were connected by anything other than the dog-eared cardboard box that they came to be in. The first pass through had shown nothing that stood out as a connection, and anyway, that would wait until Lydia had dragged every piece of information that she could from each of the photographs, noted it, tabulated it, researched it. Then, from these labours, she might possibly find the connection or find that indeed there was no connection.

*

The last time that Lydia had performed this oh-so-pleasurably private task had been six months earlier and then, as now, she found herself anxious to establish the essential first piece of the jigsaw from which she might reveal the whole picture. So she started where she always knew that she would start, with the 1911 photograph. She prepared her notepad, her laptop, and the little yellow post-it notes ready to page mark the album. On her computer she made a spreadsheet to tabulate names and comments, with columns set up ready to receive the hoped-for entries from census records, birth, marriage and death entries, war service records, address notes, even columns for as yet unknown sources. If any of her colleagues from work had ever guessed at her doing such things for pleasure they would surely have not believed it, for did she not spend the greater part of her working days entering endless information into spreadsheets? And she would do this for pleasure at home in her own time? But they would also have shrugged and put it down to Lydia being Lydia, a little off beat, a little secretive when surely she had no secrets to keep. She knew that they whispered a little about her, knew that when a casual question about the weekend was posed on a Monday, the question had been decided by committee and the answer would be reported back at the next opportunity. Like most of her sex, her work-mates had a need to chat, to check whether there was any competition around, gain some knowledge and thereby some possible advantage. Sometimes she fed them a titbit or two, sometimes they were true, sometimes they were nearly true.

First, each photograph was numbered and entered into her list. This was to be her 'A' album and when she had finished numbering she found that there were fifty-three photographs. Then each photograph was described, and the number and sex of the people it featured were carefully recorded. All this was simple mechanical work, but what followed was more satisfying. Where there was a background other than a studio backdrop, Lydia examined it for any information that might be normally overlooked. So when she did this with the Longlands image she saw that it was taken in a garden with a large house in the background which, by its style, she took it to be fairly modern for its day. Looking under a magnifying glass she also saw another figure at one of the windows, and although it was a tiny image, it appeared to be the figure of a maid with a cap and white apron. Having servants was nothing if not the norm for such a family in 1911, and most likely there would be more than one in the household, a cook at least, and perhaps a gardener.

She progressed through each photograph in this manner and then began the process of matching any information from the captions to the people shown. From there she was able to cross-reference an individual to each photograph in which they appeared. Where there was any doubt over someone being the same person as in another photograph, Lydia also noted this. It was a long and detailed process, but she had proved and enhanced it over the course of her previous investigations. She worked with an application any employer would have been proud of. And she did so in the knowledge that it was a process which could bring results.

Working on her project in this way, on and off in the evenings through the week, Lydia had gathered and recorded enough information by the following Sunday to assemble a summary of what she had found. She identified 'self' as featuring in eight photographs, based on there being seven identified as Alice and eight as 'self' or without caption. Lydia reasoned that the album maker would more likely have left herself unnamed than her sister. And then she wondered if being an identical twin might mean that 'self' was not sure whether a picture might be that of her sister or herself. Or did a twin always recognise themselves? The presumed grandchildren of 1911 came top of the list with Albert M ten, Albert eleven, and twelve each for Harriet and Phoebe. Lydia put a little note against Albert and Albert M because she could not be completely sure who was who in a couple of cases. Of Mr Melville there was but the one entry in the list, and he was joined in his solitary state by Fanny, Francis, and Edith Clopper.

According to the location of the photographer's business, this was an Essex family from the area somewhere around Colchester and Braintree. This, together with Longlands as a place name, led Lydia to believe that identifying them and finding a descendant was going to be fairly straightforward. It was this that made her pause in the project. Should she continue with her 'A' album and press on to achieve her purpose of finding that as yet unknown but surely grateful descendant, or should she take on the other albums and evaluate them also? Were they projects in themselves or was she dealing with a single enterprise after all?

As was her habit when any kind of problem needed consideration, she decided to put the detail aside and occupy herself with something completely different, allowing the issue to slip to the back of her mind from where an answer would present itself at some future point. The warmth of the day took her to her little courtyard garden and her pots and plants. It was not the best of places in which to grow anything, being west facing and overhung by too many of her neighbour's trees. Such light as it might receive was further diminished by the high fence of Miss Affleck who lived next door. But it suited Lydia, it was very low maintenance, and it was her favourite place to think, tidying up a container or two, dead-heading her roses or simply brushing up the leaves. When there were no jobs that took her fancy, she would bring out a comfortable chair and a book or magazine to enjoy the fresh air and solitude. To allow the Longlands problem to find its resolution, she chose to carefully pull out the sprouting weeds around her two pots of tulips. While she did this, Papa and Mama, Isabella and the Alberts, Harriet and the twins resolved themselves into a single project alongside Susan and Paul, with Ethel and Violet, Henry and Bertie. There was no science to this process, simply a matter of finding a course that she was comfortable with.

2

After the initial satisfaction of dragging every last piece of evidence from the collection of photographs, Lydia found her first forays into actual identification bore little fruit. She considered that her 'A' album still offered the best route in to finding the lost family. Most, if not all of its gallery of faces would have been, or should have been, present on the 1901 census, for which indexed transcripts were readily available from the comfort of her desk at home. Her quest was simply this: to find a family with a mother and father and possible children Alice, Isabella, Albert and another known for the moment only as 'self'. Since the grown-up Albert and Isabella were seated next to Papa and Mama she'd calculated they were likely to be the eldest children, and since she presumed that 'self' was also Papa's child then so too was Alice, her twin. Also possible children were Henry, James, and Joseph but Lydia realised that at least two of these were likely to be sons- or daughters-in-law to account for the supposed grandchildren seated on the ground, so for the time being she excluded them from her search.

Even as she began the process, it dawned on Lydia that the task might be beyond her. The starting point seemed naturally to be Essex, since most of the photographs had a connection to that county. A search for Longlands and Essex had brought up a couple of irrelevant bits and pieces and a link to a care home for the elderly. The photos on the web site were of a two storey block with a modern entrance, circa 1970. Reckoning that the name Isabella was the least common of those she had, Lydia tried a search of the

1901 census, guessing at an age of between ten and twenty. The resulting two hundred and seventy-six entries came as a disappointment. Extending the age range pushed it to nearer five hundred. And there was nothing whatsoever to say that Essex was the correct county for these well-heeled Edwardians in 1901, ten years before their summer gathering. Searches for Albert, Joseph and Alice were predictably even worse, returning many thousands.

Conscious she should not overlook any trifle, Lydia recalled Mr Melville, the only person at Longlands with a surname. But that very fact almost certainly meant that he was not a family member. Using the same age-range, the index returned an encouraging six results, of which the most likely, brothers Charles and Ernest, were residents of Prittlewell, but born in South Africa. Closer examination threw no further light on the Longlands family, but she noted down the details just in case they could be needed in the future, and it did reinforce the Essex connection.

After so short a time really looking, Lydia could not believe that she could have exhausted her lines of enquiry. She knew so much about these people, and yet knowing who they were was suddenly an impossible leap. What if she made an educated guess at, say, Papa's name as being the same as one of his sons, possibly Albert who seemed to be the oldest? An educated guess would be that father was also Albert. Trying this did indeed narrow the field. Only six hundred and thirty five such Alberts. Such a guess was no way to proceed, the amount of work involved in examining each of those households to see if there were any brothers and sisters with the right names would be enormous. And all on a guess at a father's name, at Essex being the right county and that Albert was living with his parents in 1901 and that the Albert in question was Papa and Mama's son. Lydia liked to work on both the possibility and probability and both were weighed so much against her that she dismissed the thought. And, such was her way, Lydia put the album aside, and put the Longlands family from her head. Given time and space the problem might find its own solution.

*

A week or so later and a rainy afternoon washed away the idea of a visit to the flower show at Blenheim. It was too wet to consider any alternative, and in any case, Lydia was more than happy to sit and read in her most comfortable chair. As she flicked through a magazine, she came across an article about wartime postcards, part of a contribution to a project to preserve memories of life in England during the 1939-45 conflict. From this she was surprised to discover that it was common practice, especially among service personnel serving away from their homes, to have postcard prints made up from personal photographs. Such cards must have nothing shown on them that would be of value to the enemy, or they would have been rejected by the authorities. The authorised cards would sometimes have 'Suitable for Transmission through the Post' stamped across them. The article was illustrated by just such a card, bearing the picture of a shy young WREN, Victoria Pleasance, posing for the camera in her freshly pressed uniform. She had apparently had several copies of the card made at the same time as having snapshots developed of herself and her friends at training school. Lydia paused after reading this and listened to the distant bell that was ringing in her head. Something somewhere was calling to her, something overlooked or misplaced.

Her gaze fell on the box of albums, heavy with unanswered questions, gathering dust where she had left it beside her desk. Wasn't there a postcard album with only a handful of cards, and none of them addressed? Was there something that she had overlooked? She put her hand to the postcard book immediately and opened it for only the second time. Empty page after empty page, then the cards of 'St James' Church, Whitehaven', 'The High Street, Braintree', and 'Christ Church Cathedral, Oxford'. The Cumbrian one had no connection to anything that she knew; Braintree High Street restated the link to Essex; Christ Church was familiar to her, but other than that was just another unattached item. There was nothing on them and when she had double-checked to be completely sure, there was definitely nothing else in the album. What was it then that had stirred in her mind? She ran back through the magazine article; postcards, wartime, forces photos, authorisation. This track took her to her 'B' album, the one with Henry in RAF uniform, casually leaning against a doorway. And the caption? She had it to hand in a moment: 'Henry at Flying School'. A little two by three snapshot. But right there next to it on the facing page, the same photo, uncaptioned but larger - in fact postcard size. She had not taken it out and looked at the reverse, believing it had no more to tell her than its captioned twin opposite. Lydia removed it from its simple slip-in mount and carefully turned it over. There it was! The stamp that approved it for transmission through the post. And posted it had been. To Mr and Mrs J D Myers at 27 Grenville Road, Braintree, Essex. Mr & Mrs J D Myers were probably the last people to have read the message it contained when they received it in 1942.

'My dear Father and Mother, All going well here, some good chaps in my section. We are all a little green but getting the rough edges knocked off! Love to V when you see her.

Your affectionate son, Henry'

Lydia turned a page and there she was, Verity. V was Verity. Now, at last Lydia had something to work on and she cursed herself for missing the detail that had been hidden there. Henry Myers, son of Mr and Mrs J D Myers, at RAF flying school in October 1942, possibly aged around twenty to twenty-five, so born in maybe 1917 to 1922. Quickly turning the page, Lydia found Henry again, standing by his plane at Waterbeach in 1943, a base which her research had shown to have been home to squadrons 99 and 514. Was it an association of ideas or did all those young men look younger in their uniforms than they really were? Maybe he was aged twenty to thirty. And, oh yes, there was that Essex link again, that Braintree link. Lydia stopped. But the Essex link, the Braintree link, that was surely all about the 'A' album, or the Longlands album, as she had come to think of it. So maybe she had been right in her working assumption that all the contents of the dusty box were linked.

Having at last found a way into her puzzle, Lydia was keen to start. She gathered her pads and pencils, readied her meticulous list of information and considered the right course to take. It would not take too long to look through the index of births for say 1912 to 1922 and list all the candidates for Henry, prioritising those with a Braintree or Essex registration. As a second line of enquiry, it seemed probable that Henry's father, Mr J D Myers, would be present on the 1901 census. A third way in would be to look for a marriage entry for him sometime in the ten years prior to the best option found for Henry's birth date. A death record was yet another route to information, and sadly, it was all the more likely in wartime. Somewhere in the recesses of her mind Lydia had an idea that the survival rate for bomber crews was lowest of all the forces, but the detail escaped her.

An hour or so later she had made a new list of all the Henry Myers registered 1912 to 1922. It did not fill her with enthusiasm. It contained thirty-two entries starting with Henry A in the September quarter of 1912, born to a mother whose maiden name was Wilson, registered in Newcastle. The last entry was Henry in the September quarter 1922, mother's maiden name Greenough, registered in Birkenhead. The ones in between were no less encouraging. The nearest to something worth pursuing were a couple of entries for Hackney and Bethnal Green, both bordering on Essex but not what she had hoped for. Almost grudgingly she made them her 'most likely', but without conviction. Again she studied Henry's face. Surely he could not be past thirty? But, to be thorough, she widened the search dates and scanned the index for 1910 and 1911. At the other end of the range she went for 1923 to 1925. This added another seven equally unlikely entries.

After studying the list for a few minutes and still finding nothing to make any one of the Henrys stand out, Lydia tried her second line of attack, which was to look for Mr J D Myers in the 1901 Essex census. Seventeen Myers with the initial J were shown, but nearly all were in West Ham, hardly the rural location she sought. Two other entries were possible. One in Grays and the other in Theydon Bois. The Grays resident was age fifty and had only his wife in the household. Her name was Isabel, which formed the most tentative of links to Lydia's Longlands album. To follow anything down that road on such a flimsy connection would be foolish indeed. Nonetheless, Lydia noted down all the details. In Theydon Bois there was also a son aged six. Yes, this family were certainly a possibility, but it did not feel right. Despite her methodical ways, her weighing of probabilities, Lydia had always found that it was important to her that such things should feel right. For her, establishing whether they were really right often came afterwards. All of which, she thought, made her third line of enquiry somewhat redundant. She could make a list of J Myers whose marriages were registered between, say, 1900 and 1924, but to what purpose? The result would be no more meaningful than her list of births from Newcastle to Birkenhead.

Perhaps Henry Myers had fallen in battle. That at least should be something she could establish. The research tools available to her were excellent and there was no better place to start than with the Commonwealth War Graves. Dozens of Myers with their graves and commemorations from Yokohama to Reichswald, but not a single Henry amongst them. If he did not fall in war then a search for Henry Myers in the national death index would provide nothing more than another even larger list to go with those of the births and marriages. Lydia examined the album again. If she had missed something so obvious as a name and address then perhaps she had missed something else. With diminishing hope at the turn of each page she checked every photograph again, checked that her recording was accurate, checked that not a ring finger or cap badge had been overlooked. It was all there. She was left gazing at the same postcard that had so energised her earlier. For all her work and excitement, progress amounted to knowing Henry's parents address in 1942 and his father's initials.

*

Lunch at her brother's house in Banbury was always an awkward and infrequent affair. He and his mawkish little wife Joan inhabited a different world to Lydia. It seemed to her that theirs was one of utter conformity. They had the regulation two children, Lydia's nieces Rachel and Samantha, they took regulation holidays in Norfolk or Cornwall, and drove a regulation Ford Focus. Brian was a regulation English teacher, while Joan maintained their regulation semi-detached house in an avenue of such houses. Brian and Joan never came to see her and Lydia felt sure that their rare invitations were offered purely out of a sense of pity and duty.

'Hello Brian, how are you?'

'Hello sister dear, nice to see you. It's been a long time.' Brian always addressed his sister in this way, always inserted an unnecessary element of formality. He had rarely used her name and when he did it was abbreviated it to Lyd, which continued to grate on her as it had done since childhood.

Lunch was a regulation Sunday lunch, roast lamb with standard accompaniments. Joan had prepared it ready to be served at precisely one o'clock; at precisely one o'clock they sat to eat it. It had been so since Lydia could remember.

'There's nothing quite like a good Sunday roast, don't you think Lyd?'

'It's lovely,' smiled Lydia, and unable to resist the temptation, added, 'It always is.'

'Do you do a little roast for yourself on Sundays, Lydia?' the little mouse-faced Joan enquired.

'No I don't usually bother, not for one.' Lydia did not like the implied criticism of her single status and threw it back openly.

'No, I can understand that,' said Joan with no attempt to disguise the pity in her voice.

It was always like this and Lydia supposed that they did not really enjoy her company any more than she enjoyed theirs. She and Brian had never been close, even when her world of married life had been more closely aligned with his. When he and mouse-face had children and Lydia did not, their differences were underlined. With Lydia's divorce had come a further distancing. The tentative closeness that had promised to grow between Lydia and her nieces was cut off, as if Brian and mouse-face feared that their regulation daughters might in some way be infected. It amused

Lydia to think that if they did but know it, divorce was quite the regulation thing now.

'Lyd, I meant to ask, do you still have all those papers you got from Uncle Bill?'

'Yes, somewhere, I haven't looked at them for ages. Why do you ask, it's not something you'd usually be interested in, is it?'

'I'm developing a project at school about wartime memories and diaries and that kind of thing. Thought there might be something you had along those lines. Wasn't there a journal or something that he wrote?'

'Yes there is, he did it for the last two years he was at sea. Would you like me to find it for you?'

'You do love your old books and papers, don't you?' Her moment of enthusiasm was seized on by mouse-face.

Lydia had inherited all the books and papers of their uncle, not by instruction but by default. She was the only member of the family likely to find any pleasure or see any value in them. Her aunt, Joyce, had assembled them in little bundles for her, all tied together with black ribbons.

'Lydia, I'm sure that your Uncle Bill would have wanted you to have his books and all his notes from his graveyard tours. If you would like to have them.'

Indeed she would like to have them, if for no other reason than that they would always remind her of those excellent times she had spent in his company. It was he who had sparked her interest in their family's history, long before the instant access that the internet now provided. He would spend much of his time on those 'graveyard tours' meticulously noting down in his perfect pencil handwriting all the details of possible value. When he worked on his discoveries in his study of an evening, he would carefully record them onto index cards and cross-reference and colour code his findings. He was as calm and considered as his gently sloping and always consistent writing suggested. Even now, although Lydia's dislike of cigarettes was intense, she was nostalgic for the scent of sweet pipe smoke in which he seemed permanently enveloped.

The greater part of the family history she had developed over the years was based on all the careful work her uncle had done so long before. How he would have marvelled at the magnificent array of tools that she had at her disposal, the ease with which such a world of records could be accessed. She knew too he would still have wanted to tour the countryside and towns of his forbears, finding the churches where they married, the houses where they lived, the roads and byways they would have travelled. He had imparted some sense of that to Lydia, and she had no doubt that on her own travels to Cornwall she would have trodden not only in the steps of her ancestors but also those of her dear Uncle Bill.

Perhaps it was with a sense of passing something down to future generations that Bill had written the journals of his sea service in the closing years of the war. Lydia had not known of their existence until after his death and had wondered if there had ever been others that he'd kept from earlier years. But all she had in the neatly tied bundles were the two books for 1944 and 1945. Much of it covered the daily routine of the kind that few people bother to record, such as a ship's log would contain, but laced into to it here and there were his own comments on the incidents he recorded. Most vividly she recalled his thoughts on the loss of a fellow seaman, not through enemy action but as a result of a simple accident. How it had made him wonder at the sheer chance of who lived and who died. She was glad that Brian had reminded her of this treasure, which had lain unseen for several years among all their uncle's other papers. She read it through again in the week following her brother's enquiry and hesitated at the thought of putting it into his hands. Instead she decided to send him a photocopy which she would carefully make using the office copier.

As she slid it into her bag in readiness, some association formed in her mind. Wasn't there another book like this, brown covered, with old-fashioned foolscap sized pages? In another instant she remembered the pair of ledgers in her cardboard box from the auction. The one with the diary, the one she had shut out of her mind for fear of intruding on private moments, surely that was the same shape, had the same feel to it. Another thought occurred. What if the diary and all the other albums really were of the same family, just as she had proposed? What if this diary was written by one of her anonymous faces? Might not some clue that would help solve her mystery lie within?

Conscious still of her previous mistake regarding Henry Myers, Lydia first examined the whole book, turning each blank page, being sure that there was nothing on them and even holding them up to the light to see if any impression of some mark or writing remained. A few shreds of white paper fluttered down as she did this, but that aside there was nothing apart from the writing on the last twenty or so pages. In her preferred way, she simply turned these over slowly, absorbing the handwriting, the colours of the ink, the odd entry in pencil, the change in appearance, until she came to the last page. She read once more what she took to be the opening lines, written in a slightly scrawling hand but legible enough. Again the sense of intrusion was upon her; again images of her grandfather and his private intimate thoughts came to her. It occurred to her that what she now had before her might not be true at all, but instead be a fiction, the workings and jottings for some unfinished novel. She read from the beginning again.

It has taken forever to get these first words out of my head onto this page in the old copy book. I have struggled so long and now they are written but none of the words are about what I need to write about. They are written now like this because a woman who I see once a week, an old woman, a volunteer at our local centre, has listened to me breaking into pieces over the last few weeks and the idea of writing out my demons has come up again today. I think she writes some stuff for a local paper and she has said that to start I should just write words, any words, any thoughts that come into my head. I have so many words swirling around they won't stay still long enough to be written. So this is an exercise, think of it as a piano player warming up before a performance she said. Are there scales for this, should I copy out lines from a book like a schoolboy in detention? Maybe a word list of love and hate and death and destruction, sights and sounds and a word I read the other day, sepulchral, which has a very good form in the mouth when I speak it. Conjunction feeble effortless timeless wisdom anxious westerly brand noxious gases bullet poison envelope powder dimension bread rabbit.

I will start again. I have to get some of this stuff out of my head and on to paper, maybe that way there will be some resolution, some means to an end whatever that may be. Writers tell of the cathartic effects of committing their thoughts to paper don't they? It is a start, the first words are out there, the rest will surely gush. But the real start, where was that? Was it way back in the mists of my other life, my other times, or, more prosaically, at the clichéd first sight from the window onto the wet footpath beyond the steps up to the house? Yes, it was that moment that sealed the future and all it has brought.

Her figure was trim but not exactly skinny. Short dark hair round a sharp face with a wide mouth. She struggled in the rain to unload her cardboard boxes from the little blue hatchback and lug them up the steps and into the house. Delivering for a friend perhaps, a new tenant? It did not matter, it would never matter, all that mattered was that that glance out the window, that fixed moment in time, had happened. The rest was decided, sealed, locked into the guidance system of life for eternity.

SDI entered my life at that moment and has been right there ever since. She should not have been, she should never have been, but she is. For how much longer I cannot now say because there is an end to this by some means.

Lydia did not know what to make of it. A novel? Notes for a novel? A diary, and if not, then what? Why the almost coded reference? Why not Shirley or Sheilagh? A shorthand perhaps, surely not a nickname. It was written by someone who was used to writing, to dealing with words and that person had a feeling, a passion even, for his subject. On balance, Lydia felt inclined to her notes-for-a-novel idea. She read on for a while until on the third or fourth page it became difficult to read and it seemed that someone else had taken over the writing. She put the book aside and gave what she had read a little more thought. It did not seem likely that it would contain anything of value, and yet she was attracted to it in a way that was hard to justify. Perhaps she would work through the rest of it. It had been written backwards, starting on the last page in the book, and that alone seemed a strange way to make notes for a novel, or to write anything else. In some places so much pressure had been applied that the writing was impressed into the page. Even on closer examination there were passages that she could hardly make out at all. The writing became more and more illegible as it progressed, so to read it all she would need to become very familiar with the writer, the context, and feel for the words as much as read them. All that would take time, a lot of time. There were more pages than she'd first realised, perhaps thirty or forty. She did not like the thought of having two projects at the same time and for all she knew she had three or four already, all of which stubbornly refused to give up their secrets. So she did what she knew she would do, put the book away in its box and let the questions slip to the back of her mind until a resolution appeared.

⋆

Even if the book should turn out to be a cuckoo in the nest of albums there was nothing to be lost by deciphering it. If in doing so some connection emerged then that would be a bonus. Besides which, the albums were hardly a full time occupation, Lydia had done nothing of substance on them for weeks. She set to work typing out the words from the journal. The going was easy enough for the first few pages, as she knew it would be, but the content of what she was transcribing began to disturb her. Like her grandfather's letters, it brought unsettling thoughts and images to her mind. Of particular worry were the last few lines of the journal, which, being written in the same clear writing of the first few pages, she'd read before starting her task.

But action will cause reaction and something will happen. The leaf will be cast to the forest floor where it will lie anonymously turning to mould. Though a million feet were to walk right by it, none would pause to remark its presence. Even I would not be able to detect it. The future at once looks crystal clear and impenetrable. The calmness of the centre has flowed out to envelop me and all around is light and clarity but the horizon remains black and infinite. This I think is the world without her even though she sleeps a sleep through this last night. Check mate in the game. Mr Punch.

She silently cursed herself for having read the end before she had read the whole. It had a lyrical quality to it, but it was also dark and sinister. And 'Mr Punch'? What was that about? Even as she worked on through the first dozen or so entries, she was aware of that final paragraph and resolved to strictly follow the sequence of the writer for the rest of the book. It was certainly more than notes for a novel, perhaps the novel itself. To make the whole thing readable, Lydia added a little punctuation where she felt it was essential, and gave numbers to each section as she detected a change in writing or the colour of the pen, otherwise she was faithful to her source. Where she came to words that defied her attempts at interpretation she left a space or put her best guess in brackets. At length she completed the first dozen or so entries, by far the easiest part of the job. It seemed to her that it would be something more suitable to read from the printed page than the computer screen, so she moved to her comfortable chair with a glass of wine from the previous evening's bottle. The words were familiar to her, as if she had written them, invented them herself, but nonetheless she began at the beginning, through the strange list of words, the finger exercises, the view from the window, the wide mouthed girl and the odd use of initials to refer to the writer's wife.

SDI entered my life at that moment and has been right there ever since. She should not have been, she should never have been, but she is. For how much longer I cannot now say because there is an end to this by some means. She has consumed me and devoured me, borne the child that we lost, transformed me and destroyed me. All this by carrying a cardboard box up some steps to her new flat. It doesn't seem likely or possible now, writing it down in this dead notebook. Surely it was not me who asked her out for a drink on our first accidental meeting on the stairs a couple of days later for it is something I had only ever done that once. Surely I did not ask her again the next day having been turned down the first time in favour of her favourite TV programme? Surely she did not grudgingly accept the offer? Did she not have a boyfriend or a real life that would take precedence? What her reasoning was for accepting the casual offer I have never known.

A drink led of course to another and another. And drinks led to meals out and then meals out led to meals in and meals in led to bed. The sheer intensity of that first joining of our bodies still tightens my muscles in a spasm of anguish. And all the subsequent couplings, however rare, however good, bad or indifferent the actual experience, they also force a stifled moan at their recollection. It is not that she was unwilling, just that she never seemed fully engaged, never one hundred percent there with me in the little single bed tucked into the corner of her bedroom beside the window. Always it seemed there was a part, sometimes a very tiny part, that was somewhere else, worrying about the marking she needed to do, or paying the rent or cleaning the bath. How I longed, still long, for her to commit completely, to lose herself in love and emotion and sensual arousal. Did she, does she, think that nice girls don't? I have never asked her, I never dared risk a word that could break the spell.

And then even when we married a few months later I never really knew if she was certain or really wanted to. Of course she said yes, eventually, when I asked her. And in the same breath said she still wanted to go away to a conference in the summer as it had been booked for ages and ages. Why did I not see the whole future there and then? Maybe I did not want to see it, maybe I believed in change, maybe I was in love, maybe I still am. And when we were to sleep together again the day after we agreed to marry, why did I not see the whole of my life stretching forward in every detail with every tiny agony like shards of metal in my eye? Why, when she said that she did not feel like it did I not say, 'no, but then you never do'? All questions and not a single answer.

And here we are today, a good day as days go, thinking like the rest of the world of signs of spring and life starting up again. Winter being pushed back into memory. We were happy today, a walk round the park in bright sunshine between the showers, once even holding hands briefly till she said it was too uncomfortable to walk like that. Out of synch, always out of synch. It is already better for writing this.

2nd entry

It is late and I cannot get off to sleep. S let me know today that she does not like me seeing her in the shower. This was not news to me. I have known this since the first time I barged in and ever since have always tried to avoid doing so. But today I needed something in the bathroom so went in, carefully averted my eyes. Even without looking I knew that she had turned round in case I should glimpse her nakedness. And now I cannot sleep for thinking about it, thinking about being denied, refused, excluded. And thinking about whether it is intentional, even malicious, or just unthinking, just how she is.

It is just how she was on our wedding day, just how she was when we took the vows and the registrar said that we were married and that we could kiss if we wished. Just how she was when she accepted my lips and returned them with a pursed peck to satisfy the tiny audience. How I wanted a full public statement of a kiss, a kiss that said 'I do' more than the simple words could ever say. And then again later when our friends wanted those happy wedding snaps the kisses were just hollow poses, as meaningless as the photos themselves are now, collected in curling bundles in boxes at the back of wardrobes. Frozen slivers of Kodacolor time telling nothing of past or future.

It was wrong to say that she has never completely given of herself. It feels as if she has never but it is not true. There was once, just once, long ago I think there was a moment, maybe longer, maybe an hour or so when another S, a different, wonderful, free as air S gave herself to me. Knowing that time, feeling that moment right now as if it had just happened only makes the rest all the more excruciating. It was me in the shower and she there with me, fixing her hair or cleaning her teeth. I asked her to pass me some soap or gel or something, half hoping that it might lead to something else but ever mindful that it wouldn't. Without speaking she came to me and started soaping me down and massaging my body. Surprise and pure pleasure rolled over me in waves. She was getting splashed and I saw that her underwear was getting wet. And she didn't seem to care. That was what was so exciting, so blissful – she didn't care. She should have been saying, no I'm half dressed, no, my hair will get messed up, no I have some shopping to do. But she didn't and it was wonderful that she didn't. S did not speak and we have neither of us spoken of it since. And it hasn't happened again.

Last time I wrote here it was better afterwards, so I'll try sleep again. I will creep in beside her warmth and be as close as I can without touching for fear of her recoiling from me. She does this even when she is asleep. At least, when I think she is asleep.

3rd entry

Today I have worked late in the office, just as I have most evenings recently. There is plenty to do, but I don't have to work in the evenings. It is not as if it is good work. I will probably have to go over the same ground again tomorrow. But it has kept me out of the way and out of her way. It has kept us apart and separate as she seems to want to be apart and separate. She is pre-occupied by school and writing reports and marking and planning her lessons. She also works in the evenings but doesn't need to go over the same ground tomorrow. Tonight she has gone to bed a few minutes after I got home.

Perhaps I should have an affair. Perhaps I want to. Perhaps I want to have an affair with P. She is young, nearly blond, attractive in every sense, thoroughly liberated and friendly towards me. She seems to have no regular boyfriend and she works conveniently in the next set of offices to mine. But I probably don't have the energy. We were with our good friends H and J at the weekend and the idea of having an affair came up. The general consensus was that it would be alright if your partner never found out and that it was not long lasting. In other words, it would be alright if nobody got hurt. Like taking drugs or speeding in a thirty limit. H declared that he didn't know where people found the time to have an affair. He has previously confided to me that he regularly sleeps with his PA and that on his occasional trips abroad he never missed the opportunity to sample the local dishes, as he puts it. I didn't remind him of this. I think J knows about H but chooses to pretend that she doesn't.

Perhaps she should have an affair, perhaps she wants me to, perhaps she was telling me that it would be ok so long as she didn't know about it, perhaps she wants me to leave her. Maybe I will. Perhaps she wants to leave me. But what do I know of what she really wants? I don't have a clue. But if she doesn't want me I wish she would say so, I wish she had said so on any one of the thousands of moments she has said nothing. The feeling of wanting to end this waiting, this hope, one way or another is getting stronger. I can feel it gnawing away towards some resolution.

4th entry

Sunday night, usually one of the worst nights, but now it is not. She is away for a whole week on a school trip. She left yesterday morning with scarcely a word, certainly not a kiss or any embrace or touch that in another life might be expected. So I have the house to myself, and this book does not need to be hidden away when I'm done. These two things have engendered in me a kind of elation. The immediate, in-your-face tension has gone with her out the door. Now I have begun to wonder if this is how it would be if we separated for good. Could we do it without speaking, without anger and recrimination and the opening up of all the past wounds and rejections? If I pack up now and was gone when she gets back then it could be that way. Inevitably I cannot do this even as revenge for all that I suffer because maybe just maybe she might still want me. Some tiny spark of hope remains and refuses to be extinguished. But even as I sit here knowing that I cannot leave now, I am closer to being able to leave than ever before. It is no longer inconceivable. The tiny spark blinks and is all but gone.

And another darker thought has skipped through my head. It came in slyly, masquerading as something quite different and while I wasn't paying attention. What if she did not come back on Friday night, what if she was not on a school trip but was gone with a week's grace before I noticed she was gone for good? And then again what if she was on the school trip but never came back because of some terrible accident? It seems that every year there is a fatal tragedy involving a school trip on a Belgian motorway or a group of children canoeing or a slip from some mountain path. I have sat here trying to imagine how I would really feel. Would I be distraught or ecstatically released from my cell? Horribly, I have concluded that I would be both, and once again trapped in the tension of diametrically opposed emotions. But even that might be better than I am now, feeling crushed under an infinite weight with life seeping slowly away.

When did we first cease any contact on meeting or parting, when did those always chaste pecks become mere approximations to kisses? And how long did it take for even those to fade away to muttered greetings half hidden for fear of underlining their insincerity. That lack of a parting kiss, that absent embrace, is another drop of acid rain slowly corroding my soul. I want to write love instead of soul but hesitated over the word. Is there love yet left? Confused by her absence, I have no equal and opposite force present to sustain my position. Maybe it is that which has allowed wandering thoughts of final separation to swim freely tonight.

5th entry

Long journeys yesterday and today and a long sleepless night ahead unless I can empty my head of some of the angst. A journey to a funeral is the worst of all long journeys. All the way to Cockermouth to stand in the grey

Cumbrian drizzle beside a grave. She was determined to go and didn't need me there beside her, after all I hardly knew the woman, her godmother, someone that S was deeply fond of. But I went, maybe I could at least have the role of sympathetic and understanding husband. So I'd booked us into a small hotel for the night, taken the time away from work and driven through the holiday traffic. A tiny room with cold beds, cold at the height of summer, at the back of the hotel where the sun never shines and the damp of winter lingers until autumn.

Eight people listened to the service and stood round the grave for the final words. How alone can a single woman of 80 odd be? How lonely a life can it be that brings but 8 people to your funeral? Perhaps it was all her own choice, perhaps she was entirely self sufficient. S was bearing up until the first handful of earth rattled onto the coffin lid. Then she wept a little and bit her lip. As the sad little group dispersed I couldn't help put my arm round her shoulders. Even in her sadness, even in that vulnerable moment of softness, she stiffened a little and her neck stretched almost imperceptibly away from me. And I made as if I hadn't noticed and waited a few moments before removing the useless arm. We drifted out of the church yard, she saying her goodbyes to people she did not know, me nodding with a dull smile in the background, thinking how much I wished I was not there, anywhere but there. Then an aimless wander round the streets where her B had lived, where S had walked and explored as a child when she stayed in the school holidays. I couldn't help but ask if it was here with her precious B, her aunt or cousin or some such, that she had learnt her own independence, her own self sufficiency. I did not think it in a kind way, I thought it in a resentful, locked out way. Drip drip more acid.

And now we are back through the remorseless traffic, exhausted and with only 24 hours before we leave for France. And she is asleep and I am awake and my mind races over the horrible possibilities of the next week or so. We are thrown together with no excuse for escape, nothing to lessen the tension I feel and which she seems to feel not at all. And dread of dreads she will make some kind advance, some touch of skin to skin and I will think how marvellous it would be at the same time as thinking why only on holiday, why not all the year, every day, every minute. And I will be cast as the rejecter, the unwilling, the cold and disinterested.

I will not try and console her for her next loss.

6th entry

Little fragments of love, mere tokens of love tossed into my begging bowl are not love at all. They are not even charity, and serve only to hint at what was, what might have been. And this is the awful dilemma now. For so long I feel like the dying man, dying of thirst in a desert of loneliness, offered the hope of life with a few drops of precious liquid at the very moment when death seems closest. Am I to take the drops and drink, prolong the death throes into a shrivelled ageing, or decline and bring forward the final ending. There that is it in a sentence. All the thinking, all the sleepless nights, all the anger and hurt, all distilled into a few words. Holidays are good for you or so they say. Maybe this one has been good for me if I can turn it all into a sentence. Or maybe it is this writing it down, here for no one but me to read that enables insight.

As ever she chooses her moments for maximum effect. A long, long drive in hot French sun all the way down to the house at La Rochelle. An early start and a late arrival, bags into the house, all unpacked, all groceries stored, pizza cooked and eaten, bottle of wine consumed, all with barely a word, all I want to do is sleep for a week. But tonight S would turn toward me instead of away, tonight she would put her hand on my face, tonight she would want contact and lovemaking. I want so much to go to sleep, so much to turn away and pay her back for the countless times that she has silently made clear that she has no interest in closeness. Through the drowsiness and the wine my tiny devil will be laughing and saying what you going to do now then, whose fault will it be when she is like ice for the next six months? Not that she is ever like ice, if only she were.

I kissed her once, in a great [despairing] effort to shake her from her indifference. Months had passed, perhaps years I can't remember, without the slightest token. I stood furious and desolate a few feet from her and could resist no longer. I took her head in my hands and kissed her hard on the mouth. In her shock her lips were still a little apart and I tasted the instantly recognisable sweetness of her mouth. Hard and long I kissed. As I pulled away a little she stood for a second and then turned and continued with the pruning of her rose bushes. There was no resistance, no pushing me away but there was no willingness, no release of tension, merely placid acceptance.

And so we continue, she apparently sailing serenely on, unmoved, unaffected by me or by us or our deadly embrace. Maybe she thinks that this is how it should be, how all marriages end up, maybe she has no expectation of any more, no hope of true intimacy. In the storm of confusion inside my head I wonder if it is I who have it all wrong, I who clings ridiculously to a Hollywood romance that never was and never will be.

7th entry

Again and again it is the dead of night when I write here. She never stirs when I leave the bed. Is she asleep? Sometimes I think she is awake, waiting for me to creep out. Sometimes when I lie there I think she is awake listening to me think, watching in the darkness for the tiniest movement, the smallest flicker, ever alert in case I should reach out a caressing hand. If she sleeps what does she dream of? These last few days have been harder than ever. Tonight a new quandary presented itself in my thoughts. What is it that she wants of me, wants of anything? To me she appears supremely self sufficient, I am completely irrelevant apart from bringing in some money and providing the husband badge. Is she waiting for the deserted badge, the separated badge or even the divorce badge? Is she looking forward to the widow badge? She may be trying to drive me completely out of my sanity. It is not possible for her to be unaware of the effect that this living death is having.

We walked together through the park to the shops last weekend. For a few moments our hands swung between us, synchronised in their movement. It seemed unnatural to do anything but touch and hold loosely together. In a few steps her stride altered a fraction and the synchronicity was gone. A few steps further and she wiped an imaginary hair from her eye and the connection was severed. This was a tiny, tiny thing, so tiny as to be invisible to anyone without a microscope. And it was a tiny drip of acid, doing just what acid does, burning, corroding the tattered fabric of ourselves. Once, many years ago it may be, when I was yet still full of hope and optimism we spoke of just such a moment. I forget the slight, the rejection that made me speak. She said that I was too sensitive, read too much into a meaningless word or action. Like a fool I was consoled and believed the fault was mine. Now, after all this time, the weight of evidence is too great, the probability too high. It is not my sensitivity, it is her indifference. Unless she is not indifferent, unless it is cunning and deliberate and designed. Unless she has the acid bottle firmly in her grasp and drips a drop here and a drop there to her own plan.

There is always a choice. Think about the choices and then decide on the best course for the chosen objective. It is easy to know this is the right thing to do and another to do it. I remain paralyzed by indecision. But there is something moving somewhere, it feels as if the log jam is subtly shifting around me. Even that dim thought is enough to satisfy me for now. Nothing has moved, nothing has changed, the scene is exactly as it was a moment ago. But there is perhaps the capacity for change.

8th entry

This is the worst time, when she is completely and utterly involved in her teaching. She has no time for anything but her class, her parents, her marking, her Christmas play, her anything but us, and certainly not me. I am here every year and the practice has made it more bearable this year. The distant S is so much better than the distant S in the same house, same room, same bed. It gives me time to think of ways to be free. And it gives me time to think of the myriad reasons to be free. The thousand slights, the million rejections, the early days and her Saturday sufferance of morning love making. I hated that so much, but like a moth I was drawn to the flame every week. Surely it would be good, or at least better than last time, surely she would lie awhile and we could doze and snuggle into each other. Surely she would not stay unspeaking for a few moments before the pretext of thirst or shopping or ironing took her abruptly away. And every week a different excuse, until I got to counting them, seeing how long before one repeated, and then checking the frequency. And I can write it here, now, but never admit before, that in the end I would reach out a hand, touch and caress her to test the excuse, to provoke the action that I logged in my survey. She never disappointed in that respect.

I think of ways out of this and every way seems as painful as going on. Suppose at the last moment, she dissolved and wept and said how much she loved me really, and how it would all be different and let's try again, suppose that happened and I'd already said I was leaving her. And if I was leaving her, where would I be leaving for? There are no friends I could suddenly announce myself on. And to plan it all beforehand, without telling her would be my betrayal not hers, I would be the deserter when all along it [was] she who left me. No, I have always been here, she is the one who left slowly and agonisingly over the years. Why couldn't she talk to me or accept my love that I so wanted to share when that tiny scrap of a person, that dead, dead baby lay for a few hours in his Perspex crib, for all the world peacefully asleep as any other baby on the ward except that he wasn't breathing.

9th entry

Across to H and J for a meal tonight. They were their normal selves, perhaps a little more tension in the air than usual. All explained when after the cheesecake J said they had something to tell us. I thought they were having a baby, people always seem to find that a very hard thing to tell us. A few of our friends have told me quietly when I have been on my own, as if it only S who would find the news brought back dismal memories. But not so tonight, instead H and J are to split. Needing their separate lives and space to live them in. Quite astonishing how little we know of what happens in other people's private lives. or how little I know. They seemed to have the perfect solution to their infidelities, ignore them. And we were the first to be told, we who are so 'good together', we who have known them for such a long time and who are so 'close' to them. Close? Listening to H's detailed stories of humping in the capitals of the world is not 'close'. Embracing J when we meet and planting a playful kiss on her cheek is not close. Do they have any idea what close means? Can people be close when the closeness is entirely one sided? Did they love each other in the same way? Did they love entirely by their own definition of what that was, unconcerned about the other's notions or feelings on the matter?

S was completely unmoved by the news and she has known them longer than I have. I might have appeared unmoved also but I felt convulsed. I wanted to know how they had even approached the subject. Did they just one day wake up and say ok that's over, lets move on. They apparently plan to split when H finds somewhere to live. No emotion, no tears, so casual it was painful.

Which has left me more angry confused and inadequate than ever. S did not even mention it as we walked the few streets back home. And was she surprised? No not really it happens to a lot of people these days she told me almost disinterested. Is that how she would be, calm and matter of fact, so we're splitting, so what? It seems that I am the one who is completely out of step with the world, if I was like the world then I could be as casual, I would count love for so little. But there is the bind, I don't and I can't. I do not begin to understand how she can be so cool. Not cool, tepid more like. Ice or flame would be easier, I could cope with that. But tepid, so you don't know if your hand is in the water or not, is impossible.

10th entry

All is confusion. I want the world to stop and let me catch up, instead it swirls about me teasing with opportunities and maybe's and if's and then as I reach for the idea it dissolves and laughs at me for thinking that I could grasp it at all. Does she laugh at me I wonder, do they exchange little jokes in the staff room about their husbands or is the indifference total and utter, beyond the slightest emotion? Would they want their partners at home when they got back from school? I have had a silent plan forming somewhere in my head that I could work more from home, increase the amount of time that we share the same space, increase the opportunities for meeting, seeing, even touching. How this was to happen I have no idea, but until tonight it seemed like an idea, like a step, a movement that could offer something in the bleak log jam. For a tentative floating of the notion I could not have chosen a worse moment, but of course I chose it just so that she would not be put in a corner and have to respond. A more careful plan was needed but I seized on an instant, so no surprise it was wrong. H and J continue their bizarre cohabitation and as still a couple, they visit as a couple. H spoke of working from home a few days a week when he finds his new flat. It was the moment that my silent plan found voice and I suggested that I might do likewise. J was in like a flash, saying how it was a good job he hadn't tried that on before now as she wouldn't want him at home in her private time and didn't S agree. I could not even look at her as she said how much she agreed, certainly couldn't have that, how would she get anything done. That was her time, her own private time, those few hours between our different returns from the work day. I want to tell them, to scream at them, that they are selfish bitches uncaring, unthinking, blinkered cows. I don't, I scream in my head while H says how he wouldn't want to interrupt anything, get in the way of anyone's fun. If I had a gun I could shoot each of them right there.

Now that she read it through properly for the first time, Lydia found herself slightly stunned. She had focused largely on the accurate copying of the words for many hours, sometimes spending several minutes on a single phrase, now their flow and meaning came to the fore. Fact or fiction, this was a man struggling with his life, maybe struggling for his life. That idea, a man, a male, wrestling with emotion and feeling, came as a surprise. It was so long since Lydia had come anywhere near to such strength of feeling herself, she had to make a conscious step to reach into her memory. There on the page was some of the same pain, but more intense than the passage of time now rendered her own. The shock, revelation almost, was that it was a man's voice crying out. She wanted to reject it as being fiction and fiction written by a woman.

Lydia's own marriage had ground to a halt after nearly ten years. Michael had lost interest in every part of it until, as the cliché has it, Lydia had been traded in for a younger model. The end had been relatively swift, more depressing than acrimonious. She was cast as the wronged party, he the infidel. They had settled with a clean break, probably to her financial disadvantage. Without children to complicate the arrangements, she had been keen to cut the knot with a single stroke, where he might have wanted to stay in contact. Now she could look back objectively, as she thought, at a time which may have been her life, but might just as easily have been someone else's. Had she ever thought that he might have felt any pangs, any anguish? He had always been big, bluff, uncomplicated Michael, not too troubled by the deeper things in life. Suddenly, and to her shame for the first time, she contemplated the idea that she could have played a part in driving him away. Had she ever had such passion, been as consumed by him as the anonymous author was by his 'S'? Maybe it had simply faded away, dulled by the everyday routine of marriage. At this distance she found that she could not remember.

Lydia slept badly, her normal peaceful night disturbed by unseen demons relentlessly hunting her down through twisting mazes, past the mindless stares of a cast of characters from ten and twenty years previously.

3

11th entry

S sent me a Valentine's card yesterday, just as she always does. She always signs it 'love ????' which I once knew meant love from guess who. For years it has meant simply 'love?'. I send her one also, which I don't sign at all and never had. This exchange of cards defies all reason. Today they sit on the bookshelf between the photo of her mother and father and a souvenir ivory elephant she brought back from Thailand a thousand years ago. Is it not peculiarly perverse to kill an elephant to carve [an] image of the dead animal from its remains? Not so perverse as the two mute valentine cards which will sit there for a week and then be put in the bin. They will sit and stare at me for that week in silent rebuke. And they have their matching partners at Christmas and on birthdays, except that they are signed and signed 'with love'. I want to not do cards any more, I want to not keep up the niceties and the pretences, I want to stop it all for ever and ever. I want her to go away, and I want her to stay, I want it to be possible. But that is the horror of it now, it remains just that, possible. Better impossible than eternally possible, and never realised.

Our neighbours had a grand shouting match this morning, not loud enough to hear the words but enough to feel the anger. Enough to hear the silence when it was finished with a slammed door. How I wish I could have that row, provoke that reaction, engage that emotion. Not that we have never rowed because we have. Precisely three times. And now that I come to think about it, to write about it, to define it and consign it, maybe we have not. She has not shouted at me once. But we did row on our first holiday together after we were married when she took some [   ] at something that I know not what and did not speak to me for a day until I refused to go further until she told me what was wrong. And we did row a year later when the same thing happened for a week with just monosyllabic grunts instead of speaking. That time she took herself away to some spot until she came back and said she was sorry and that she would try again, whatever that meant. For a couple of weeks she was sweetness and light, but it all seemed such an effort and I was just holding back waiting for the spell to be broken, until it was. Maybe five years ago one night when I drank a little too much, defences lowered I complained of feeling as if I were dead and wanting a life again, and she with a little drink inside her too, wept a little and said how she knows it has not been very good but she would try harder and she was scared to lose me. There was a difference for a few weeks before the indifference seeped back. I think I tried to respond but I was too wary, suspicious, untrusting of this artificial attention. Now a bloody good row seems like a good thing to have, a thunderstorm to clear the cloying air. I can hardly bear to look at her any more, she just looks away.

12th entry

I went to the centre again today to see if I could make an appointment with the woman who listened. I didn't even remember her name and couldn't say why I needed to see her. Then I needed to go to the office but could not work out the best route to take. There are two obvious ways, each really as good as the other, but I needed to take the best one and I could not decide. I know the best one from here, but not from the health centre. So I sat in the car unable to move until rudely prompted by the person waiting to get out of the car park. Panicking, I drove home, to where I knew I could choose the correct route. I think this is the start of madness. It may be beginning of the end of madness or it may be too late for anything. Tonight I have waited a long time after she has gone to her bed to write this. First I got this book out and two pens set beside it. One works well but I don't like it. The other works less well and blobs ink from time to time but it sits well in the hand and is comfortable. Now I have waited, deliberately letting myself think about which pen I should use. I am testing whether or not I can make a simple decision, one of no consequence whatsoever. There is ink now on the page under the very tip of the pen that writes this but it is from neither. I have become transfixed by the choice and put it off by choosing neither and hunting until I found a biro that neither works well nor is comfortable in the hand. I know that the pens still sit here beside me, each unused, each with its virtues, each its faults. The third way is the worst of both pens. I look at them and think that I may never use either again. I see that this is strange behaviour, but I cannot control it only observe that it is odd. Even the observation of it is odd and I can see that too.

13th entry

She is asleep and has been for more than an hour. I have not slept at all, I have been waiting for her to give me an answer to the question. By chance, certainly not by design we got into the same bed at the same moment. After a few minutes of darkness and silence as if in a trance, someone who might have been me, said that they wanted to make love and had wanted to for ages. Then in a slow-motion parody of conversation someone also said that they loved the other. And someone else replied that they loved the other. And then me, probably me, asked what did love mean? And yes, there are many kinds of love but what kind is yours. And I listened for an answer as she [breathed] slower and deeper and [snuffled] in a way that she only ever does when she is asleep and I waited and listened again until there was no possible [mistake] that she had gone away into whatever she dreams of and there was still no answer.

But I do have an answer. It is the kind of love that cannot see how important it is to give an answer. It is the kind of love that does not see love coming the other way. It is the kind of love that cares not a jot for the other, that can't smell the burning flesh. It is a [destructive selfish loveless] love that wears the clothes of love over the [torso] of a corpse. It mocks the word and the feeling, laughs at sentiment and anguish. When did it slither in and make its rotten home in that other love that once was there, I can't see through the fog. I need an [antiseptic aerosol] spray to clean it away and wipe it clean again.

14th entry

It doesn't count if you have to ask for it. Love doesn't count as love if you have to ask if you are loved, even if the answer is yes. I do not want a love that is there when [demanded] but absent otherwise. I want her love and everything that goes with it completely unasked, completely voluntary and more than [volunteering] she must want to give it. I dream of making love in a million places in a million ways and I dream that she would have those dreams too. Not because I dream them, but because she dreams them, not because I have a [fantasy], because she does. My fantasies can only come true if she shares it without knowing that I have it. It is a cruel fantasy to have, it can never ever be made real. I am [marooned] on an island from which there is no escape, never a hope of escape, and I cannot even wave at the [passing ships]. I must hide from them and wait for them to check my island for lost souls because they want to, because they see the island and think that there could be someone there in need of [rescue]. And while I wait my mind becomes fuller and fuller of every thought [imaginable] until it is unable to cope with volume, the [complexity] of every tiny nuance of every particle of thought and races madly away in a [vortex] of [ ]. And amazingly there is a tiny cold [unblinking] point in the centre which sees all this chaos of thought and [synapses] sparking. And the tiny cold centre does nothing, can do nothing to stop it relentlessly churning in my head.

Is it the tiny cold centre that does this scribble in the journal? It seems not, it seems as if that is another person altogether, the scribe who works once removed from the [master's] hand. The master watches this pen write and these hands move just as it watches everything else. Sometimes it does a little more than watch, sometimes it plots and schemes to free itself of the chaos, to do away with the [cacophony] of nerve ends spitting their messages to and fro.

15th entry

Sleep. There is no sleep, only snatched minutes in the darkness. I want to sleep a dreamless, blank, dead, numb sleep for a hundred years. I want to lie in suspended animation, maintained but [comatose] like the film, hanging by a wire unseeing and uncaring and unthinking. How long would forever be? Until the electricity failed or the wire broke. Or someone got bored with the idea.

I half fear and half relish that I will lose the job soon. It is becoming so difficult to [concentrate] on, to make sense of the [nonsense] that I write and the nonsense I am asked to write. It is trivial beyond imagination, who gives a shit about anything that comes out the process. It pays the bills and there is not another single thing that can be said for it. And this nonsense, this blurb for today's rubbish, today's toothpaste, tomorrow's [ ] [ ], just words jumbled and mixed and their tiny [nuances] pored over and poked and examined and [user trialled] and they are still just words. Once I must have cared, must have been able to put them together how people liked them put together. Put them in just the right order with just the right amount of this and not too much of that so people would rush out and [cover themselves] in the cream or the lotion. But probably that was someone else completely. And if they were to fire me that would be excellent in a way, it would change things as I cannot change them, the whole set up would be different, we would need to speak of things, many things like [walruses] and sealing wax most likely. There's a [cabbage] and a king in there somewhere too. Would we speak? Maybe, maybe the loss of income would force her to speak, if I were to tell her. How would I do that when I can tell her nothing at all. Tell her that there is no money, no job, no sleep all for thinking of how it was or how it might once have been or how I dreamed it once was.

16th entry

S is away. Brighton or Bournemouth or somewhere. A conference. It is easier when she is not here. She is not right there where I see her at every turn, doing the things that she does, solitary, [undemanding], single in every respect bar my presence. [Supremely] self-contained, an ocean liner ploughing serenely onward looking neither to left nor right, unaware and uninterested in the drowning man thrashing in the swell. In the empty space I can float on the waves, breath air a little longer, until Friday when she will return.

Conferences are meant to be made for affairs, breathless tumbles and [blushing] mornings. Does she have that in her any more, did she ever? At 31 you'd think so, but how would I know, how could I judge. There is nothing there, nothing I recognize any more. There is a great big space where the spark and fire and interest used to be. Or else it is a face turned away from me, but I don't think it looks upon anyone else. And all this in a body that seems much as it has always done, you can still see that she was very pretty once, still see that she has a figure, still goes in and out at roughly the right places, still takes some care over her hair, even though it becomes ever shorter. You can still see it through her clothes but not otherwise she was never one to prance about the house naked, and now there is neither prance nor nakedness. I remember dimly a picture with a caption 'when did you last see your father?' I could paint one that said 'when did you last see your wife?'

17th entry

Just a few days back from Brighton S announced that she is going away again in a couple of weeks, this time to [Harrogate], a training thing she signed up for a last minute place, something important to her promotion prospects or some such. It is almost certainly true, she is almost certainly going to [Harrogate] and will almost certainly be trained. Just for a millisecond of hesitation it could have been a lie. Or it could be both true and a lie. Maybe the lie is in what is not being said. Did she give me too much information, did she speak too quickly, what caught my attention. I [feigned] disinterest. Or I didn't [feign] it at all. I am disinterested, I am completely and utterly without interest. Does this mean I am dead, drowned already? Maybe part drowned. I will have a few more days to float and breathe in a calm sea.

18th entry

While she was not looking I checked her suitcase. Don't know what I was looking for, but I had to see if she was taking anything that she might not usually take. Whatever that might be. I was looking for something, something out of place, something extra or something missing. There was no book. And she scuttled out of the house, couldn't wait to be gone. I would imagine the scene but I see nothing at all, a completely blank space. If she is with someone else, it is just as if she were dead, I cannot feel how it would be, am I [ecstatic] or beyond [despair]. If I stay still and be nothing at all then it will stop. I will drift on my back on a slow ocean.

19th entry

If I were to be gone from her life what would she do? I think she would do nothing at all, just carry on with her daily routine, take her little conference trips, tend her patch of garden, read her books, mark her homework, plan her lessons. She would say how she missed me when it was [appropriate] to do so, and say how she had got over it when that was more so. I could be gone before she even returns, just open the door and walk out into the summer air and keep on walking. Walk down to the river and walk right into it until it just floated me away downstream, gently bobbing until I was lost from view. It is a very soothing thought. My still centre can see the river weeds waving as I float past them, free to float and drift with the flow while they remain anchored to the river bed, [doomed] to ripple forever as the water floods past them, never to [join] the flow themselves. But even as I see this, write this here, I see her drifting along with me, now a little ahead, now a little behind. We say nothing, do nothing.

20th entry

The peace of last week is destroyed and turmoil takes its place. A greeting of sorts, a tentative, almost touching, excuse for what might once have been a kiss, no more than an acknowledgement of existence. An insult to every kiss there ever was. There was a time when we kissed to part and kissed to meet, kissed goodnight and kissed awake. There was a time when a longer absence made for more than kisses, made for hugs and squeezes, touching and stroking. If that was not someone else altogether. Maybe it was in a dream or a book or a film. Which day was it that she first turned her cheek a little to [subtly] change that kiss to the [proverbial] peck? And then that became no more than a touch, then even the touch was gone, not even a pretence of a kiss. And now she is back from her training and it is barely a nod.

There is a darkness, a [blackness], that is spreading [relentlessly] outwards from the [diamond] bright pinprick at its centre. When it covers me completely I will be gone. But if it reaches her first then she will be gone. Absorbed, [dissolved] and gone as if we had never ever been. Nothing nix null absolute zero on anybody's scale. There is a curious [disembodied] interest to see which of us disappears first. It is of no consequence to me nor to anyone else which it might be. It [is] just conceivable that it could embrace us both in the same instant. A final togetherness.

21st entry

I watched her eating her breakfast yoghurt and wondered if it might be poisoned by some random serial killer. People do that, they buy a load of yoghurt then inject poison into each pack and put it back on the shelves. Or Marmite to hide the taste. They do it. You never know how it will get you or who it will get. Nobody ever knows not even the one who puts it there. And why did they buy it, because I wrote some little [jingle] that tickled their taste buds just enough to increase the sales by a [decimal] dot. And it was full of poison. How do you like that, then. Or shampoo that makes you come out in blisters. There are a million ways it will get you.

Shoot a dozen people who you don't know, then shoot the one you do.

That's the way to hide a body, with a lot of other bodies. Want to hide a leaf, then drop it on the forest floor. They can see all the leaves but they can't see yours and after a while neither can you. Clever [brains] but not that clever. But if you shoot a dozen people where would you put the one you know? Not number one for sure, never number one remember. No and not number twelve either. Maybe number eight or nine or ten, but how to decide which number? Or make a pattern that does not really exist just to throw them off. Invent a pattern of Sundays or Fridays. Maybe Tuesdays. I can't work out a pattern that does not exist. Some very careful thought needed to do that and that needs a focus of energy. Which I may have tomorrow or the next day. A lens to focus energy is needed.

It had taken Lydia nearly two weeks working most evenings and weekends to get this far. Only where she needed to refer back to compare a word with another version of it did she read back anything that she copied from the book. She was perhaps two-thirds of the way through. She needed a break and there was no reason not to take one, her rules were no more than a self-imposed discipline. The results puzzled, depressed and fascinated her. Gone completely was the feeling of intruding on a private grief, of looking through the keyhole. Whatever these words might be, their underlying meaning seemed clear. For her puzzle of anonymous faces she had swapped a greater mystery, and one that she was sure would haunt her until she could unravel it. And all the while that she was reading through her finished work, the words that ended it all, the words to which she was slowly moving, hovered over the pages, a mystery in their own right.

Without any warning one fact about the book jumped into her mind. If this were fiction, carefully crafted by a writer, considered prose that might be a novel or used later in a story, then it would not have been physically written with such passion and aggression. It would not have so many changes of style from the barely legible to the clear; it would not be lightly scribbled in one section and practically gouged out of the paper in the next. It would be written so that it could be read. Here, in this oddly chosen book, the words of passion were written with passion, those of anger were written with anger, words of calm were written with clarity.

Lydia let the idea sink in. A real person, a man, had written all these secret thoughts out on paper. A real man with a real wife. A real man with real demons in his head. A man who called for help or a man who found help through writing them out? He did not seem to be finding help, on the contrary he seemed more in need of it that ever. Although she knew the ending, knew that it would provide no ultimate answer or satisfaction, she had to follow the narrative through. But even before Lydia had the whole thing in front of her, a part of her mind began to consider how she might identify these people, date the events, discover hard facts. And that small part of her brain also realised the task might be impossible, something which would dwarf the difficulties she'd encountered with the Longlands family and Henry Myers.

⋆

Evenings flew past, Lydia labouring with a growing intensity as the end came into sight. Words began to form themselves naturally in her mind as she copied the scribble, so much so that on a couple of occasions she had to stop and retrace her steps to feel sure that she had not invented anything of her own. The twenty-fourth entry had defeated her completely, extracting no more than a few words with any certainty. At length her task was completed. She knew the story, as far as it went. The Saturday evening after she had finished she printed out the remaining pages, settled to her favourite position in her favourite chair and read the whole thing straight through. Even though she was now intimately bound up in its contents, the anguish flowed undiminished from the pages. The twenty-second entry had been easy to interpret. It had been written with clarity, written slowly, Lydia thought.

22nd entry

S can see my ideas and she does not think much of them, they are pathetic to her and inside she is laughing at them. She has her own plans now and they do not involve me, at least not as far as I can see. Her self-sufficiency is complete. I have less bearing on her life now than the smallest and most insignificant piece of chalk in her classroom. She does not talk to me any more and I do not listen. She nods sometimes and her smile once so open and beautiful, once lighting up her face, is reduced to a twisted smirk. If I am careful I can avoid her nearly all the time now. She does not see me in the mornings when she goes to work, leaving me undisturbed on the sofa where I spend the nights drifting in and out of sleep with the world service. We have not spoken of this separation and I am sure we will not. It gives me time to think of the end game. It is at a critical stage, and the pattern appears to be coalescing into a uniform whole. I can't see the shape or the details yet but I sense their formation. There is a flow and method just hidden beneath the churning surface. Resolution beckons but the direction is not yet determined. I may need more time to work it all out, it is getting harder to think in the office, too many interruptions and the thread is lost before I can hold it. If I spend more time at home and then go to work late and stay when the rest have gone home then there will be less distraction, give it a chance to become clear. And I must speed the process before it is all taken out of my hands. I must choose the weapon, the weapon of choice, before one is chosen for me. Choose the time and place, the hour and the minute, down to the second, before it happens without me. As each thought becomes ordered I will write it down so as not to have to keep it in my head. It will relieve the pressure, make room for analysis and focus the rest. Thought number 1 – find a calm point from which to order the thoughts. And number 2 – decide the order in which they must be written.

23rd entry

Too much time is spent ordering the details of how to avoid her. It takes my energy so there is none left to work out the bigger picture. Anticipating a potential contact, [sidestepping] the chance of meeting, the dangers of having to speak. So tired tonight that I can hardly write. I could stop the writing that would give more time, but only a little, it is weeks since I had a thought that was finished and ready to write down. And now I have all this extra planning to do and each thought is getting [thinner] and [thinner] as they are all squeezed together. I can barely see one from another they are all packed in so tightly and now with so little room to move they are stuck in limbo. Would it be possible to do something without a plan, to act just randomly, step randomly off the kerb, eat random products from random cupboards in a random house. Say random things that just happened to be there at the moment of speech. It would certainly be easier than this. She spoke to me this morning and I was so surprised that I did not recognise her voice, couldn't determine what the sounds meant, hadn't accounted for any meaning, couldn't speak. Every angle was meant to be covered and one was missed. Sloppy thinking, sloppy planning. But I was reminded of her. I sneaked a look to be sure I would know her again. She seemed to be smiling. I am not sure whether she could see me or not. Probably she could and as I could see her then we were both certainly still here this morning.

From the twenty-fourth entry Lydia saw that she had managed only the words *'Xmas'*, *'mother'*, *'probably'*, *'vomit'*, *'black'*, and the initial *'S'* appeared three times. Even then 'vomit' was almost purely guesswork. From some conversation she recalled once being told that Christmas was the worst of times for family tension. With more food, and more drink came unwanted relatives, and enforced togetherness. Lydia wondered if it could be a tipping point for someone already struggling to hold on to their sanity.

25th entry

The first day of a new year and unfamiliar calm has settled on me. It is such a strange feeling, at once both liberating and suspicious. There seems no rational explanation as to why this should be. I have looked diligently and found nothing to explain it. I know she is out of the house and this book is opened for the amusement of writing the diary. I can sense a storm a little way off, but it does not concern me at present, even though it may swing my way later today or tomorrow. I cannot focus on that or worry about it right now. And that feels odd in itself, I think I should be working out what to do. Perhaps it is just that convalescent feeling after illness. I caught something horrible over the holiday, I don't remember a doctor but she says that she called one. And for once the pills she left seem to have been of use. But it has been said a million times that I must finish the course, not that S would allow anything else, all measured out for me and then watching as I take them. She has been quite attentive while she has been here and not out visiting. All visitors barred from the quarantined house. There may be a sign on the door I don't know. I will go and look later.

I have even thought about work today and I may be fit to go back in a day or so if I can shake off the drowsiness that pervades me. It may be the pills and they will be done soon. If I can write this then I am sure I could write something for them. I forget exactly what it was that I was working on before but there was certainly a lot going on. Enough for now it is hard to concentrate.

26th entry

S has taken to hovering around me, not exactly checking on what I am doing and not leaving me alone either. I don't know what she wants, something she is not telling me, even though she talks to me a great deal more than usual. She doesn't seem to want any answers though and I am being careful in what I say. I think she has a scheme and I will wait to find out what it is before giving anything away. It has begun to be the same at the office since I have been back, there is a scheme in [train] there too and I am not included in the planning. It might be a coincidence but probably not, they are hatching something together most likely, but I am on my guard, I see them coming. When I know what they have in mind I will make a plan and [sidestep] their scheme, but it will take a lot of effort, I must stay [focused] on the problem. First I must work out what it is they intend. They may mean to remove me somehow, give themselves a clear run and if so then I may play them at their own game. Now I am recovered, a little more like my old self these last few days, more alert and able to think. Whatever bug it was that struck me left a big [hangover], weak and swimming in a mist for days afterwards. Thankfully that has mainly cleared and things are back in a sharper focus, there is power and energy flowing back into me.

The nonsense of the pathetic cards appeared again yesterday, hers with two hearts linked together. I could not make out what it was at first, couldn't understand what it was or what meaning it had or indeed if it had a meaning. I was off guard, surprised by this foreign item that she clearly expected would cause some response from me. Catching my struggle, she explained it was a valentine card. Yes, yes, I knew that, of course, but then reaching into some imagined past came up with "I thought we didn't do that any more", to cover my incomprehension of it. It worked well enough she did not see the chink that had let her slip past the defences. But it shows that I must be more careful, have a bland and non committal response prepared for absolutely anything that she might throw at me. And it is so devious, hiding her plans behind such a thing, she had even signed it. And only the night before I was feeling very pleased with the way that the office people have accepted the new me, it hasn't taken the effort I thought it would. Maybe I was getting complacent, too clever by half. I have learned the words that make them happy, make them leave me alone, let me write the words they want to read. Let them think that I don't know how they scheme and whisper, titter in their corners from the sides of their mouths, turn away when they speak on the phone about me. To her I am sure, reporting back, logging movements, and when they are done they'll casually ask if I need some more water. I feed it to the plants when they are not looking or tip it out the window. It is not possible to see if they put something in it, it is too clear to see.

27th entry

Now I am redundant in every sense. Today found that I was no longer required at the office. Now I will have time to think of solutions. A whole pile of stuff is redundant too, all the thinking for the office is gone, there is room for everything now, space to get it straight once and for all. Complete concentration on S and her plans. She has no chance to get past me now all my power can be channelled right to the very centre. Enough money to see my [me] through, not a lot when you think of the millions my clever little words brought them. They'll pay more one day for sure. Goodbye for now Pink [on] Pink your turn will come. They will probably go to the wall anyway. I must repay them before they do. Eight years of my life redundant. Most likely she has a similar scheme but without the payoff. She will not be allowed to do it, I will stop her before she can push me out or she slips off to another bed in another hotel and slides back through the door all smiles and guilty hellos. She is so far away now she is like a little dot on the horizon but I can still see her if I strain my eyes, still hear her if she speaks above the static. Not that I let her know that, better she thinks I am not aware of her at all. I see her hollow smiles and fake tenderness, I see them for exactly what they are, I wanted the real one the one who used to live here, not this imitation, this [stepford], this [deceitful] hideous parody. She must go away from here or be made to before she breaks my head and the void consumes the every part of me. There is still a refuge at the bright centre of everything but it is harder and harder to get there, like walking through a black [whirlwind].

28th entry

She really is very good at what she is doing, but not as good as I am at seeing the truth. She makes out that I am short of vitamins or some such and this is to be remedied by some new pills. I took one the other day when she was watching, but not till I had seen her take one herself. OK one won't kill me, I'll take it. Then when she was out I checked the bottle. Sure enough the label showed they were just what she said. But they are making me feel sick and I have a constant headache. It seems that she has swapped the bottle with an old one that she had. I checked the date on it and sure enough it is not new, she has had it for months. But I am keeping this to myself, I will not challenge her, I will be the compliant fool that she takes me for and let her think that I continue with the taking. But in one thing she is right, I do not eat well, it is of no interest. And she thought that she could take that little [observation] and use it to poison me. I must be very careful of what I eat from now on.

29th entry

It has taken a huge effort but I see the way now. Still a few things that have to be planned the little details of the timing. I will write a list elsewhere for safety.

30th entry

Now I have the time and the place and the means all neatly arranged it is sometimes a struggle to keep them in order. Right now I want to write them all down again to be sure that I have them but security is an issue. I know them off by heart and write them easily but must destroy them once written. I will write them again to be sure, I have purchased a notepad for the purpose. Always use the back page straight onto the cardboard cover so as to leave no indentation. Written. Read carefully, yes all there all in the right order. Neatly torn off from its spiral binding, all the little flaky pieces removed. The page was never there. Chew until dissolved then spit into the toilet. So long as I can hang on to that sequence and repeat it [faultlessly] that will be the way to do it. Mr Punch I think.

31st entry

I am at once calm and excited, nervous and elated. [It] just occurs to me as I write those words that it may simply be a migraine in waiting. Or the [vicious indigestion] that wrecks my snatches of sleep. All is ready and I have everything in [perfection] in my head. Rehearsed and rehearsed until I know it in my sleep, can walk with my eyes tight shut. This book has done its job, been the space needed. It seems certain that this will be the last entry, something I did not realise until I wrote it out now. Maybe a new book will be needed another day. Tomorrow is another world a new world a better world. Or it is oblivion. Which would be its own peculiar blessing. But action will cause reaction and something will happen. The leaf will be cast to the forest floor where it will lie anonymously turning to mould. Though a million feet were to walk right by it, none would pause to remark its presence. Even I would not be able to detect it. The future at once looks crystal clear and impenetrable. The calmness of the centre has flowed out to envelop me and all around is light and clarity but the horizon remains black and infinite. This I think is the world without her even though she sleeps a sleep through this last night. Check mate in the game. Mr Punch.

The effort of transcribing these words had left her tired enough, now reading them through as a whole proved just as exhausting. She was bound up with them, part of them in some inexplicable way. Nagging away at her was the growing belief that what she had found were the terrible cries of a man who meant to kill his wife, or at least be rid of her by some sinister means. Whether a plan to do so existed in reality, or simply as imagined events was far from clear. But some event had caused him to stop writing, and to stop at a point which he knew was the end. Stopping had not been forced upon him unexpectedly, he had not stopped mid sentence or mid thought. The author's mental breakdown, for surely that is what it amounted to, was laid out in the pages for anyone to see, even though Lydia was sure that she was the first to see them. If not, then how else would they have come to be sold as part of a job lot from some house clearance. A house clearance! Why oh why had she not thought to go back to the auction rooms months ago and check where the albums had come from? If she knew the house, the family whose house her assorted box of books had come from, she would finally be on the track.

Lydia slept soundly for the first time in weeks, content to have a plan of action that held out the promise of resolution to her puzzles. Yet the question of puzzle or puzzles remained to be answered. She would contact the auctioneer on the Monday, then gather together all her facts, prioritise her searches, sequence her actions and move forward with purpose.

4

The auctioneers were closed on Monday and when Lydia called the following day she found them less than helpful. She had not realised it had been so long since the sale until she found the catalogue still crumpled in the recesses of her bag. It would take them time to find the records and after all, they complained, it was nearly six months ago. If she came over on the Wednesday someone might be able to find something for her. When she presented herself at the office it was only to be told they had no record of where her purchase had come from. Since it had been described as a mixed lot it could be a collection of items left over from another sale, possibly even from another sale room. Her last hope of a real helping hand to get her started had evaporated. Driving back to Oxford she weighed what she might do next. One option was clearly to put the box and its contents out with the newspapers for recycling. But that would go right against her grain, for she was still convinced that someone somewhere would be pleased to have the photographs, to be introduced to their lost family. And there was that other puzzle to be solved, the one that went beyond family history, the one that might be far more important than finding a distant third cousin.

'Lydia, when are you going to really do something?' Gloria asked. 'You need to get out more, get in the swim.'

'I do lots of things, I'm busier than you think.'

When Gloria suggested, as she did regularly, that she should 'get in the swim', Lydia knew that what she really meant was 'get a man'. Getting a man had never been high on her list of priorities and never lower than it was now. She was completely focused on her box of treasures and every hurdle that was put in her way only made her more determined than ever to unravel their mysteries.

'Busy? Come on, what've you been busy at? We'd love to know, wouldn't we?' Gloria included the rest of the section, all female, all younger than Lydia by a decade or more, in her question. Nothing would have pleased them more than for Lydia to be having an affair with a man, maybe a married man. That would have made her conform to their norm, put her back in the swim. She was tempted to hint at what they wanted to hear, for she grew as weary of their continual goading as she did of the chatter about their own sex lives.

Instead, a thought popped into her head and before she knew it, it had found voice. 'I'm busy with a murder,' and then, quickly to cover her folly, 'It's a family history thing.'

Gloria rolled her eyes. 'Typical Lydia, that's just you isn't it? You need some real interest in you life. I could fix you up with someone, anytime you like.'

Lydia smiled her thank-you and shook her head. She knew that she was going to be busier than ever for a while, far too busy to be thinking about being fixed up by Gloria or any of her workmates.

The spoken words crystallised what she had been gradually working round to ever since she had finished the transcription. Saying out loud what she had not fully admitted to herself, suddenly made it true - she was busy with a murder. But she needed a new approach instead of repeatedly banging her head against the same brick wall of unanswered questions. She reasoned that if all her puzzles were to be solved then there was no hope of solving them individually. She would look at all her evidence again on the assumption that it was a single puzzle, that all the main players were related in some way, even the tormented journal writer and his misunderstood wife. She'd look at all possibilities and probabilities and see if a coherent picture could be made from the pieces.

As a first task Lydia let herself become familiar once again with all the photographs, feeling for the lives, absorbing the scenes. At the same time she kept her detailed notes handy for reference. Then she opened the journal alongside the printed copy she had made and read through them, taking from the original where it was easy to do so and from her copy where it was not. By putting all the photographs, the captions, the notes and the journal into her head as a whole collection she hoped to gain a different insight. If she absorbed them as a single entity then perhaps she might begin to see where they joined. But instead of seeing where they joined, a solitary thought jumped into her mind as she read the thirtieth entry of the journal. A thought that fixed the journal as being fact and not fiction. To be certain, she read the words again:

'. . .Always use the back page straight onto the cardboard cover so as to leave no indentation. Written. Read carefully, yes all there all in the right order. Neatly torn off from its spiral binding, all the little flaky pieces removed. The page was never there. Chew until dissolved then spit into the toilet . . .'

Carefully turning the same page in the journal itself, she examined where it was bound to the spine. Three or four of those tiny little flakes were still there, just the few that had not fluttered out as she had held the pages up to the light. A surge of triumph and excitement swept through her, it was so small a thing and yet it was real physical evidence. This was not a fiction, no author would have gone to such lengths, it was not sheer coincidence, it was real. The probabilities swung in her favour.

With her fresh conviction about the journal, Lydia set to work drawing up a list of possibilities for the names and faces in the albums. To begin with, she concentrated on those who might reasonably be regarded as the core family, who appeared repeatedly and whose names were common to more than one volume. From the Longlands album she had already drawn a rough family tree with Papa and Mama as the head and with the definite children 'self' and Alice, and probable children Albert and Isabella; then, in order of probability, Beatrice, Joseph, James, and Henry. Finally, there were possible children or grandchildren Phoebe, Albert M,

Albert and Harriet. Clearly Albert the son, who looked about thirty-five, would not have a brother Albert, more likely his own son Albert. Albert M, who might be around six or seven, was differentiated by the letter M, possibly suggesting a different surname than the others. If that were so and Albert M were a grandchild, then he was the son of a married daughter. Beatrice and Isabella were the obvious candidates, but that might also imply that their husbands were in the photograph and that did not quite tally with the count of adults. Lydia did not spend any great time considering this, instead she moved back to her original purpose.

The next album was devoted almost entirely to James, the second 'self', the son Henry, and presumed children Verity and Bertie. James was the tentative link to Longlands. In this second album, or as Lydia had come to think of it, her 'RAF' album, James could be between thirty-five and fifty. The Longlands James might be twenty or so, a difference which was consistent with him being one and the same person. Lydia examined them both under her magnifying glass. Nothing to say they were and nothing to say they weren't, just a family likeness that could be her imagination. She did the same with 'self' from the RAF album and the possible females from the Longlands album with exactly the same result. The RAF album did have the huge advantage of a family name, the Myers name, to give her Mr & Mrs J D of whom the J was surely James, plus Henry, Verity and Bertie. She looked closely at Henry and Verity. Similar ages and brother and sister she was sure, but there might be more to it than that. Might they be twins, and if so then did twins not run in families? She was positive that the Longlands 'self' and Alice were twins. Another possible link danced elusively in the mist.

According to her notes, the next album in sequence would be the one without photographs, her 'VE Day' album as she had christened it. From the little she could gather from the brevity of the captions, it covered the years from the late 30's to the early 50's. Albert needed no prompting to be considered first. An Albert who was present in the captions before 1945 but not after, so an Albert of an age to have died in the war, one who might have had children called Ethel, Violet and Rose in the 30's. Assumptions certainly, but the name Albert was a link with Longlands. Either one of the Albert grandsons would have been in their mid twenties and perfectly placed to be have children at that time. The Essex connection was there again, in the name Coggeshall. Lydia checked her gazetteer. Sure enough there it was, just a few miles from Braintree. The idea that three random photograph albums should all have links to so small an area and end up together in an Oxfordshire saleroom was unlikely. Once again, Lydia considered the probabilities to be favourable.

The last album, her 'sandcastles' album, had no discernable reference to Essex. But it did have a Fred to go with the pictureless caption '*Ethel and Fred, Chelsea August 1952*' in the VE Day album. It also had Susan and Paul and yet another 'self', plus the usual cast of extras, a handful of appearances by Tommy and Mick, and various picnics with 'the Arncliffes'. Although the 'self' in each of the albums was certainly not the same 'self', Lydia wondered how unusual it might be to caption a photograph in this way. How did people identify themselves, if not their name? Might 'self' be something unconsciously learned from a mother, or was it so common as to be unimportant? Having no way of answering her question, Lydia let it drop. The dates and places identified were those of holidays such as '*Margate '58*' and '*The Dales*". The possibilities for this album amounted to just one; Fred was the same Fred as the Chelsea 1952 Fred in which case it was just conceivable that 'self' was the Chelsea Ethel. Lydia reminded herself that 'just conceivable' did not offer the balance of probability she was seeking, but she still noted it down.

Finally she gave similar consideration to the journal. In doing so, Lydia realised that she had only looked at words and handwriting, trying to decipher their sad and seemingly awful meanings. She hadn't really thought about dates, places, and clues to identity. It seemed clear that the book itself was a good deal older than the handwritten entries within it. The author had used at least four different ball-point pens for the most part, with a sprinkling of pencils which had their points broken at regular intervals. Now she read the whole account once more, looking not for clues to the outcome, but to see if people, dates and places could be narrowed down. The author was educated, had a good vocabulary, worked with words, wrote jingles or advertising slogans. The use of '*jingles*' suggested a date after the 1960's, but it was a tentative marker at best. When she read the reference to a film about suspended animation and the word that she'd interpreted as 'comatose', a quick search on her computer came up with '*Coma*' which dated to the late 70s. There was a reference to '*user-trialled*' which she felt must be later still, possibly a buzzword from the 80's. The only places mentioned by name were Brighton, Bournemouth, La Rochelle, probably Harrogate, and Cockermouth. As for time span, she noted a summer holiday and two distinct references to Valentine's Day, and one between them to a Christmas, although admittedly that was in the least reliable entry, the illegible twenty-fourth. But it was followed by a reference to New Year, so a year had passed between the eleventh and the twenty-sixth entries. If that was the pattern for the whole journal then it covered about two years. Some entries, she was sure, were only a day apart, may even have been the same day, others were more separated. By how long was uncertain but, if she needed to, Lydia reasoned that she could get a closer approximation. The company that made the author redundant as his illness - it was surely an illness – progressed, he'd referred to as 'Pink on Pink' although on checking she saw that the tiny scribble she'd read as 'on' could be any single letter or two letter word. It could also be 'and'.

Of the people who featured, none were named. They were identified only by an initial and even those single letters might not represent names but codes. H and J might be Henry and June just as easily as a fevered mind might have them down as Handsome and Jealous. It was clear that his wife became S after that initial entry and she was specifically noted as being aged thirty-one. There was also the funeral of 'her precious B' in Cockermouth, or at least somewhere nearby. It was the only fixed event in a specific location, yet it too suffered from the individual being identified by yet another initial. In her road atlas Lydia noticed that it was on the same page as Whitehaven. Three postcards, Whitehaven, Braintree and Oxford. If instead of 'Whitehaven' and 'Cockermouth' she read 'Cumbria' then there was a glimmer of a connection between every volume in her collection. Just how tenuous can it get? She could not suppress a smile at her own devious thinking.

*

'How's your murder going, Lydia?' Gloria hissed in a mock whisper, loud enough for all to hear.

'It's ok,' was the guarded reply.

'Found your man yet?'

Lydia could see the conversation was about to turn abruptly in another, all too familiar, direction. 'More a case of finding the victim,' she countered.

'You can't have a murder without a corpse can you, I mean they can't get you for it without a body, can they?'

Lydia was about to correct this widely held belief but stopped herself in time. 'Oh, all this happened a long time ago, I'm just trying to put the story together, that's all.'

'So, what's the next step?'

For once Gloria sounded interested, but Lydia was not ready to let anybody else, and certainly not Gloria, into her private world of puzzles and mind games. For one, she doubted there were many who would remotely understand her fascination, and for another, the history that she was constructing would sound too far fetched in its present tentative state.

'C'mon Lydia, tell us the juicy details,' she pleaded, which only made Lydia all the more resistant.

'I have some more checking to do. I'll see how that goes.'

'What're you going to check then?'

What indeed. Closed up in her back room with her notes and files and her laptop, she'd had run low on inspiration if not determination. She needed somehow to find a new spark, something in the real world away from her census searches, her trawling through dozens of pages of Google results with their inevitable meanders and sidetracks.

'I'm going to look at a care home in Essex,' Lydia replied, for no apparent reason that she could think of afterwards.

Gloria pulled a face of absolute exasperation, an expression that she had practised almost to perfection on Lydia. 'You want to watch out, you'll be in one yourself before you know it.'

★

The Longlands Private Residential Home was located in Bocking, a village close to Braintree, Essex. The pleasant-sounding manager had been very happy to have Lydia visit to see what it could offer when she had called to make an appointment. She may have been less accommodating if she had known the true purpose, although even Lydia was unsure what that was. It had been surprisingly easy to lie in explaining that she was looking for a home for her elderly aunt and Longlands was a possibility. She reconciled these lies with the fact that her grandmother had spent her last years in such a home and that Lydia had helped her select it, so that her lies were not really lies, simply displaced truths.

The journey from Oxford was slow and Lydia was grateful to arrive in Bocking in the early afternoon. Following the directions she had been given, she turned left into Bovingdon Road, past the splendid edifice of St. Mary's and then immediately right into the short driveway of Longlands. The building was obscured by trees until she stopped outside the modern block, easily recognisable from the picture on the web site. Before going in, Lydia paused a moment to take in the whole aspect. A modern wing had been added to an older building, built to the west and extended more recently across the original frontage. It was not easy to tell the age of that original, but there was nothing to suggest that she had come to the wrong place. Even then, as she stood on the driveway, she was not entirely sure what she was doing there, other than playing detective. For an instant she wobbled, feeling fraudulent and foolish in equal measure.

Celia Barnard was most welcoming and over tea in her little office asked Lydia all the questions she'd anticipated. They were the same questions she'd been asked years ago so with the simplest of adjustments to her supposed aunt's age, Lydia was able to answer them all truthfully. In her turn, Lydia was able to ask the right questions of Celia, questions recalled from those previous interviews. The home had the same air of quiet that she remembered from those other visits, the same scattering of residents, some asleep, some simply gazing out across the front lawn, perhaps recalling pleasures of younger days, or regretting the loss of someone to share the memories with. Two or three looked up and smiled, pleased at the prospect of a new face, a conversation with a younger mind. But the tour did not include a chance to chat with any of them. Neither did it encompass any part of the old house, which was a great disappointment to Lydia. The manager explained that it held only the offices, staff accommodation and a few larger rooms, reserved for couples. When they passed a corridor into that original Longlands, Lydia could see it was entirely painted white with all the old doors and their frames replaced by the mandatory fire-resistant variety. Perhaps she had lost nothing by being excluded. After what she calculated was a suitable amount of interest, Lydia asked if she might see the gardens, as her aunt was particularly fond of flowers and sitting out whenever possible.

'Could I have a little while to walk around, try and get the real feel of the place?'

'Oh yes, of course. There's not much to see, I'm afraid. It all takes so much to keep up that we don't have a regular gardener anymore, just someone who comes in to cut the grass and keep it tidy.'

'I'm sure that it will be fine. I'm quite happy to spend a few minutes out there on my own, I'm sure you must have things to be doing.'

'Well, I do have a phone call to make, if you're quite sure. Let me show you out. I'll need to collect you in a few minutes, the security locks won't let you back in again without your necklace.'

Celia Barnard indicated a little tube on a loop of cord round her neck. 'These let you back in to the building without the need to press buttons.'

And, thought Lydia, are probably a very handy way to keep track of exactly who is exactly where. This was a new surveillance method since her grandmother's time.

When she was a little distance from the house, Lydia looked around to see if she was being watched before pulling the folded copy of the *Longlands 1911* photograph from her bag. From the lawn at the back of the house there was no mistaking it, she was standing maybe twenty yards from where the photographer had stood to capture the family. She adjusted her position as near as possible to align picture with reality. Then for a few moments she stood with her eyes closed, listening for family chatter and summer laughter, the bounce of tennis balls, the rustle of dresses too warm for that baking hot season. When she looked again through half closed eyes a figure was busy adjusting the window in a room on the upper floor, top left as she looked. An elderly resident? Or perhaps the maid in the picture, eternally airing Papa and Mama's bedroom. In the corner of her eye, the twins leaned towards each other, whispering of Papa and how stuffy he was about Mr Melville coming to visit unannounced. Two of the grandchildren walk hand in hand beside Mama as she points out insects busy in the flowers. A woman's voice calls for Harriet to come and taste the cool lemonade, freshly made. A tranquil scene, a family at ease with themselves, all is harmony despite the sultry heat. Another voice calls 'Hello, how're you getting on?' and the sounds and images of 1911 slip abruptly away. Celia Barnard had come to collect her visitor.

★

The trip to Bocking had been most rewarding. Despite the fact that it hadn't advanced her quest by a single inch, Lydia had found a real connection to her subjects. Prior to those few minutes in the garden at Longlands she had begun to doubt if anything that she was doing was more than a mental exercise with no place in the real world at all. And she had also begun to feel confined, chained to her desk for want of a concrete action to take. Now back at that desk with her senses sharpened, her next idea was to try to fill in a little of the background to the journal's author. She had read his employer as 'Pink on Pink' but whatever word she might place between the Pinks, it still amounted to a strange name. But a jingle writer, a blurb writer, would be working in advertising, in the media, and such companies often went by the strangest of names, designed to draw attention. Perhaps, Lydia thought, like the coded initials, 'Pink on Pink' was not the real name but his slang, his code for them. If so, then why not 'P P' or 'P on P' or even just 'P' which would have been more consistent with his way of writing? No, 'Pink on Pink' held within it some significance to the writer, not met by using simply initials.

Her first searches of web sites produced little encouragement. 'Pink on Pink' brought her ninety-nine thousand results, other combinations brought several hundred thousand more. Predictably, a high percentage appeared to concern girls and clothing. Lydia was also a little shocked to find that many had a sexual undertone, and the word 'lesbian' appeared more than once. She quickly qualified the query with 'advertising'. This severely reduced the results to a few hundred, as did using the word 'media' instead of 'advertising'. But even though she carefully scanned anything that looked promising, nothing of any value emerged. Most likely, she thought, if there ever had been such a company, it had long since been dissolved or renamed. If she were to follow this any further, what she really needed was a directory of businesses for the 1980's. But for what area? She was familiar with finding old trade directories for a hundred years ago, but not for modern times. She searched again, and yes, there were dozens of trade directories covering every town in the country, but apart from the ones people had neglected to update, they were all for the present or the more distant past. Quite reasonably, there were none for the dates she was interested in.

The question of where the journal writer had lived re-surfaced in her mind. Cumbria had been a long drive, an overnight stay. To go on holiday to France had been another long drive but doable in a day. So somewhere in the south of England pleased her sense of probability. Essex would fit well enough, as would anywhere in the south-east. He'd lived close enough to be able to walk to the unnamed river. Unnamed because to him it needed no name. There was a park nearby and convenient shops. It could fit a hundred or more towns. But not a village, no, it was an urban area. There was nothing to prompt her closer than that. Except that the journal had been sold to her in an Eynsham sale room. Where better to start a search than right there on her doorstep. And what she did have access to, thanks to the world's unquenchable thirst for information, were some of the old telephone directories, scanned and made available to her right there in her back room in West Street. She started with 1980 because it felt right, no science to the choice, just her sense for the possible and the probable. Oxford Area September 1980 could not be any closer. Page 477 Pilling to Pitcher contained the Pinks. There jumping right out at the top of the list was the entry *'Pink 2, Adv. Agts, Seacourt Tower . . . . .Oxford 402291'*. A direct hit in one try? Well, she was certainly due a little luck. And why not Oxford, the choice was not random, and the chances of getting a hit from a random list would have been very great. This was a good omen. And when she looked further, the latest available was for 1982. Sure enough, Pink 2 were still there, still in the tower, less than a mile from where she sat. It remained a hideous building whose only nod to Oxford's classic skyline was the addition of a steel pylon to top out the roof. For this reason it was sometimes referred to with a certain irony as Botley Cathedral.

If the tormented author lived in Oxford, then so too did his wife, and H and J. In itself this was not hugely significant, they had to live somewhere, so why not Oxford. But it if she were to find a little more concrete evidence then some lines of enquiry might be undertaken far more easily right there on her doorstep than at even a modest distance. Popping in to the local library, newspaper office, or even the record office could be done in a lunchtime and would not involve planned expeditions, too much cost or tedious correspondence. Should she need to, it would also give her the chance to browse for some event, when she did not know exactly what she was looking for.

Lydia knew very well that, pleased with herself as she was, all she had done was take the seemingly obscure reference to '*Pink on Pink*' and make a tentative link to another name. Simply finding the name of a company that fitted, at least to her own satisfaction, a reference to the author's employer amounted to nothing at all in the larger scheme of things. As with her visit to Longlands, it advanced her enquiry hardly a jot. But, taken together with the Oxford link, it gave her encouragement to continue, and in her own mind it all fitted. She was lining up the possibilities so that when a sufficient number of them were all neatly arranged in a row, the whole became a probability. Any one of them could be wrong, they could all be wrong, but it seemed highly improbable that all those wrong things would come together and still fit the picture she was building.

With these small progressions, and being overdue a little leave from work, Lydia resolved on her next course of action. Even as she considered it and sketched the outlines of her trip, she smiled at the prospect of explaining herself to her colleagues in the office. What she was going to do was on the edge of ridiculous, and to say it out loud would make it even more so. She was going to Cockermouth to see if she could find a grave, the one that the journal writer and his wife had stood beside, watching the earth rattle down onto the coffin lid. She would make a list of all the graveyards near the town centre, map them all out and plan a day's tour of them all. The priority would be church burial grounds since the journal specifically mentioned a church and a burial. The reference had been in the earlier and, dare she say it, saner, part of the journal. The writer had been quite specific, and no attempt had been made to obscure the name of the place with a cryptic reference. It was the one solid event in which she could put any faith. All this she would do while staying in a modest country hotel she would find nearby, and from there perhaps she could also do a little walking, a little exploration, once her detective work was done. She would take the whole week as leave and stay for as many days as she wished, recharging her batteries. She might even find time for a little reflection on precisely where she was in her life, and what she might do with it between then and the care home that Gloria had predicted for her.

5

There is nothing at all to commend the drive north from Oxford and Lydia was tired, relieved to leave the incessant traffic behind her by the time she turned west at Penrith. From there it was not far to Keswick, where again she would turn from the well-trodden route to climb through the Winlatter pass and head cross-country to her destination. All this was courtesy of the route planner from which she had printed a detailed itinerary. The little hotel near Loweswater had been chosen with considerable care, although in truth the selection hadn't been that inspiring. It was small and family run, but offered all she thought she might need. Cockermouth would be just a short drive away and, when she was not looking for graves, there was the spectacular countryside where she would take a few walks, perhaps even read a little. If the weather held out as it was forecast to do, she might even consider a picnic lunch or two. In case of rain there were the scattering of pubs in the villages around. All in all, it was a break she had looked forward to from the moment that she had decided upon it. Now she was nearly there, the landscape unfolded before her and mile by mile she could feel the little tensions of her life slipping from her.

As she passed Keswick, cloud gathered in the west ahead of her, the first change from the hazy sun that had accompanied her from Oxford. Climbing steadily through the darkening forest, the thickening mist began to leave drops of moisture on the windscreen. A flicker of concern passed over her, the first real worry she'd had over her hare-brained scheme. The evergreen gloom of the trees closed round her, full of the demons of doubt. Then, as the impossible notion of turning and running straight home crept into the corner of her mind, the descent began. After another mile, a bend in the road revealed a glimpse of distant sunshine through clear air. A few minutes later she stopped to check her notes of the journey, just to be sure that she was on the right road. She took the opportunity to step out of the car and stretch her legs a few steps, taking in the massive scale of the hills rising around her, relishing the prospect of the week ahead. Her confidence restored, the fears of the dank forest were forgotten as quickly as they had arisen. A few miles further and she was hugging the shore of Loweswater, then she swung the Nissan to the right, into the drive of the hotel, black timbers and white walls through the screen of trees, exactly as she remembered from the photos on the web site. The original house had been added to over the years and the result was something of a mish-mash, unified by the black and white paint. Only two other cars were parked by the entrance as if to confirm, as she had hoped, that there would be few holiday-makers so late in the season. A collie with colours to match the hotel came wagging round to greet her as she took her bags from the car. A call from the hotel owner's son sent it scurrying away as he came out to meet her and exchange pleasantries about the journey, the weather and the prospects for the week.

The Water End Country Hotel met Lydia's requirements exactly. It was comfortable in a somewhat faded way, friendly without intrusion, had a small dining room and even smaller bar, but a big welcoming drawing room with large old-fashioned sofas, a few shelves of books and a writing table. She'd ordered an evening meal for her arrival, and after a little freshening up, chose to walk in the neat gardens, contemplating her stay between sips of an expensive glass of inexpensive red wine. In part her plans depended on the weather, but in essence she intended to complete her checking of graveyards before any other recreation. She'd not much idea of how long it would take her, even though it seemed that there may be very few burial grounds within the area she had decided upon.

There was no point in leaving her search for eighty-something year-old spinsters who were buried in the 1980's and might have a first name beginning with B, until the last day. The very thought of what she had embarked upon struck her as faintly ridiculous even as she stood on the threshold of doing it. Having deemed it unnecessary to mention the details to anyone, she was determined that it would remain as her private secret, at the very least until she had answered her own questions. Perhaps then, success or no success, she would be able to laugh at her own foolishness. To all enquiries she had answered quite truthfully that she simply fancied a break in the Lakes.

The following day dawned as fair as had been promised. An indulgent breakfast, a hotel breakfast, far bigger than anything she would have prepared for herself, was tucked away as an insurance against missing lunch. Then through the lanes to Cockermouth where, armed with a town map from an estate agent's office, Lydia set about her task. She had identified seven possible churches and two local authority cemeteries as prime targets, but she well knew that her list might not include all the possible sites. Many churches had closed in the last twenty years and these might not be so easily referenced by the simple web search that she had done. So, to her nine identified sites Lydia would add anything of interest that she might find as she walked the streets of Cockermouth or the villages of the immediate area.

It was easy to become distracted from her purpose, looking and listening to the Saturday morning bustle of the little town. Walking down the rather prosaically named Main Street, her mind wandered to the journal and the words describing the visit by its unknown author. *'A tiny room with cold beds, cold at the height of summer, at the back of the hotel where the sun never shines and the damp of winter lingers until autumn.'* Passed the Globe, the Wordsworth and The Fletcher Christian she wondered if he could have been referring to any of those places, if he had walked down that very same pavement, walking beside S, a hand half looking for hers. Or the Trout, surely too upmarket to be described in that way, but then again, perhaps more than twenty years ago it had been much less than it appeared now. Lydia quickly reminded herself that the journal was only one side of the story, and a very peculiar side at that. And then another thought struck her, one that she would need to check when she was back at the hotel with her precious laptop. Did the journal not also add at that point something about leaving the churchyard and walking round the streets where B had lived, where S had spent holidays as a child? Why had she only just thought of this, when it surely meant that her search would be a short one, and that if anything was to come of her quest then the answer most likely lay within a mile or so of the place where she stood.

Just as she had anticipated, she was quickly able to cross off the United Reform Church and St. Joseph's, both without any sign of a burial ground. At Christchurch Lydia found even less encouragement. Not a single gravestone, or sign of there ever having been a burial in its mainly tarmaced grounds. Resting for a moment in the entrance Lydia questioned her criteria and her sanity. At this rate her search would be over by Sunday evening without a single name to which she could attach the slightest hope. From Christchurch she walked along South Street towards All Saints, up Lorton Street to take in the equally barren Methodist chapel, then wound round to Kirkgate. The Friends Meeting House was also grave-free, as she had expected, but at last she saw gravestones in the churchyard of All Saints. It took no more than a minute to realise that nobody had been buried there in modern times. So much for a short search, so much for relying on the journal in every detail. The dark thought that none of it might be accurate, the whole concoction might be pure fiction, re-entered her head. She fought back the thought. Had she not already found the evidence that it was real? No, she must simply interpret what might be a way of speaking, from that which might be used as evidence to investigate. Nonetheless, her journey was becoming more foolish with every moment that passed. The picture that Lydia had drawn from the words of the journal was clearly wrong. There was no churchyard that fitted the description that she had worked from. For a few moments she stood undecided about what to do next, the disappointment hanging heavily around her. Yes, she had other paces to visit, she had a list of them already made, but in her mind's eye they were not supposed to be needed, she was supposed to have found the elusive 'B' in a churchyard right there in Cockermouth.

The drive to the cemetery in Lorton Road was shorter than she'd imagined, and she was surprised to discover it was really a part of the town, not separate, as she had supposed. Two things struck her immediately upon entering; the driveway was a gorgeous blaze of colour from the late summer flowers, and, more relevant to her mission, that this was a large cemetery which more than compensated for the scarcity of burials in the town. There seemed to be miles of pathways through the carefully tended grounds, and so many inscriptions to study that from being depressed at the absence of information, Lydia became equally despondent at the size of the task before her. But this was what she had come for, this was exactly what she wanted to find, even if it was not a churchyard. To allay that thought, right in front of her were twin chapels, one either side of the arch. One of these might easily be referred to as a church and this cemetery as the churchyard. Even if it was a stretch too far, the thought consoled her. She set about her task, methodically walking each path, looking in vain for a name and dates that met her criteria.

After half an hour or so there was a single entry written on her notepad: '*Beatrice Alexandra Grant 1902 – 1984*'. Unfortunately, also written on the page was the additional note '*and her husband!*' She had added this comment as a reminder of her own folly. Lydia sat to rest awhile, and to contemplate her task, to question if it was even the right task. It had seemed so much the right thing to do, and she remembered it was the only real line of enquiry left open to her, all else had failed. If she widened the date range and made allowance for 'in her eighties' to mean between, say, seventy-five and ninety-five, and then also allowed 'spinster' to mean 'widowed a long time', it would certainly net some extra names. But then again perhaps it would be better to keep the spinster aspect and ignore the need for a first name that started with B. She sat a little longer, taking in the deep sense of peace and tranquillity that pervaded the place. Changing the criteria would mean that she must re-visit the paths already travelled. She smiled to herself at the thought that at least there was only one part of one cemetery that would need revisiting.

The pause and the rest served her well. She turned over the whole investigation in her mind, reasoning with herself, re-assembling her arguments and evidence that were in such disarray before she'd found that spot overlooking the bubbling stream below. Around her the unmistakeable tints of autumn had started to creep across the trees, the smell of the earth hung in the air. A place of stillness, a place to weigh and consider. Perhaps the journal writer had written in cipher after all, perhaps he had simply misremembered the name of the town where he had driven so far to go to a funeral, perhaps, perhaps. It was all perhaps. But if memory served her right, the journal was quite sane at the point of the funeral entry, the writer had not only driven there but also booked a hotel, and his wife had spoken of childhood holidays spent there. She and her husband might have stayed in Cockermouth, walked round the streets where she holidayed with her 'B', but they could quite easily have attended a funeral somewhere else, somewhere beyond the confines of her arbitrary search area. And there were other places yet to be visited. The afternoon had worn on and Lydia was tired, her legs aching from unaccustomed walking. She decided on a new tack; all her research had been done via her laptop, but this was not a virtual world in which she stood, this was the real world. With her slightly revised criteria she would make one more visit today, to Brigham. But first she would walk back into the town and purchase a proper detailed map that she would put to good use later.

The parish church of St Bridget's was easy enough to find, and no more than a few minutes drive. Now that she had revised the supposed events of the day of the funeral, it fitted quite easily into the picture, and Lydia's spirits rose as she wandered round the overgrown graves in the churchyard. For the most part they were far too old to be of relevance and there seemed to be little order to them. Tucked in a corner down a slope she found some more recent burials, but none that came close to adding to her list of one. In the warmth of the late afternoon sun her chosen task was pleasant enough now that she had freed herself of doubt, now she began to sink into the feeling of place, of lives long passed. Right next to the churchyard, almost as an extension to it, was a newer municipal burial ground. Before she walked the neat rows with their polished headstones, Lydia sat in the cool shade of a beech. Her eye was taken by the line of the grass cuts to the row of cypress with St Bridget's tower peeking above them. Somewhere to her right in an unseen field beyond the stone wall, the bleating of sheep floated above the distant hum of traffic on the main road.

By the time all the inscriptions had been inspected Lydia was content to find that she had no less than three additional names in her notepad. '*Beryl Jane Poulton 1903-1978 Beloved Wife and Mother, Much Missed*' satisfied the 'B' and the extended dates if not the spinster element, as did '*Brenda Simpson 1906-1986 wife of Michael Simpson 1904-1988 who also lies here*'. She was careful to make a note of not just names and dates, but the whole inscription, knowing it would be of value later. Of more interest was the simple dedication '*Betty Ann Garth 1902-1982*', although in the absence of any additional information, there was nothing to indicate spinster, wife or widow.

After her evening meal she took advantage of the empty drawing room and spread out her new map. She had not studied one with such detail since she had been at school and had paid it little attention then. Now she needed to re-acquaint herself with the scale and the symbols, to understand the differences between contour lines and paths, between power lines and railways. With her notepad beside her, she slowly worked outwards from the centre of Cockermouth, marking the map and writing the details in her notepad. Each symbol for a church or a cemetery acquired a circle and a number on the map, each number was listed together with the location. Deep in concentration she'd been unaware of another guest entering the room.

'Are you looking for something in particular?'

Lydia's head shot up and she looked directly into the face, into the dark grey eyes of a man.

'No. I mean yes. Well not really, just places to visit.' She was flustered, caught off guard.

His eyes did not leave hers as he smiled a warm and open smile. 'I would be happy to help if you should need any. I'm not a native but I have some knowledge of the area.'

'No. I mean, no thank you.' For no reason that she could think of she felt the colour flood her cheeks and the more she felt it the hotter they became. 'I mean that's kind of you, thank you, just a little project that I have, that's all.' Suddenly she felt like a schoolgirl again, awkward and inexperienced in speaking to an older man. And he was, she thought, a much older man, perhaps twenty years her senior, although in her confusion she could not be sure.

He took her embarrassed rejection of his offer with ease, simply adding that should she change her mind she should feel free to speak to him. 'Free to speak to him?' What an odd way to put it, Lydia thought afterwards, surely most people would have said 'feel free to ask', or more likely simply closed the conversation.

He settled himself in the corner of one of the sofas and opened a book. Lydia had almost completed her list of places to visit but she pretended to study the map a little longer than was strictly necessary. It gave her the opportunity to glance sideways at the stranger, to gain a better impression of him. He appeared completely relaxed, sunk into his book. It seemed to be a novel, or rather, it was a paperback and she assumed it was a novel. Although she would never have openly admitted it, Lydia realised that she was checking to see if he was actually reading and not just sitting there secretly studying her. But his eyes flickered over the print and he turned a page at regular intervals, his interest in her apparently at an end. After a few minutes, shame got the better of her and she went out into the garden to catch the last of the evening. She was satisfied with the improvement to the plan that she'd left Oxford with, but disconcerted by her childish reaction to a casual exchange of words with a stranger. She felt quite odd, but did not recognise the oddness nor see any reason for it.

After a more modest breakfast on Sunday, Lydia checked her route one more time before heading to Lamplugh on the first leg of her zigzagging journey through the rolling countryside west of the fells. Again the sun shone on her throughout the day as she travelled through the little villages scattered across the landscape. On several occasions she found no need to stop as she passed a chapel that was no longer a chapel. Her greater wonder was that so many of these out-of-the-way buildings were still used for their original purpose. At Bridekirk she thought better of wandering the churchyard while a service was in progress and postponed her visit in favour of Great Broughton where the smell of the coal-field hung in the breeze. She paused a while to watch the bubbling Derwent, clear and swift beneath the bridge at Isel, and was blessed by a glimpse of a kingfisher as it flashed under the arches. From there it was but a few yards walk to the tiny St. Michael and All Angels, as peaceful a place as was imaginable, and likely had been for a thousand years or more. An inscription in the perfectly groomed churchyard of St Philip's, parish church of Mosser, caught her eye. It wasn't relevant to her search but seemed worthy of anyone's attention. *'In Loving Memory of A Dearly Loved Lady ENID MAUREEN McLEAN'*. What a lucky woman, Lydia thought, to have such a memorial. Who could want for more than that?

There wasn't a single place where Lydia stopped that she didn't meet a friendly face and a friendly word. Most enquired if she was 'doing her family history', to which she replied that, yes, it was something like that, and they would fall in to brief conversation about such-and-such a name or family. Recollections of a Norwegian wedding, the number of parishes with woman priests, the tidiness or otherwise of the churchyard; these subjects and many more were touched upon. At Lorton a biker, leather-clad with helmet beneath his arm, stood alone and silently wept, lost in memories of a loved one who lay at his feet and oblivious to any other person. Having approached more closely than she might have otherwise done, Lydia saw his grief and slipped away as unobtrusively as she could. Curiosity as to whether it was mother, wife or child that brought him to that place went unsatisfied, for she could not bring herself to go back and look at the grave to hazard a guess. It was a public place but the tears were private.

Lydia drove back to her hotel tired but content with her day. The notebook at last had some entries in it, even if some were unlikely. It had been all too easy to lose the focus of her quest in the tranquillity of the hidden places she'd visited, but she'd changed from being driven to being relaxed, enjoying the task and all it had brought. And now she had a clear plan to complete her search. The Lorton Road cemetery she would leave until last, now she knew exactly the extent of the work involved there. It would not be difficult, just lengthy and she would need to concentrate on the job in hand and not get sucked in to reading every word etched on the stones. She'd leave Lorton Road until Tuesday or allowing for poor weather, the next reasonably fine day. For Monday, Lydia had decided that she would explore the last of her churchyards, the one at St Bartholomew's, just down the road at the other end of Loweswater. She would make a visit there as part of a gentle stroll right round the lake, treating herself to lunch at the village inn en-route. For two days running she had missed lunch altogether, although she'd had the benefit of a full English to keep her going. Monday would be almost a rest day, a day of holiday, one she felt she could afford now that she had a better picture of the remaining work in her search for 'B'.

As she exchanged a few words with the hotel owner, the man with grey eyes also returned.

'Have you met Stephen Kellaway?' she said, introducing him. 'This is Lydia Silverstream. Stephen is one of our regulars, how many years is it now? Ten or more I should think.'

'We met briefly last night,' he smiled, holding out a hand.

Lydia might have smiled back but she could not remember. Again she felt the tingle in her cheeks as their hands met. His were big and dry and warm, hers suddenly small and clammy. 'I must get on, get myself changed before dinner', she blustered and turned away to scuttle up the stairs to her room, leaving Stephen and the proprietor to their reminiscences.

The bath that she ran was plenty deep enough but as she settled in, it felt too narrow to stay for an enjoyable soak. Could it be that she was too wide, rather than the bath too narrow? Lydia pondered that unwelcome thought for a few moments, contemplating the excess inches that she carried on her hips. No, she was sure it was the bath at fault in this case, even allowing for the inches. And they were her inches, nobody else's to see or criticise. Like her hair and the absence of make-up, the inches were another line of defence, a reason for nobody to take any interest, and without interest there was no need for any reaction to that interest. She might as well be a spinster herself, like the elusive 'B'.

It struck her how difficult it had been to find any memorials to aged spinsters, never mind ones which fitted the description she was working from. '*Loving Mother*', '*Sadly Missed Nan*', '*Beloved Wife*' and their like were everywhere. '*Beautiful Daughter*' was predictably reserved for the young. How unfair life was, even the wrinkled and decrepit had been somebody's beautiful daughter at one time. Maybe the aged spinsters had no-one to bury them, no one to compose a loving thought for their headstone. A simple plaque might be the best that could be expected, quickly overgrown with grass. B's grave might never have been marked, an idea Lydia had all along sought to suppress. Was that how it would be when her own time came, an unmarked grave or scattered ashes, with no one to remember her as '*A Dearly Loved Lady*'? Lydia regarded the prospect briefly, not wholly with indifference. If she survived her brother, then who would there be to bury her with anything like interest, not to mention affection or loss. There was no sister, no parent, her nieces were growing distant, and certainly there was no man. Which brought her back to Stephen Kellaway and the unsettling effect that he had had on her.

*

After a leisurely start to the day, and a little less breakfast than previously, Lydia set off with her already familiar new map and her notepad stuffed in her bag, along with a little fold-up umbrella. As she emerged from the drive, Stephen Kellaway appeared from the path to her right.

'Good morning. How are you this morning?'

'Oh, hello Mr Kellaway,' Lydia began with a little more confidence than the previous evening.

'If it's all right with you, please call me Stephen.'

This put Lydia back in her unsettled state. She had half surprised herself by remembering his surname, and thought she'd taken control by using it with assurance.

'Stephen, yes. I am well thank you,' and thinking it only polite to add her own enquiry, 'and you, Mr Kel . . , er, Stephen, have you been out walking already?'

'Just a few steps up the hill. I'm just popping back to my room to collect my backpack and then I intend to walk round the water down to the village. And you, are you headed far?'

Lydia's heart did an uncomfortable somersault as it tried to be both excited at the prospect of this man's company and deflated at losing the planned solitude of the walk. The result was Lydia swallowing hard, thinking of lying, thinking of changing her plans, thinking of waiting for him or walking quickly so that he would not catch up. But 'Oh' was all that she managed to actually say.

'Enjoy your walk, we may see each other later,' and with that he was walking away up the drive to the hotel entrance, patting the black and white collie on the way.

Momentarily paralysed, she stood staring after him before she gathered her thoughts and set off along the farm track opposite the drive. After a short time it began to climb steeply, seemingly taking her away from the lake. The gradient clawed at the backs of her legs and doubting her route, she stopped to check the map. From her higher vantage point she could see the expanse of the lake before her, cupped between Burnbank and Darling Fells, fringed with woodland. She could not resist a look back to the hotel where a figure she knew to be Stephen Kellaway was walking down the drive. Would she wait until he caught up with her or walk on? In either case he would certainly be faster than she would be. She waited a little longer to check his route. He was not following her, he was taking the opposite way round, taking the road to the village. And again there were conflicting sensations in her chest. Relief and disappointment combined into one unfamiliar feeling.

Once through the farmyard at the crest of the rise, the stony path descended as steeply as it had risen, back down towards the lake and the cool Holme Wood that borders its western side. Then she was walking on the flat, her view of the water again obscured by the hedgerows. It was easy going and, under the brightest of blue skies, Lydia began to relish the day ahead. Lunch at the village inn had been recommended, the walk was relaxing, the scenery spectacular. And there was the possible bonus of adding to her list of candidates for 'B'. Not that she really held out much hope, Loweswater was right on the outer edge of her area, and if she'd not been staying so close by, then most likely she wouldn't have included it. But it was only a twenty minute drive to Cockermouth, so not entirely out of the question. These thoughts were running through her mind when a voice from close behind interrupted them.

'Hello, again.'

Startled, Lydia turned, knowing before she did so that only one person in the world could use that phrase to her this morning. Stephen was about ten yards away, emerging from a little-used path between two bushes.

'Oh, hello. I thought you might have gone a different way.' The sensation in her chest was more muted this time.

'No, I have always preferred the anti-clockwise route, don't know why, just seems more natural. Which is a little silly, as whichever way you go the sights and sounds are very much the same.'

'It's just that I thought I saw you on the road.' Lydia did not want to give him the idea that she might have actually watched him.

'Little path across the fields. Strictly speaking not a public path, and it can get rather wet underfoot close to the water. It just means that you don't climb up to the farm and then down again.'

They had both stopped walking and stood right at the very edge of the wood. Lydia was sure that if she set off again then he would accompany her, but if she stayed where she was then he might just go on without her.

As if to read her mind Stephen said, 'I'm sure that you planned to walk alone today, as had I, so if you like, I will head off. But if you would like some company then we could continue together. I certainly would not be offended if you were to choose to walk alone.'

His direct manner of speaking, delivered in his soft and even voice left her both disarmed and confused. He had a way of leaving doors wide open when he finished speaking. Now she had a choice to make. How long since someone offered her even such a trivial choice as this. If she waited and said nothing he would walk on alone, if she said yes, let's walk together, would he take it the wrong way? If she said no, she preferred her solitude, would it be true?

'That's ok, I do completely understand,' he said as she dithered, and made to leave her side.

'No, it would be fine to have some company, it would be nice,' and then as if to cement her decision she added, 'thank you, Stephen.'

So they walked through the woods together, she at first full of anxiety that she could think of nothing to say while he strolled easily beside her, or in front or behind according to the width of the path. After a mile or so she grew more comfortable with silence, so that when they stopped to enjoy their surroundings at a little pebble beach she was almost at ease with herself. Stephen tossed a few pebbles into the lake, skimming them and counting the bounces, saying how he could never resist the temptation of rekindling childhood memories. He pointed out a farmhouse high above on the opposite side of the lake, telling her how that house had looked upon the water for more than four hundred years, and asking how that made one think, did it not? Which chimed immediately with Lydia's own sense of history and place, though it made her think less about the house and the four hundred years than it did of this easy-going stranger she found herself with.

It took well over an hour for them to complete the first half of the walk. While Stephen collected a menu for lunch and bought some drinks, Lydia sat at a table in the pub garden. She was enjoying the day, the change of scene, and even the company. She had almost forgotten that she had a little work to do in St. Bartholomew's churchyard and wondered how best to explain without going into detail. But whereas before her walk she would have fretted over revealing her ridiculous enterprise, now it did not disturb her. If it all came out then so what? It struck her that neither Stephen nor she had indulged in any of the small talk usually associated with such casual acquaintance, no questions of occupation or age or children and certainly not of marriage, no urgent need to find common ground to enhance conversation. In fact they had spoken little, and after her initial anxiety it had been a companionable silence, a silence that did not cry out to be broken. Which did not mean that Lydia was not curious about this languid man, she most certainly was, but there seemed no urgency in discovery.

'Shall we have the time-honoured argument over who pays for lunch, Lydia?'

'No, Stephen, we will not. I will pay for mine, and you will pay for yours,' she replied, a little more firmly than she had meant. She had been ready for his offer to pay, but not in the way that he had done so.

'Fair enough, Dutch it is. Quite right too.'

Lydia rummaged in her bag and passed him a note while he found some coins to give her the exact change. While this was precisely what she had said, it left her a little uncomfortable. She had expected him to counter with at least an 'Are you sure?', instead of which he had simply agreed and that was the end of the matter.

'Will you take the walk straight back?' she said, somehow needing to approach the question of her graveyard detour.

'Probably sit here for a bit, and then, yes, a gentle stroll back. There's a path down by the water for much of the way, although the road is fairly quiet. Did you have something else in mind?'

'Well, I would like to spend a while at the church.'

'Religion or architecture? Or maybe both?'

'Oh no, not religion, I'm not religious. No offence to you, if you are, I mean.' Again she had been wrong footed by his directness and by her own perverse wish to keep her motive secret.

'Nor me, so no offence.' He said it with a weariness that hinted of faith lost, rather than faith never held. 'I might join you, if you don't mind. In all these years I have never been inside the place.'

'No, no, that would be fine, er, nice.'

Now there would be no getting away from it, she could hardly walk round the churchyard studying the memorials, maybe noting some down, then not go in the church itself, without offering some explanation as to what she was doing. And if she lied or told half the truth, then that would only invite another question and another lie.

It was no more than a few steps from the Kirkstile Inn to St Bartholomew's and whatever she might find it would not take long. Modern graves had been placed in a small extension to the main area and for the most part they were arranged in chronological order. A matter of minutes Lydia imagined. While she started her inspection, Stephen tried the door of the church, but it was locked. By the time he had wandered round the exterior without finding anything to take his interest, Lydia was almost done. One name had been noted, one that she was feeling quietly optimistic about. '*Beatrice Jinifer Wright, 1903-1984, Benefactor of this Place, Much Loved and Much Missed Friend*'. To Lydia's mind it was as near as any inscription she'd read had come to saying 'spinster'. And everything else worked beautifully, not that she allowed herself to get carried away and think that this Beatrice must be the one she was looking for.

Stephen rejoined her as she was approaching the gate.

'Well, not much of interest here, at least not for the casual observer,' he suggested.

'Nothing in the church to draw the eye?'

'Locked. And you, did anything draw your eye?'

'Yes, well maybe. Something of interest, but it might be nothing.'

'Not a wasted trip then.'

'No, not wasted, and even if there had been nothing at all, it wouldn't have felt wasted.'

'Indeed not. Apart from what you are doing with your notepad, you are also here to enjoy the place, so no, not wasted.'

So, thought Lydia, he is not going to ask me what I am up to, he's probably just not that interested, no curiosity in him. But as soon as the thought came, so she took it back. Perhaps his apparent lack of interest might be simply reserve, an old-fashioned politeness, a reluctance to go where he was not invited. Her story, the whole reason for her being there, was entirely contained within her head, wavering daily from conviction to far-fetched fantasy. Inviting him to share that story would not make it any less than it already was, he could only laugh. Not that he was likely to, far too polite. Maybe too considerate also. If he thought her foolish, saw huge flaws in her theories, he was after all just a stranger she happened to have met and would never see again. To share it with another, put her ideas and logic into words, that would also test it out for herself, would it not?

'Have you ever had any interest in genealogy, family history and the like?' she ventured as they climbed up from the village.

'No, it's not really something I've ever considered. I have an interest in history, or rather the sense of history in places, in events in ordinary people's lives. I suppose that would touch on family history, or do you mean strictly the 'who begat who'?

'I wondered because of the way you spoke about that house this morning, and your interest in the church. And yes, 'who begat who' is a part of it, but there's a lot more to it than that.'

'Well, the church was no more than idle curiosity I'm afraid, something to fill a few minutes while you were busy with your notepad. I had rather assumed that you were looking for an ancestor.'

If Lydia was going to tell him her story, she would not have a better opening than this.

'An ancestor, yes, but not one of mine. And funny you should say that because the person I am looking may not have been anyone's ancestor.'

'Curiouser and curiouser. Will you tell me about it?'

Just below the house he had pointed out in the morning they paused by a gate. Between them and the lake an emerald pasture sloped gently to the water's edge. A half dozen horses grazed, the sound of their cropping the grass drifting on the breeze to the two observers.

'It's a long story.'

'We have the afternoon, will that be long enough?'

So, almost to her surprise, Lydia told the story of the box of albums, of how she came to have them, what she would do with them. She told of her investigations, the frustrations, the visit to Longlands. She told him about the journal, about the feeling of intruding in something private. She even told him of her suspicions of the unknown outcome, and of how she came to be walking down a lane in Cumbria telling a perfect stranger about her foolish obsession. Not everything came out in the exact sequence it had happened, and she could not instantly recall every detail or tally of the abortive census searches. But the few items that she was fairly sure about, the Myers family, Longlands, Cockermouth, Pink2, she related in detail. She had finished her tale before she remembered the postcards, unconnected to anything else she could find and yet a real physical link between the places of the story, between Braintree, Cumbria and Oxford. And while she spoke, Lydia had a growing belief in her story, the more she put it into words the less ridiculous and fanciful it felt. It was the first time that she had assembled and recited the whole thing, even though she had picked over the detail endlessly in her head, and it was plausible, her box of albums could all be linked, they could be different parts of one whole. Stephen appeared to listen intently throughout, once or twice interrupting her to clarify a particular point.

The little hotel was in sight by the time Lydia fell silent. They walked on another dozen steps before Stephen observed, 'Well, that's quite a puzzle you have set yourself. But a fascinating one, nonetheless.'

'To be honest, you are the only person I've told. I think I've used you as a sounding board, to try it all out in words and see if they made sense.'

'And now that you have, what do you think of it all?'

'I feel ok about it. It sounded better than I thought it might. It doesn't seem completely foolish now.'

'I will take that as a compliment, that you risked looking foolish by telling me. But tell me, why do you think that the journal is real? I mean, that its contents are not fiction?'

'Oh did I not say? If it is fiction then it is a most elaborate hoax or an amazing coincidence. First, I was, well, pushed in that direction, not by the words so much as their physical appearance. The writing varies enormously and in places the sheer anger of the words is right there, etched into the paper where the writer pressed so hard. And there are sections that I can't make out at all, so scrawled is the writing. I think that no fiction would be written like that, even if it were a draft or something like that.'

'Ok, I can accept that, it's a good conclusion. Or at least, a reasonable inference that you take from the evidence.' He spoke with mock formality, as if correcting a junior, but his open smile told Lydia that he was mocking himself not her.

'No, there's more. There's the little bits of paper that fluttered out of the pages,' Lydia was back into her stride again. 'Near the end there is a passage about how he has written a plan and a list in a notepad and to keep it secret he has torn the pages off and destroyed them once he is sure he has it memorised. Look.' Lydia took her notepad from her bag and turning to an unused page near the end, ripped it from its spiral binding. 'See, there are little pieces that fall away as you do that. Well, right there at that page in the journal, right in the binding, there were little fragments like that.' She offered a few specks of paper to him in the palm of her hand.

'I like that, that's very good. You have a passion for this. I like that too. I'm convinced, even though I haven't seen this journal. From all that I hear, I agree with you. And what have you to lose anyway? You will either prove your theory and have a most satisfying outcome, or you will not, which may be unsatisfactory, but you will have had much pleasure in trying. Surely that is far from foolish? And if I may offer some advice from my own experience, then it would be that not every puzzle has a solution that can be found, too many of the pieces have been lost or rotted away, for anyone to discover the truth. Sometimes we can only throw a little light on one tiny part of the whole.'

'I know, and as you say, much of the pleasure is in the trying. But you sound as if you know something about puzzles like this. Have you done something similar?'

'Well,' began Stephen a little sheepishly, 'my life has been full of puzzles for many years, because you see I am, or was, an archaeologist of sorts. The proper name is forensic archaeology. These days I'm semi-retired, just do the occasional lecture, I don't get involved in the . . . er, field work.'

Lydia was a little taken aback by this revelation, even though she was not sure why. She had idly speculated that he might be an academic of some kind, maybe a mathematician by his precise manner of speaking. But to find that he was one of a select few in this lately glamorous field of investigation, a real detective as she saw him, well, that just added weight to his earlier comments about her own little project. Suddenly it did indeed seem insignificant, and she merely a clumsy amateur when put beside such knowledge and experience as he must have.

After a few moments silence she said, 'That's rather daunting, you know.'

'Yes, I can see that you might feel that way. It always has been a bit of a conversation stopper. But look at it from my point of view, I know next to nothing of the world in which you are working, and I find your puzzle fascinating. And for many people I suspect that what you are doing would also be a conversation stopper.'

'Forensic archaeologist. That would be examining bodies? Buried, murdered bodies?'

'Not always murdered, not always bodies, but always buried in one way or another. It's a lot more besides, but it's only the bodies that ever get any attention. It's really about examining very carefully anything buried to see what can be found relating to that burial. So in some small way my work has been similar to what you are doing. We can find out many facts, but it is the joining of the dots that makes the picture. Sometimes we cannot and no picture emerges. When you said about how you like to immerse yourself in the subject, to feel your way into the lives in your photograph's, I thought how lucky you were to have that opportunity and freedom to imagine. I have often felt that there are times when we lack that creative thinking when we are wrestling with a few fragments of someone's life.'

'Perhaps you don't have the time to sit about thinking, immersing, like I do.'

'Maybe we should make the time.'

Before Lydia slipped into a deep and long sleep that night, she dreamily reviewed the unexpected turn that the day had taken, enjoying a small contentment with her new friendship. It seemed to demand nothing of her, was wonderfully free of overtones or undertones, and was as refreshing as the cool drink that she had shared at lunchtime. And there was the promise of tomorrow.

*

'I see what you mean about this place being more like a park than a cemetery,' Stephen said, as they entered through the little side gate in Strawberry Howe. He had readily agreed to her invitation to join her expedition to Lorton Road and by mid-morning they were ready to begin systematic inspection. Stephen had offered to help, thinking that they could halve the time needed, but thought better of it as Lydia tried to explain the criteria that she was using.

'The thing is, Stephen, yes, I have these dates in mind and this age of person to go by, and a name that might start with B, but, well, sometimes there's something else.'

'Something not quite definable, something felt?'

'It sounds daft, very unscientific to you I'm sure, but yes, something felt.'

'And I might not have that feeling?'

'No.'

'Ok, I understand, but as we walk round and you make a note of someone because of that feeling, someone who falls outside the dates, will you tell me? I would like to know.'

The morning passed as they ambled along every path, cutting

across the grass where there was no path. For reasons that Lydia was not quite sure about, she was always careful to avoid treading directly onto the actual plots. With the handful of other visitors they exchanged only a smile and a nod, apart from one talkative woman clutching a tiny mongrel of a dog close to her chest. She was anxious to tell them how she came every day what with nothing else to do with her days now that she had buried her parents at one end of the cemetery and her husband at the other, and how John kept the place so nice that you wouldn't think it was a cemetery if it wasn't for the graves, but it was a pity she couldn't let her baby onto the ground as it wasn't allowed but it was probably for the best really, and she didn't mind that much. As rapidly as she had talked, she turned and walked away. There was a huge sadness in her desperate desire to talk to strangers, to talk to anyone probably, and they were reminded that pleasant though it was in that garden of rest, it was a place of accumulated sadness, year on year adding layer upon layer.

After a couple of hours they settled themselves on the same bench that Lydia had occupied on Saturday. She had written down just three names, Muriel Plunkett, Rhoda Senior and Doris Dickson, to go with Beatrice Grant from her previous visit. If only Beatrice did not have that annoying addition of '*and her husband*'. Her presence on the list was incomprehensible to Stephen. When he had asked if this was one of those that she had a special feeling about, Lydia had simply replied 'No, was just that her name was Beatrice.' Muriel, Rhoda and Doris were not much to show for their morning.

'I think that there were some other Dickson memorials too.'

Lydia looked at the page, then at Stephen and then back to the page. Her stomach turned to water and her chin sank to her chest.

'Something wrong, something about Doris Dickson?'

'No, not Doris. Something wrong with all of it. You see, I should have been taking a note of every memorial to them all, to Plunketts, Seniors, Dicksons and even Grants. If one of these is my missing 'B' then it would be invaluable to have other family details too. And if she isn't, then those same details could help eliminate her. I've done it all wrong, it's all wasted.'

'Well no, not wasted, with four names to look for we can speed round again and collect the extra information. You could say that we have narrowed it down and now we can refine the list.'

Lydia looked up at him, looked at his encouraging smile, and wondered if his students had been inspired to great things by him. She was his worst student, she had got this exercise wrong, easily rectified by an hour's gentle stroll, but there was more.

'Yes, Stephen we can, thank you,' she said quietly. Should she tell him the awful truth or quietly slip away tomorrow morning and leave him none the wiser?

'Something else is a problem?'

'You could say that.'

'Will you tell me? I won't tell anyone else, honestly.'

She saw his wide imploring eyes, his smile, his open hands palms up in supplication. Was he gently mocking her or himself? Either way it broke her depression.

'Yes, I'll tell you. You see, I have made the same mistake not just today, but everywhere I've been. To do it properly I must retrace my steps not just here but over half of Cumbria.'

'Ah, I see,' and then after a moment's thought he added, 'Well, you have the rest of the week and from what you have told me there are not that many names. How many places to revisit, not more than six or so? We could do that this afternoon. The cause is not lost, Lydia, just a slight adjustment and you are off and running again. You have come a long way, I think you would regret throwing it all up now.'

'No, no, I wouldn't give it up, I will go back. You're very kind, but I'm sure you would not want to traipse round with me all afternoon,' she said, but she was thinking, 'how did he know that for an instant I thought of throwing it all up?'

'It's interesting, I'm enjoying myself, I have no commitments and I'm in good company. I'll manage.'

By the time that they returned to The Water End, Lydia too was enjoying herself. She had relaxed into this amiable man's company as if she had known him for years. More than once she had found herself smiling for no particular reason. As he drove back from their last port of call at Brigham, she had reviewed her new information. Once home in Osney she would tabulate it, and then search for details of these eleven women who, by whatever route, had come to rest in Cumbrian soil. Most, she supposed would have been raised here too, but possibly not her 'B', if indeed her 'B' were amongst them. The fact was that Lydia had no great hopes that she was. The list contained a distinct shortage of plausible 'B's.

'Stephen, do you have anyone who is known by just an initial, a friend or a relative perhaps? You know, like my 'B', maybe a Dee for Deirdre?'

He thought about this for a moment. 'Well, I have a niece who her friends call Fee, any help?'

'Is that Fee for Fiona?'

'No, confusingly it's Fee for Phoebe.'

'I have a Phoebe,' Lydia quickly turned the pages in her notebook. 'Phoebe Marshall. She's at Bridekirk.'

'Is that where the ruins of the old church are?'

'Yes.'

They were on the last stretch, down into the valley, the hotel flickering into view above the hedges, when Lydia thought out loud, 'Phoebe might just as easily be called B.'

'She might, yes she might.'

'All this time I have only thought of names starting with the B sound, never of something ending with it.'

'Then it proves you were right to include everyone else, and not just the Bs.'

Lydia slid her notebook back into her bag, hugging the warm thought that she had found a real possibility for her B. Phoebe Isabella Marshall, 1902-1983, had been promoted to top spot on the list. She would shorten her stay, that she had already decided, but if the weather held she would relax for another day or so.

A tremor of anticipation rippled briefly through Lydia as she got ready to go to dinner with Stephen. He had suggested that they extend their shared time as far as an evening meal together in Keswick. It had been easy to accept, why not prolong a pleasant day? Single men in hotels have but one thing on their minds according to Gloria, but Lydia had detected no threat. His company was enjoyable and he was interesting. More than that, he seemed interested in her. As she selected something to wear, Lydia realised that it was the first time in a very long time that such a thought had crossed her mind. Pulling on the nearest sweater did not seem like an option. She saw her shabby clothes for what they were and her enthusiasm for the evening waned. It was one thing to be dressed as a scarecrow for a graveyard tour, quite another to be dressed as such for an evening meal with an interesting man. And make-up. She had none bar the stub of lipstick buried in the debris at the bottom of her bag. She put a tiny smear across her lips, the once familiar smell and texture now strange to her mouth. The usual single pull of a brush through her hair made no difference to the dowdy image reflected in the mirror. Neither did a dozen more strokes, but she was what she was, and in the long run, well, what did it matter? A cloud of depression passed across the sunny prospect of the evening. Maybe it would be better to go home tomorrow.

6

Back at her desk surrounded by her familiars, Lydia completed the methodical tabulation of all the details she'd gathered from Cumbria. There were the eleven females on her candidates list with as much information as the memorials had given, plus another twenty-six inscriptions for those with the same surnames. These twenty-six records covered fifty-eight people who might in some way be related to the eleven. Or rather to ten of the eleven, as there was but one other Marshall inscription, that of a nine year old boy buried in 2006 at Lorton Road. All these possible connections would wait until Lydia had researched the eleven, then, if a candidate stood out, she would look for links beyond the coincidence of name and burial.

It was impossible not to start with Phoebe Marshall, even though Lydia felt sure that a dead end with her would probably mean disappointment with the whole list. There was a moment when she thought she would save Phoebe, her best prospect, until last, as a child she used to do with the food on her plate. But the temptation was too great. She had begun to think of Phoebe as 'Fee', just as Stephen's niece was thought of by her friends. Try as she might to think otherwise, recording the results of her research, recalling the places, inevitably it all took her back to her time with Stephen. They had parted with smiles, he a little surprised at her sudden decision to leave, she blaming the poor turn in the weather. He had given her his email address but asked for nothing in return and Lydia had not offered anything. Yes, she would tell him the end of the story if there was one to be told, and yes, she would be sure to contact him if he could ever be of any help. But these things were said because the opposites could not be said. She had set her mind firmly against any idea of maintaining their friendship, it would be too difficult and all too probably end in an unsatisfactory way. She had no need of any complications in her life, least of all a man maybe twenty years her senior, however pleasant his company might have been for a couple of days. No, she had opened herself up to him all too easily, which hardly mattered for so brief an acquaintance, but long term it would leave her too vulnerable. Hadn't he called her passionate?

The first port of call was obvious enough: check the index of deaths for 1983 with a registration district in Cumbria. Sure enough, there was Phoebe, without the Isabella, recorded in the September quarter of that year, the date of birth shown as 29th May 1902. With the information fresh in her mind, Lydia clicked the link to order a death certificate, confident that at last she had found the key to open her box of mysteries. Now, with this precious detail, finding Phoebe in the birth index should be straightforward. Marshall was a common enough name and Marshalls were breeding as fast as anyone in 1902. She took the precaution of including the first quarter of 1903 in her search of the index. Even though she searched for both Phoebe and Isabella as first names, the result was a satisfyingly short list of three, one in Lincoln, another in Devon and, most satisfying of all, one for Braintree, Essex. No need to check her notes or a map or anything else to recall instantly that Longlands was but a stone's throw from Braintree. She carefully opened the album and studied the family group intently once again. With fresh knowledge she looked at little Phoebe in a new light. Are you perhaps Phoebe Isabella Marshall, are you Mama and Papa's daughter or grand daughter? Are your mother and father in the picture with you, is that your brother sat beside you on the grass? Oh! She looked again, Albert M, could that be Albert Marshall to distinguish him from Albert something else? And if the something else did not need saying, then did the rest of the family bear that something else name? After all this time, all the searching, all the brick walls, Lydia felt something close to ecstatic that she might really have found a way in to her puzzle. Quite unexpectedly, the thought that she should tell Stephen popped into her head. In an instant she rejected it on the extremely sound grounds that in fact there was nothing to tell. Lydia knew that between these happy discoveries and final resolution lay a long and twisting path. But it would have been good to tell someone, and for Lydia there was no-one else who could be told, no-one else who might share even a small part of her pleasure.

With Albert Marshall a tantalizing possibility, already to Lydia a probability, she was tempted to search through every index she could find to look for a Marshall marriage that could conceivably be Phoebe's parents. There was no justification in doing so, nothing she found would be of value until it was matched with a birth certificate. But she was desperate to build on her discovery, without the enforced wait while the certificate was acquired. Again she sat with the photograph, drifting back into her own afternoon at Longlands, the lawn, the laughter, the smallest echoes of a distant summer. What had Phoebe been doing before she was called to pose with the family? Had her mother insisted on brushing her hair and tying the ribbon just so? Did she tease her little brother? A search for Albert M might not be wasted effort, he was someone that she could profitably explore. How many Albert Marshalls were born between say 1903 and at the latest 1906, to judge by the image of the boy? Already she knew that there were a lot of Marshalls and Albert would be a challenge, still one of the most popular names in the early years of the century. But it was certainly worth a look, especially if she confined herself to possibilities in Essex, or better still, in Braintree.

Within forty minutes she had the answer she sought. Of seventy-nine Albert Marshalls, a mere four were registered in Essex. Of the four, a solitary Albert William F Marshall had been registered in Braintree in the last quarter of 1904. She was triumphant, her theory all but proved. Now she would send for both Phoebe's and Albert's birth certificates, and resist all temptation to investigate further until she had them. The moment they were ordered, she closed all her notepads and albums, shut down her laptop and put everything out of sight under her desk.

Resolve is one thing, but a racing mind requires an immediate occupation. She still needed something to take her right away from Longlands, Marshalls and maybe's. She had been home less than a day, and one way and another that elusive unnamed family had occupied her for nearly a week. There was plenty around the house needing some attention, including the unwelcome consequences of returning to an empty fridge with no more than a bag of dirty clothes. For the greater part of her single, divorced life, such domestic tasks had never bothered her. They had always been done without much thought or interest, in a mechanical way that demanded little. But at that moment they were distinctly unappealing, yet nothing else attracted her. Her mind swarmed over the prospects of solving her self-made puzzle, anxious to be getting on with the story, establishing the characters. Yet there was nothing that she could sensibly do except wait.

By Sunday, the need to be constructive got the better of her. What if Phoebe was not the golden ticket after all? Surely she was duty bound to follow up on her other ten candidates who, in her excitement, she had completely forgotten. One by one she looked up their death entries and made notes of the references. So simple was the exercise that in no time at all her list was complete. It had filled an hour of her time but without any satisfaction. She was left staring at the notepad, completely at a loss as to what she might do next. The grey and dreary day beyond her window had seeped into her home and with it a great wave of depression, a deep anticlimax, swept over her. The excitement of the chase, the clear purpose and direction, both had vanished, leaving her adrift and rudderless. The pleasures of her stay in the lakes each turned to dust as she recalled them, a deceptive mirage of happiness dissolving as quickly as it had appeared.

Lydia remained enveloped in this cloud of gloom for the next two days as she fiddled her way through work, avoiding any chance of direct conversation with Gloria until the Wednesday, when she was cornered by the coffee machine.

'Meet anyone that took your fancy then?'

'I don't think I know what my fancy is these days,' she replied with as light hearted and uninformative an answer as she could manage.

'No, Lydia, I don't think you do. What did you get up to then?'

'Oh, you know, walked a bit, read a bit, just pottered around really. It's a lovely area.'

Gloria shook her head to emphasise just how hopeless a case Lydia was. 'I bet you found time to check out a few tombstones though. Met a few dead people, eh? Go on, say you didn't.'

God, she hated Gloria, hated her shallow monochrome view of life, hated her trying to foist it on the rest of her narrow world. Mostly she could tolerate the stream of nonsense, the fixation with sex and shoes, the daily recounting of the gruesome details of the previous night. Oh how she was tempted to shock her once and for all, if only she had something to shock her with.

'No, no meetings with the dead,' and then added straight faced, 'but you know, they often have a lot more of interest to say than some of the living.'

'If you say so, Lydia,' Gloria retorted as she flounced off, the sarcasm passing her by completely.

It was no better at home where she could settle to nothing. No sooner had she sat down than she needed to get up and prowl the house, which for the first time in the eleven years that she had lived there, felt cramped and unwelcoming. Like her clothes, all her other possessions had acquired a shabby second-hand quality. Once, for no apparent reason, Lydia found herself suddenly close to tears as she washed a few pans after her supper. Her meals, repeated with little variation for so long that she could not remember a different time, became tasteless. Her sleep was punctuated with fearful dreams, waking her with no memory of their content, only the fear. Each morning she blinked into the day as tired as the night before, so that by the end of the week she did not know whether the weekend was a blessing or a curse.

It turned out to be a blessing. Saturday's post brought three letters and Lydia knew instantly from the colours of the paper showing through the envelopes that these were a death certificate and two birth certificates. Before she opened them, she sat at her desk and carefully arranged her workspace. If they contained what she so fervently hoped they contained, the day ahead of her would sweep the week's depression away. The death certificate would be opened first because that was the order in which she had done things. Carefully she flattened the folded document. It was as sad in its way as everything else Lydia had come to understand about Phoebe Marshall. The date of death was given only approximately: *'About 17th July 1983'*. And under cause of death *'Myocardial infarction, Ischaemic Heart Disease'*, which was certified by the coroner *'after post mortem without inquest'*. The informant was a police constable, the date of registration 23rd July, the place of death Bride's Cottage, Bridekirk. The place of birth was given as Essex, confirming it was almost certainly the Phoebe whose birth certificate she would be reading in a moment. Heart failure, a coroner, a police constable, these new details only served to underline the air of melancholy that surrounded this lady. Lydia could see her body in the cottage, or worse, in the garden, discovered by the milkman or a neighbour. The police are called, an ambulance arrives shortly after, no sirens or lights. Days later a doctor examines the remains and a constable is despatched to the registrar. Later still, the neighbour goes through her things, sorts through her papers, and finds some reference to S. It could even have been S who arranged and paid for the funeral. A will! There might be a will, the thought had not occurred to her until that moment, but now she had the details of death, finding a will would be a real possibility. And that might tell her much about this Essex girl who came to final rest in Bridekirk.

Lydia opened the two birth certificates and knew in one glance that she had a brother and sister. Here was Phoebe Isabella and her younger brother Albert William Francis. Both born at Coggeshall, Essex, both born to Isabella Marshall formerly Joslin and Francis Marshall, an insurance agent. *'Formerly Joslin'*, she savoured the two words that could unlock the Longlands picture. Lydia felt a smile on her lips for the first time in ten days. She took great care to record the details from the certificates into her table of information. Then, in a most deliberate manner she opened the Longlands album. Second left in the second row there is Isabella, but there is no Francis recorded in the caption. Are these the Joslins in their Edwardian prime? A search through the 1901 census would surely establish the family once and for all. And then there was Isabella and Francis' marriage to find, and after that maybe other children.

So totally had Lydia become engrossed in Phoebe, her death and her place in the journal, she almost overlooked her original purpose. All those months ago she had set out to re-unite the Longlands album with some yet to be found family member. If she could truly establish the surname, then reunion would surely follow. She set about her task with renewed vigour. First stop were the Marshalls, Isabella and Francis. Plenty of matches in the 1901 census to Francis but none that were married to an Isabella, so she turned to Isabella Joslin. Two possibilities in Essex, one of which was in Bocking. There she was, she and her parents Albert and Pitternelle, her brother Joseph and sisters Alice and Aletha. Aletha! Alice's presumed twin now had a name, and an unusual name at that, maybe a mistake in the record, but in due course a birth certificate would establish that. Now Lydia could put a name to 'self', something which gave her a huge sense of achievement. And because she was thorough, she also noted another Alice, Alice Speen, domestic servant recorded on the census form. Could she still be with the family ten years later? Was it Alice Speen who forever adjusted the curtains at the upstairs window? The address was 'Bocking End', no mention of Longlands. It did not matter that every name from the photograph was not represented, what mattered most was that nothing in the census contradicted the theory that Lydia was building. Census and photograph were entirely consistent, only when theory and record disagreed would she question that theory.

Saturday morning turned into the afternoon and evening before Lydia rested from her searches. Even then it was only because her eyes were sore, her back and shoulders ached and she felt faint from hunger. She was completely satiated with Joslins and their variants. From census to census she had worked back to Joshua, born around 1800, a farmer at High End Farm, Bocking in 1841. And then with no census to rely on she had used all the other sources she could find to look for Joshua's marriage to Constance Jolly in 1825 and from Constance she found her parents John and Martha. They in turn gave her Constance's sister Prudence and brothers Nathaniel and John. Lydia had to keep reminding herself that all this was provisional, all depended on the actual records, but it didn't dim her enthusiasm. At every generation, every change in circumstances she had trawled through the birth and marriage index to find likely entries for her subjects. Killing them off would come later, even though it ran the risk of false trails now. In the fullness of time she would need to see copies of the critical entries in the registers to verify the picture that she was building. At least a dozen of those entries appeared essential even at this stage, which could be costly. She would start with the most important and order the certificates one by one, so that not only would the expense be spread but she would not waste her money if there was a broken link in the chain. And if the certificates endorsed her work, then it would be time to think of studying the actual parish records, not just other people's often faulty transcriptions.

Not content with the Joslin and Jolly ancestors, she started working with the children of the marriages. It was not with huge success, but she found that Prudence had married a James Dix. Then by pure chance as she entered the wrong dates into a marriage search, she noticed that 'Papa' had apparently been married before he and Pitternelle had wed. And his first wife was Isabella Dix, daughter of Prudence. She went through her records and repeated all the relevant searches. There was no mistake. She knew the information could not always be trusted, especially where some of her sources were sloppy researchers who posted their guesses as fact. But, if the records were to be believed, then 'Papa' Albert's first wife was a close cousin. Lydia sketched out the relationships and yes, sure enough, first cousins once removed. Nothing unusual in that in 1874, no more than her probable death a year later, which would make Isabella Dix only one among tens of thousands of women who had not survived their first pregnancy. Perhaps that was why, when Pitternelle had borne his first daughter in 1881, he had found it natural to name her Isabella. Such things escape the parish record and the census enumerator but Papa can scarcely have plucked the name from thin air.

Some food, her first glass of wine since Loweswater, and a dreamless sleep set her up for more of the same on the Sunday. She turned her efforts to finding likely identities for the remaining faces in the Longlands photograph. Gradually she made her lists and they were satisfyingly short. In part she relied on the Joslins having their children in and around Braintree and in this she was not disappointed. The family appeared to have been successful farmers, well established in the surrounding area for several generations. No '*Ag Labs*' amongst the Joslins. A likely date for the birth of Albert and maybe even his marriage would be easily verified with yet another certificate. Likewise for Beatrice, another Albert, and Harriet, children or grand children perhaps, but most importantly, with names in the album. Late in the afternoon Lydia prioritised her list of critical certificates to be ordered. She decided on three to start with, 'Papa' Albert Joslin and his marriages to possibly Isabella and certainly Pitternelle, together with his probable eldest son Albert's birth certificate. With nearly twenty more 'criticals' on her list Lydia was sincerely hoping that these three were not duds, she could hardly afford expensive failures at this early stage.

*

In the weeks that followed, Lydia found her normal equilibrium restored. Even Gloria became, if not likeable, then at least bearable. She continued her researches, doing at least one thing nearly every day. Over this time she sent for and received fifteen certificates of Joslin birth and marriage. She allowed herself just one death, that of Nathaniel Joslin in 1887. To her immense satisfaction the informant was 'Papa' Albert, doing what an eldest son has to do. Each of the envelopes was eagerly anticipated, and much to her relief only two appeared to be irrelevant to her immediate quest. Nonetheless, she still tabulated the information they offered, knowing that one day they might fit into some obscure corner of her jigsaw.

Before she knew it, the calendar had clicked into December, which was not so much winter as an endless extension of autumn. Warm damp days followed one another in a clammy cycle. The annual invitation to her brother and his family to join her for a Christmas meal was met by the annual polite refusal. This in turn was followed by Lydia agreeing to spend Christmas day with Brian and Joan and their girls. The enforced ten-day break from County Council payroll administration, or 'Human Resources' as they currently liked it to be known, loomed ahead of her, an unwelcome gap in the routine of her life. Worse still, before that lay the drudge of shopping for a few gifts, and the prospect of the Christmas meal with her colleagues from the office.

*

'No, Derek, you squeeze in here between me and Lydia.'

Derek was Gloria's current infatuation. The meal was strictly 'no partners', just the eight women from the section, but an evening entirely without male company had clearly not been on Gloria's agenda, so Derek turned up just as the dessert was being served and dutifully squeezed in where he was told. A big man, well over six feet, and heavily built, maybe in his late forties and certainly a good deal older than Gloria. He nodded a half smile before turning his attention to Gloria and his back to Lydia. This was a relief, since an hour and a half of full-on Gloria was about as much as Lydia could stand, and she had just calculated that in another twenty minutes she could safely take her leave.

'Derek, say hello to Lydia. Lydia, this is Derek, he's a detective, a real detective. You two should have plenty to talk about. Lydia's investigating a murder, aren't you?' Gloria was extremely pleased with herself, although Derek was less taken with the idea.

'Oh, are you?' he offered lamely, with no hint of genuine interest.

'No, not really, just a little project I've been working on. Anyway, it was all a long time ago.'

'Oh I thought she meant now.'

'No, the, er, death was a long time ago.'

'That would make it all the harder.'

'It's for fun really, I enjoy the puzzle and seeing if the pieces can be made to fit. I suppose that would be a luxury for you.'

'Yeah, it's not all Morse in Oxford. Paperwork mainly, bloody great mountains of it. That and computers. It's all computers, analysing this and checking that. If not computers then it's boffins, forensic stuff, little wisps of chemicals or a hint of DNA. Don't matter if you get caught in the act, no little wisp then you're off. Not many puzzles left in the job now. Only how to work the bloody computers, eh?'

'I can imagine,' said Lydia, and she could. She looked at this big dull man breathing beer in her face and wondered if he had ever solved a puzzle in his life. Perhaps he hadn't needed to. 'That's a pity if you don't enjoy what you do,' she added, before remembering her own far from interesting employment.

'It's a living, pays the bills.'

'That's something.'

'You two having a good chat, then? Comparing notes?' Gloria interrupted. 'How is it lover, shall we go on somewhere in a minute?'

Oh yes please, thought Lydia, go on somewhere right now, take this guardian of the peace and go anywhere. The opportunity for her own escape soon presented itself, as other members of the group began talking of one more drink and then which club to go to. No one expected Lydia to join them and she was able to slip away without any fuss, as relieved to be gone as she imagined her workmates would be to see her go.

The night was cold, St Giles still glistening from a shower as she made her way towards the lights of the shops. Crossing Beaumont Street she turned to walk down past The Randolph. A few steps from the entrance she stopped. Ahead of her Stephen Kellaway was getting out of a car, the door held open for him by the hotel porter. Lydia stared in astonishment, jostled by the others on the pavement as she stood in their path. There was no mistake, the black tie and dinner jacket could not disguise him. He would not see her if she did not approach him, she could turn away or walk right up to him. He would be friendly and greet her warmly, take her in for a drink, enquire about the journal, encourage her, take an interest. It would be the second time that they had met in a hotel entrance. Lydia moved to the side, closer to the building, steadying herself against the brickwork with one hand while the other went to her hair, a damp and frizzy mop. As she stood gulping air, a woman, radiant in evening dress and million-dollar hair-do over shimmering earrings, descended the steps to welcome Stephen with a kiss on each cheek. Taking his arm, she guided him up and into the Randolph. The car drew away. Beaumont Street returned to its business. Of the scene that had played out, only Lydia remained, pinned to the wall.

The walk to her little house in West Street took no more than fifteen minutes, but it might have taken an hour for all Lydia knew. She travelled in a daze, her footsteps mechanical, the direction instinctive. Her breathing was all wrong and she could not find its proper rhythm. Confused thoughts and contradictory images flickered through her head one after another. After a while she began to berate herself for such stupidity, what on earth could she have been thinking about? To have simply said hello, to have just acknowledged the happy chance would have cost her nothing, now she could never contact him or meet him, the burden of her shrinking into the shadows at the sight of him would be too great. If he knew how she had reacted there could never be even the most casual of friendships.

*

On the Tuesday after Christmas, Lydia decided on her next course of action. Quite deliberately she had pushed the whole business of Joslins and journals out of her mind and enjoyed herself more than usual with her brother and his wife. She even agreed to stay over for a night, something she'd done only once before and that when the girls had been mere toddlers. Joan was a little less condescending, Lydia's presents a little more appreciated, the scarf and gloves from Brian and Joan a little more appropriate.

Surprisingly refreshed, the dead days until her return to work no longer threatened. She would be occupied by the belated Christmas present that she gave herself. It took the unusual form of four hundred stamps and envelopes. These would be used to send letters to two hundred Joslin households in the hope of finding a link from the living to the Longlands album.

Her researches had included placing messages on the half dozen or so relevant family history message boards. They had never previously brought her much joy, dominated as they were by Americans looking for grandparents in Kentucky or a link back to King Arthur, but she did find one message relating to a Joslin family in Essex. It was not her family, but the chances were that they would be closely related, and from that might come information that would lead her to one of Papa Albert's descendants. Some messages remained on these sites for years without reply, but there was always a chance that another researcher with common cause would stumble on her postings. While they sat there waiting for the right person to read them, she would adopt the old fashioned method of sending letters, 'begging letters' her uncle used to call them.

Finding the names and addresses of likely Joslins was not easy. Ideally, she would wish to contact one of Papa's grandchildren, a cousin to Phoebe, but the chances were slim of such a person remaining alive. There was more probability of a great grandchild. So, with an educated guess, she reckoned that any still surviving were likely be sixty-five at the youngest or as old as eighty-five. As part of her research armoury Lydia had previously acquired a wonderful computer based people-finding tool. It became more out of date with every month that passed, but nonetheless it still enabled her to find a large percentage of the addresses of everyone with a particular name in the whole of the country, or if preferred , a smaller area. Out of date it might be, but it had served her well in the past. The initial list of Joslins shown as over the age of sixty was quite daunting, but by carefully selecting the information and removing all those who shared an address she was able to reduce the list to two hundred and seventy households. Where both male and female were listed she chose only the man's name. They were spread across every corner of the land, with particular concentrations in Essex and Sussex.

It took her an hour or so to finally settle on the wording.

Dear

I hope you will not mind me writing to you with a slightly unusual request. I am researching a part of the Joslin family and have information regarding Albert Joslin and his wife Pitternelle White who were married in Coggeshall, Essex in 1878. Their children were Albert, Isabella, Joseph, Alethia and Alice.

I am keen to contact any living descendants of this family. If you are, or think you might be, a descendant then I would be extremely pleased to hear from you. You will see that I enclose a stamped addressed envelope for that purpose. If you are not a descendant, but have a family member who may be then I would appreciate your passing this letter to them or giving me their name and address so that I may contact them.

I do not ask for any private or confidential information and any information that you are able to supply would be treated with respect. Lastly, if this letter is addressed to a former resident then I would appreciate it if you would forward it on my behalf or simply return it to me.

Should you prefer to reply via email then please feel free to do so by writing to me at lydia.silverstream@gmail.com.

Thank you for taking the time to read this, I do hope that you can help in my enquiries.

Yours Sincerely

Lydia Silverstream

Lydia chose her two hundred according to their first name, starting with Albert and ending with Ursula. It meant that no Veras or Veronicas or Williams would be included, but they might be an Easter present to herself. The name of each recipient she wrote by hand and addressed the envelopes likewise. On the inside of each of the reply envelopes Lydia wrote a reference number in tiny writing so that if she had any replies she could easily reference the original recipient. Each of these envelopes she carefully folded and included with the letters. By New Year's Eve all two hundred letters had been posted.

7

Responses to Lydia's two hundred letters began to arrive within a few days, but they were not what she had hoped for. After a week she had thirty-seven letters back, all marked as 'gone away' by the post office. Then a solitary reply envelope landed on her doormat. At first sight the contents were puzzling, for inside was a letter and a shower of torn squares of paper. The contents of the letter were shocking to her. Michael J Joslin, writing on behalf of his mother Mrs K Joslin, abused Lydia in no uncertain terms for trying to scam money from old and vulnerable people and enclosed her disgraceful letter in pieces. Mr Joslin also threatened police action and even a personal visit to teach her a lesson she would 'not fucking forget'. Lydia found the whole thing disturbing, dropping the letter as if it were contaminated by some contagious disease. Her first thought was to go to the police herself. She had done nothing wrong whereas this man appeared to be a raving lunatic. Surely he could not have read or understood anything that she had written. Regaining her composure, Lydia checked the envelope for its tell-tale number. Eighty-three. After carefully noting it down, she tore the letter into small pieces and consigned it to the waste bin. If fate should take her down a path to eighty-three, she would certainly be forewarned.

In the following week her email produced two replies, both interesting but with no apparent connection to the Longlands family. Lydia recorded the information that they gave, and made special note of one writer's belief that his great great grandfather

Joshua had emigrated to America in the 1860s. Lydia checked her record and there was a Joshua Joslin, uncle to Papa, of about the right age. One day such information might have value, but she had no intention of following that track immediately. Along with the emails, eight more gone-aways and four more postal replies arrived. Lydia opened them with caution, half fearing a tirade from another maniac. Two were polite notes explaining they were unconnected to Papa Albert, but demonstrating that there were still some who felt it a duty to respond with a letter when written to. A third was comprehensive in its listing of a completely different Joslin family tree. At first sight the fourth had little to commend it.

5 Orke Road
Worthing
West Sussex

Dear Miss Silverstream

Thank you for your letter about the Joslin family. Let me say straight away that I have no real knowledge of my family, but I would like to find out more. My mother was Fanny Joslin, she was born in 1915 and died in 1963. She was born in Essex, Colchester I think. Unfortunately I have lost her birth certificate, but could probably get a replacement. That is about all I can say with any certainty. I know that she had cousins but I have never been in touch. I still have some of her papers and other things which I will try and get down and have a look at. I am getting on a bit and your letter made me think that it would be a good thing if I could find out something about my family.

Yours sincerely
Dorothy Joslin (Miss)
PS I am sorry to waste your time and I don't have a computor

It probably was a waste of time, but such a letter deserved a reply at the very least, though she couldn't add much without knowing Dorothy's father's name. Lydia referred to her records to see if she had noted one of Papa's children marrying a Fanny. Albert she knew about, which left Joseph and she did have a note of a possible marriage in 1914 to Holland. Her other note linked back to the

Longlands album and the fact that it contained a photograph of a Fanny. Probably not Dorothy's mother but it was a tentative connection. It was enough for a talking point in her reply to Dorothy and at the same time she could ask for her father's name. Lydia took out the album to find the photograph in question. Midway through there it was, a studio portrait of a plain woman, perhaps twenty-five or so, standing posed with an umbrella in one gloved hand, the other resting on a chair back.

Dorothy replied almost immediately to Lydia's second letter, although without much encouragement. She wrote to say that she thought her mother's birth certificate would be with her other papers in a suitcase in her attic, but that she was not able to get to it. Dorothy also wrote that she thought her father's name was probably Weston, but that she was not sure that she remembered correctly something her mother had told her a long time ago. The significance of this little snippet was not lost on Lydia, for if Dorothy's mother was born a Joslin instead of marrying a Joslin, with an Essex connection already hinted at, then there was a better chance she could be directly connected to Longlands. In the absence of anything more concrete in the post and silence on the message boards Lydia decided to follow this wisp of a trail. Clearly Dorothy was unable to retrieve her mother's papers without help and presumably had no-one she could turn to. Nor did Dorothy appear to have the wherewithal to do any investigations of her own. It would be Lydia or no one.

After a third exchange of letters they arranged for Lydia to travel to Worthing on the first weekend in March. The Saturday arrived full of driving wind and rain, which made the prospect of a two or three hour drive to the Sussex coast particularly uninviting. But Lydia had committed herself and to judge from her letter, Dorothy was very much looking forward to the visit. To let her down at the last minute would certainly be a huge disappointment, and besides, there remained a small hope that the journey would prove to be of value.

Orke Road and its Victorian terraces was easy enough to find, tucked in between the railway line and the Tarring Road. Number five was distinctly less smart than its whitewashed neighbours and retained a front garden with a privet hedge behind the wall, whereas nearly all the others were paved over for cars and bikes to stand. Lydia desperately needed a cup of coffee, the journey having been as wearing as she had feared. For the time being, the box of albums were left safely locked in the boot, to be brought out only if it was appropriate. There was little point in starting with them since they might occupy a great deal of time and need unnecessary explanation, all wasted if they were unrelated to Dorothy.

A curtain twitched in the front room of the house. Before Lydia could set her hand to the knocker, the front door swung open and a woman maybe somewhere in her seventies greeted her. She partly supported herself with a walking stick telling Lydia instantly why her attic was out of bounds.

'Hello Lydia, I hope you are Lydia, please come in.'

'Dorothy, thank you, how nice to meet you.'

Dorothy led the way into her front room, clearly reserved for visitors and just as clearly rarely used. Dark velvet curtains, sun bleached at the edges, were drawn back while a film of greying net ensured privacy. Two shelves of long-unread books slept behind the sliding glass of a bookcase while a pair of china spaniels sat begging on the mantelpiece above an ancient coal-effect electric fire, one bar of which glowed a meagre warmth into the room. The whole impression was to have stepped back in time forty or more years.

'Now, you've had a long journey and I expect you would like a drink. It really is so good of you to come and see me. Tea or coffee, dear? I have both and it's no trouble.' Lydia wondered if she always had both, or whether the coffee might have been a special purchase for the visit.

'Coffee, please. Let me come and help.'

'Oh, its an awful mess out the back, dear. But come through if you like.'

Lydia followed and stepped from one world to another. The back parlour-cum-kitchen was as littered as the front was tidy: piles of magazines on the floor, tins of food with doubtful dates on an old dresser, a selection of plates stacked loosely on the draining board next to a deep square sink, possibly the original fitting. On the yellow formica-topped table were a plate of sandwiches tightly covered in cling-film along with a packet of individual apple pies, two plates and two knives. The whole scene was barely illuminated by a single bulb casting its yellow light from beneath a once tasselled shade. The single sash window grudgingly revealed a dark yard with brick cobbles, grey with age and green with moss. Beyond the overgrown fence at the end of the patch an electric train rattled into the station.

'Have you managed to find anything of your mother's, Dorothy?' Lydia felt it was time to turn the conversation to the purpose of her visit.

'No dear, as you can see I don't get about too well these days. To be quite honest with you, I had thought that you might be able to get some things down for us to go through.'

'I might. Where are they exactly?' Lydia had anticipated such a possibility and worn a pair of trousers that she thought might be suitable for scrambling about in an attic.

'Have your coffee and then I'll show you, dear. I haven't been up there for years and I don't know if you'll manage.'

The trapdoor to the loft was above the top of the stairs on the tiny landing. From the back bedroom Dorothy retrieved a pole with a metal hook on the end. She opened the catch with some difficulty, releasing a shower of dust and cobwebs as the trap swung down to reveal a narrow opening. Then with Lydia's help she pulled a crude ladder from behind a wardrobe.

'It was made for just this job,' said Dorothy as they hooked the top of the ladder over the side of the opening. Two hooks on the lower section steadied it against the banisters. It reminded Lydia of the climb up to her bunk bed in her childhood bedroom. Dorothy handed her a torch. 'I bought some batteries just in case,' she said.

Lydia barely fitted through the gap and had doubts about escaping when it came time to descend. In the blackness a few chinks of daylight pierced ill-fitting roof tiles. There must surely be better things to do on a Saturday morning than explore a freezing attic in a stranger's house with a tiny torch looking for an old suitcase. Not that it took much exploring. A couple of old tennis rackets, a backpack, a box of shoes, bundles of magazines tied up with string, a rug, rolled and similarly tied, and there, under a wooden clothes horse, a solitary suitcase. Lydia retrieved it and carefully passed it through the hatch down to Dorothy.

'Oh yes, this is it I'm sure, dear.'

'I hope it's worth it, Dorothy,' was a sentiment truly felt.

'I'll let you carry it down, if you don't mind.'

Lydia squeezed back through the gap and they put the pole and the ladder back where they belonged. Downstairs, Lydia took herself into the little bathroom behind the kitchen and did her best to clean herself up. When she returned to the front room, Dorothy had the suitcase open on the coffee table and was poring over a handful of papers.

'I cleaned it off a bit, dear, come and sit down and we'll have a look at what there is. Look, I have her birth and death certificates. They were right on the top.'

The death certificate gave no family details, simply the date 20th March 1963 at Southlands Hospital, Shoreham-by-Sea. Dorothy was the informant. The birth certificate was an original, not the full copy of the registrar's entry, but the short version given 'on request to the parent or informant' and stated simply the name, Fanny Joslin, the date of birth of 19th April 1915, and the date and place of registration as being 20th May 1915 at Colchester.

'Dorothy, this is wonderful. From this we can find the registrar's entry and from that we'll see if there is a connection to the family I'm looking in to.'

'That's good, dear. I haven't really understood why you are looking in to anything.'

'It will sound a little silly to you I'm sure. Sometimes it sounds a little silly to me, but I have a photo album, in fact I have more than one, and I started off with the idea that I would like to find the family, someone who would like to have it, someone who's grandparents' or great grandparents' pictures are in the album.' Lydia thought the explanation simple enough, it would not raise Dorothy's hopes too much and avoided the convoluted story of the journal and all its intricate detail.

'I see, dear.' Probably not, thought Lydia.

'You have a lot of stuff here, what else might there be to tell us about your mother?'

'Well, I have a few photos, here. I don't know who the people are. Except this one, this is my grandmother, look you can see on the back where it's written.' Dorothy turned the photo over to show Lydia the words 'My Mother' in a female hand written in faded blue ink. When Lydia turned the photo face up it was with the shock of recognition. There was the same twenty-something woman, the same umbrella in the same gloved hand. She was looking at the photograph of Fanny from the Longlands album.

'Oh.'

'It's a nice picture, isn't it?'

'Yes, very nice.' Suddenly she could see the end of her journey, handing over the albums, and she did not want it to end just yet, it was her story as much as Dorothy's. Lydia chose her next words very carefully. 'Dorothy, I have seen this photograph before. It is in one of the albums I told you about. Her name was Fanny, the same as your mother. It is possible that you are directly connected to the family I have been looking into. But it's not certain, just a possibility. Or maybe a probability.'

'How is that then, dear?'

'All I can say for certain is that your grandmother is in the family photo album, but she may be a cousin or just a friend of the family. I should be able to find out quite easily if she is closely related. If she turns out to be a friend or a distant cousin then that will be harder to work out. But Dorothy, it is very exciting.' Lydia was not sure that Dorothy shared her excitement. 'I must start making a few notes.'

For the next hour or so, Dorothy mulled over the contents of the suitcase, while Lydia took notes and asked questions. Dorothy's own memorabilia were mixed with her mother's. As she leafed through the papers there were long silences as she read long forgotten birthday cards, re-took the maths test in her first school exercise book, mouthed the words of the hymn in the order of service for her mother's funeral. As something took her particular interest she would pass it across for Lydia to inspect it more closely. For the most part there seemed to be more of Dorothy's paper's than her mother's. Lydia decided to venture onto the potentially delicate subject of Dorothy's own birth.

'Do you have your own birth certificate in there?'

'Yes, here in this pile I've looked through. I didn't think you'd be interested in it. Here have a look if you like.'

Lydia took the paper and unfolded it. *Dorothy Joslin, born 14th May 1932 Downland nursing home Broadwater, Worthing, Sussex. Father Byron Weston, Seaman (RN) Deceased, mother and informant Fanny Joslin, registered 9th July 1932.* She looked up at Dorothy with what she hoped was a reassuring look. 'So you kept your mother's name. Not easy for her then, I should think.'

'She never talked about it much, people didn't in those days, dear. She once told me he died at sea, but I don't know if that's true. She'd no parents herself and I never questioned it. You don't, do you, not when you're young.'

'Why do you say she had no parents?'

'Well, I don't mean that, what I mean is that they died when she was young and she was brought up by aunts and uncles. I think when she was older she lived with her cousins for a while, then I came along and they packed her off here. Not that she ever said as much, just a feeling I got. I think that's why she never talked much about family and that. Funny now, isn't it, me getting interested in it after all these years. It was your letter what set me off. Now here's you looking for someone today and me looking for someone from yesterday.'

'I may be able to find out something about your father, if you wanted me to.'

Dorothy hesitated and looked down at her hands for a moment or two. 'I don't know really, might be better off left the way it is. Some things better left buried. What do you think?'

'I think whatever is right for you, is right, but if you change your mind, you'll let me know?'

'Yes, dear I'll let you know.'

While they ate the carefully prepared sandwiches, it occurred to Lydia that there would be no harm in letting Dorothy see the Longlands album, she was sure in her own mind that one day it would be Dorothy's anyway, and there might be a name or a face to jog some long forgotten memory. Dorothy seemed pleased at the prospect, although not as excited as Lydia had anticipated. There was something slightly unworldly about Dorothy, something almost of innocence. Lydia had warmed to her, she was open and friendly, and they smiled a lot at each other. It took Lydia a while to recall who it was that Dorothy reminded her of, not physically, but in her ways. It was Lydia's Aunt Sarah, not a real aunt but a close friend of her grandmother, who was by persuasion and manner a Quaker, strong on belief and short on shouting about it. When Lydia's thoughts did turn to god and religion, which was rarely enough, it was Aunt Sarah who came to mind. With Dorothy's firm jaw, wisp of grey hair at the sides of her mouth and complete absence of make-up, Lydia imagined she might so easily have been a nun. Even as she thought such a thing, her hand went involuntarily to her own cheek - how rarely any cream or lotion was applied there. Might the casual observer place her in a similar category? She was reminded once more of how little she could really know of another's life however deep she delved.

Once the sandwiches and remains of fruit pie had been cleared away, Lydia fetched the album from her car, leaving the others tucked away in the boot. There would be another time for those. Together they looked through it, Lydia pointing out Joseph, who might be Dorothy's grandfather, and of course Papa and Mama, who would be her great grandparents. Dorothy was much taken with it and lingered over each picture, but there was no hint of recognition.

'And you got all that family worked out and sent me a letter from just looking at these pictures? I don't know how you could do that.'

'Well, no, not just from these pictures, there were other things too, other pictures which even now I don't know if they're connected or not. And a kind of diary too,' she had been going to say journal but changed and quickly moved on, 'and mention of a funeral. Really the family is not all worked out yet. I think it will though, I think this is your family.'

'Who's funeral was that, dear?'

'I think it was her funeral,' Lydia turned the pages back to the summer of 1911 and pointed to the seven-year-old Phoebe. 'If we're right, if I'm right, then she would have been one of your mother's cousins. She was Phoebe Marshall.'

'Marshall? I worked for a Frank Marshall for years at Bentalls.'

'Where was that?'

'Right here in Worthing, they had a store here. He was one of the big bosses and his father before him. I worked for Frank Marshall just like my mother worked for his father. I forget his name. It was a big store, they had branches all over.'

'Did you work there for long?'

'Left school at fifteen and never worked anywhere else, nor did my mother.'

'What did you do at Bentalls, Dorothy?'

'I did all sorts over the years, but mainly I was in drapery.'

Lydia could not help but wonder if Fanny, just seventeen, had indeed been packed off to Worthing and given a job by one of the Marshall family. As is so often demonstrated in life, it is not what you know, but who you know. Or better still, to whom you are related. A private birth for Dorothy and a job as a shop girl for Fanny, well away from her former life and courtesy of a little family connection organised by the aunt and uncle who brought her up. Lydia ran ahead of herself, enjoying the speculation, but she chose not to share it with Dorothy.

'You never married then?'

'No, never married. I might've once, but he was all for going to Australia, and I had mother. You know how it is.'

'No, but I can imagine. Did you stay in touch?'

'We was at Bentalls together, that's where we met, but he left a bit after that and I never saw him again. I think he went, someone said he did, and then not long after, mother died. Just how things turn out isn't it, dear? What about you, are you married, got children?'

'Once married but not now, and no children.'

'Like I say, just how things turn out, but I'm sorry for you, dear,' Dorothy said with complete, almost childlike, acceptance. No wistful regret of what might have been, simply that things were as they were and that was an end of it.

Lydia had exhausted all possible lines of enquiry and she was far from displeased with the results. She knew when she had the copy of Fanny's birth registration in her hand she would see that her father and mother were Joseph Joslin and his wife Fanny, the proof that Dorothy was Papa's great grandchild. The Longlands album would find a home, here in this house, but not before she had wrung every last secret from its pages.

'I'd like to hang on to this for a while, Dorothy, if you don't mind. I think it will be yours soon enough, but we'll wait to prove it, if that's all right.'

'No dear, anyway its yours, not mine, it's been lovely to see these people, lovely to know something about them. Thank you so much, coming all this way to talk to me like this.'

'Just one more thing, going back to Marshalls, does the name Bee mean anything to you, someone's nickname or pet name? I think that Phoebe Marshall was called Bee.'

'Bee? I was at school with a Bee, that's what everyone called her, but she was Beatrice really. Bee Worthington, yes that was her name, nothing to do with the Marshalls. You'd think Bee would be Beatrice wouldn't you? But not now, I don't know anyone called Bee.'

'What about your mother, was there anything your mother might have said about Bee?'

'Oh there might have been. One of her aunts, one of the ones who she lived with, I think she called one of them Auntie Bee. It might've been Bee. I know she did have some people come over once, cousins or something, came over for the day. There were some children I think too. Its going back a long way you know, dear.'

'How long would you say, Dorothy?'

'Oh, I don't know, maybe I was twenty something, I never met them, I remember mum saying she didn't know what they came for. Hardly worth taking a day off work for, she said. Like I say, dear, that's a long time since them days.'

'Yes, I know. I was hoping there was a letter or something, maybe something about Bee's death.'

'No, but could there have been something about a god-daughter? It was a while after mother died. Probably a good while. I know what it was. It's Oxford, you're from Oxford aren't you dear, and it was that what made me think, yes it was Oxford, a letter from someone's god-daughter. Or maybe it was from someone's daughter, I know there was some connection in there somewhere. Someone had died, but I didn't know who they were. Could that be it?'

Lydia knew well enough that it was hard going, trying to remember things long past, remembering things without significance at the time, and Dorothy was clearly getting tired. But another small connection was made, still as tentative as so many others, but a possibility. Hadn't she linked the journal to Oxford, wasn't the whole box of albums purchased a few miles from her own home? And now here was Dorothy Joslin making a similar link without knowing it.

'Dorothy, that might be something really important. It might be all part of another bit of the story, your family story. Was there anything else, might you still have the letter do you think, could it be in these papers?'

'Well, it might be but more likely it got thrown out. It was good long while ago you know. But I do remember it being Oxford,' she paused a moment and then added doubtfully, 'or maybe it was Oxted. Now I'm not at all sure.'

'If you think of anything you'll let me know?'

'Oh yes, dear. Its been so lovely having you here, talking about old times. And this might all be my family, I just don't know what to think about that.'

'I think that Oxford figures somewhere in the story, your family story, but what about other places? Does Whitehaven or Chelsea mean anything to you?'

'I can't say as they do.'

It was late afternoon before Lydia set off for home with her spirits high. Even so, that unexpected tinge of disappointment when she realised that she would have to part with her treasures remained with her. If the day had not run on as it had, curiosity might have taken her into the town for a stroll, then maybe a walk around Broadwater to see if the Downland Nursing Home still existed. Not that it would, sometimes Lydia knew her imagination wandered further than facts would dictate, but it was her way, and hadn't someone said how they envied her creative thinking? A smile crossed her face as she savoured the thought that it was creative thinking which had brought her to this point, on the very brink of solving that first part of the puzzle. And with one part solved the others might fall neatly into place.

As to what she should make of Dorothy, Lydia was still not sure. She knew that she liked her, but all day she had been unsettled by the connection she had made to her Aunt Sarah, a connection that was probably just a trick of the light. But even allowing for that, Dorothy was still a little unworldly. Perhaps living alone with her mother for half her life had left her ill-equipped to deal with people and relationships when Fanny had died. If those supposedly swinging sixties had passed anyone by, it was surely Dorothy Joslin. Sat in the time warp of her back room, apparently unengaged with the world around her, everything since those far away days seemed to have gone unnoticed. It suddenly occurred to her that she had seen no television in the house, a rarity indeed. One day, Lydia thought, someone would find her dead or dying and questions would be asked as to how it could be, how someone could fall through the safety net of social security, how was it that there were no friends or relatives that took any interest. Had it been that way for Phoebe too? And of those other Joslins, what had happened to them and their bright confidence of the summer of 1911? Had it all dissolved, lost in war and misfortune?

However it would all turn out, whatever she might find, Lydia resolved that she would stay in touch with Dorothy. Not simply to present her with the album, which she knew for sure would prove to be Dorothy's family, and not because there might yet be more to be gleaned from some snippet in her mother's papers. More because she did not want to hear one day from one of Dorothy's neighbours that Dorothy was dead and that a police constable had notified the registrar.

8

Tired from her travels, Lydia indulged herself in a long lie in bed on the Sunday morning. Half awake and half asleep she dreamily considered the pleasures yet to come and those already taken from her box of albums. The trip she had taken to Longlands persisted in her mind, as did the delights and surprises of her stay in The Lakes. Underneath it though, was the gnawing angst of the journal, its secret story still undeciphered. Glad that she had kept the journal and its contents from Dorothy, she was still a little uncertain of its meaning herself, not really daring to trust her ideas, still hoping that in some obscure way it might be a fiction. Had Dorothy seen it or known the detail, Lydia was not sure how she would have responded. Perhaps she would have thought it best to leave well alone, let the past remain undisturbed, as was her attitude to her father. When Lydia started her day she would write at once to Dorothy to thank her, knowing well it would bring her pleasure to receive such a letter. That done, she would track down Fanny's marriage to a Joslin and fit those pieces into the jigsaw. On second thoughts it would be better to wait to write to Dorothy until she had something more than a simple 'thank you' to say. But then again it might be better to wait until a certificate had been obtained. The sequences swam round her head until they were a blur and she sank back into a deep sleep until late in the morning.

Once she had her wits about her and a coffee or two inside her, Lydia set about the day's jobs without hesitation. First, the little note to Dorothy, thanking her for the visit and all the information and the trouble she had taken, together with a promise to write again as soon as she had any new discovery. Then immediately she set about confirming the marriage for Joseph Joslin to Dorothy's grandmother Fanny. If Dorothy's mother had been born in 1915, and there was no reason to doubt what the abbreviated certificate stated, then she should find her answer easily enough. With the aid of her previous notes she found the entry right away in the September quarter of 1914. *'Joslin, Joseph married Holland, Colchester'* followed by the reference in the register, which Lydia carefully noted. She would order the certificate later, with any others she might need, once the day's investigations were done. The next step was to cross-reference the entry by checking the other side of the marriage under Holland. As she was about to start the search it occurred to her that she'd arrived at one of those vital moments, a critical confirmation of her theories. Or, dread the thought, the first indication she was completely wrong. As the image of the index page formed on the screen, she fervently hoped that there would be an entry for Holland, Fanny, marrying a Joslin in Colchester in the summer of 1914. Anxiously she scrolled down the Hollands to F. The poor image and the smudged typeface made it hard to read. She clicked to enlarge the page. *'Holland, Fanny, married Joslin, Cochester'*. It was there, right there in front of her, with the identical reference. Lydia realised that she had been holding her breath for too long.

Next in Lydia's mental list was confirmation of Dorothy's mother's parents, though she hadn't the slightest doubt that they would be Joseph and Fanny. It was a matter of moments to switch her searches from marriages to births and look for Joslins in the June quarter of 1915. There was baby Fanny Joslin's entry. Again she noted the reference details. That was another certificate to be ordered. Now, on to finding the truth about 'having no parents', as Dorothy had put it. It was no great leap of imagination to think that Joseph might have died in the war. And if not in the war then perhaps of wounds shortly afterwards. If he had been pensioned out of the services then she might find such a record, and if he was one of the casualties then he would be recorded somewhere for sure. It was at moments such as this that Lydia remembered to be grateful for all the work that had gone in to providing the millions of pieces of information that she relied on, trawled through, sorted and sifted to throw a little light on past lives. The Commonwealth War Graves search was instant and enlightening. *'Joseph Joslin, Serjeant, Essex Regiment, 09/05/1915, Ypres. Memorial at the Menin Gate.'* Other Joslins too, but no other Josephs, and no other match more likely than the first that she found. For a few moments Lydia's vision switched to that memorial, and to the figure of Dorothy, supported by her stick, reading her grandfather's name amongst the thousands of others. If Dorothy would like to go one day, then she would go with her.

Lydia checked the notes from her visit to Worthing. What was the date of birth she had for Dorothy's mother Fanny? 19th April 1915. So, baby Fanny had a father for just twenty one days, and most likely father and daughter never laid eyes on each other. Did her mother even know that Joseph was dead by the time she registered the birth, or was he still 'missing in action'? Maybe he was still missing to this day, a name on a stone that marked no grave. Lydia tried hard to feel that loss, to try to understand how hard it would have been, how crushing to the spirit. Was it any easier for knowing that so many other wives and mothers shared the loss? Some sense of it came to her, sitting alone in her little house in Osney, but the distance in time and space spared her true knowledge.

With Joseph lost at Ypres, Fanny's fate remained to be discovered. When had Dorothy's mother become an orphan, farmed out to aunts and cousins? As methodical as ever, she started her search through the lists for 1915 in the same quarter as Fanny had registered her daughter's birth. Most likely it would be found sooner rather than later, probably no later than 1925. The index images flickered in front of her well practiced eyes. On each page she ran down the whole list and then to be sure that nothing had been missed she checked the bottom of the page to see if a stray entry had been added. And for every search for Joslin, there was one for Jocelyn and Josslin too. Fifty-eight pages into her search came her reward. December quarter 1922, Joslin, Fanny, death registered in the Colchester district of Essex. Another set of references was added to Lydia's list of certificates. When they all arrived she would have much to write to Dorothy about.

Such was the volume of notes and information of one kind or another, Lydia set about reviewing it all in the week that followed. She resorted all her data, removing to a separate list all those individuals she had collected as being possibly connected to the family, and prioritising those she was sure of. Then she turned to the budding family tree she'd begun and entered all the additional information. This prompted a list of data yet to be gathered and questions yet to be to be answered. Finally, she arranged those questions into an order of importance. Laid out before her she had Papa and Mama's family, the five children that she knew of, Albert, Isabella, twins Alethia and Alice, and Joseph the youngest. She had a tentative line back from Papa through Nathaniel and Joshua to John Jolly, Joshua's father-in-law. And from John Jolly there was a second line through his daughter Prudence to his granddaughter Isabella Dix to Papa Albert. Coming forward from Papa there were his grand children Phoebe and Albert Marshall, and the orphaned Fanny. Most of these characters were no more than names on a page, but for some she had uncovered something of their lives and their loves. And everything she'd found had been touched by sadness, as if the Great War had cast its shadow down the generations. It was all good, all believable, all corroborated by the records. But still it only satisfied her original objective of finding a descendant who would be interested to have the album. The mystery of the journal remained, as did the possibility of connecting the faces from the sandcastles and the RAF albums to the whole picture. Their places in the puzzle remained to be found. In finding them Lydia was convinced she would also find the key to unlock the journal.

To her surprise she realised that although the family had been established, she had completely failed to follow up on Albert junior and more surprisingly she had made nothing of discovering the 'self' of Longlands was Alethia Joslin. Neither had she properly studied Beatrice, James or Henry, teenagers in the Longlands album, nor the youngsters Albert and Harriet. Who first? It was no choice really, the male name does not change on marriage and her theme was clearly Josilin, so Albert, the eldest son, it had to be.

★

West Street
Osney
Oxford

4th April

Dear Dorothy

How have you been getting along? I was sorry to hear of your head cold and hope it is all cleared up now and that you will be able to get out a little more now that the weather has cheered up. I would be very happy to take you to the gardens that you mentioned the next time that I come down to see you. I can imagine the view is as lovely as you describe.

You will want to know how I have been getting along with the Joslins. Of Alice (your great aunt) I can find nothing, no marriage and no death and no other record. Albert junior (your great uncle) married Beatrice Pelham on 3rd February 1902 and they had at least three children - Beatrice, who died aged 6 weeks in January 1903, Albert born 6th August 1903, and Harriet, born 7th July 1905. You will see that I have copied the main photograph that we spent so much time over and written this information on it, so that you will be able to put faces to the names and dates. I'm guessing a little about Beatrice in the photograph being Albert's wife but I think it is a reasonable assumption. Likewise with their two surviving children Albert and Harriet being present.

Since I wrote to you last I have received the certificates that I applied for, that is for your grandparent's marriage and your grandmother's death in 1922, together with your mother's full birth certificate. All confirm our expectations. I am making up a new 'album' with all these documents in it so that when you have the photograph albums you will have all the certificates too.

I am still no further forward with the other albums and have yet to look into what may have become of Alethia, another of your great aunts. By the way it is Alethia and not Aletha as I had originally thought. I will probably find that she becomes Althea somewhere along the way. I hope she is not as elusive as Alice!

I do hope that this finds you well, I will be pleased to hear from you. Or give me a call anytime.

Your friend
Lydia

As good as her word, Lydia began searching for Alethia before the letter was even posted. By the time she reached 1920 in the index she was beginning to think that, like Alice her twin, Alethia would disappear from the record. She would have been twenty-eight in that year and becoming less marriageable by the month. Lydia re-checked and then, sensing the Joslin malaise of sadness, looked right through the death lists to 1930. Nothing. Not even an Althia or an Aletha, not a Jocelyn or a Josslin. Pausing in her enquiry, Lydia pulled out the Longlands album once again looking for an answer to the disappearance of the twins. They were pretty enough, surely? Well nourished and clearly from a comfortably placed family, they would have been a catch for anyone. Her eye rested for a moment on the other two faces as yet unaccounted for, Henry and James. Seemingly they were not Alethia's brothers, but most likely family since they were not 'Mister' anything, in the way that Mr Melville was described. If not brothers, then cousins? Tracking that possibility would be a mammoth task without some further clue. And even if she should find them, they might easily have been devoured by the coming cataclysm. Which reminded Lydia quite forcibly that twenty-eight was probably no age at all for marriage, if war had snatched four years of your prime. Might even have snatched your husband-to-be.

She returned to the lists, determined to take her enquiry to 1950 if need be. Her endeavour was almost immediately rewarded. In the three months ending in March 1922 there was her prize. *'Joslin, Alethia, married Dix-Myers, Chelmsford.'* Now that, thought Lydia, was really worth waiting for, here was the door to a new path. And then she stopped still and closed her eyes for a moment to assemble the jumble of thoughts into a meaningful pattern. 'Dix-Myers?' Wasn't the RAF album about a Myers? But there was more to it than that, something else above and beyond. Quickly she opened her list of family names. A couple of clicks and there she was, Isabella Dix, Papa Joslin's ill-fated first wife; Isabella Dix, Papa Joslin's first cousin, removed by one generation. And J D Myers was the name on the postcard in the RAF album. Now here was Alethia marrying a Dix-Myers. Lydia's fingers flew across her keyboard to see the other side of the entry. March quarter 1922, '*Dix-Myers, James married Joslin, Chelmsford.*' The circle was complete.

All those frustrating early searches to try and find something, anything, for Myers, would need to be done again, this time for Dix-Myers. If what Lydia just knew must be true really was, then she would be able to prove it from two directions, taking Alethia forward through her marriage and her children and working the names and places of the RAF album back to join them. Not only that, but there was Papa's marriage to Isabella to reconsider. The Jolly's and Joslin's might have entwined their families more often than appeared at first sight. With so many avenues opening, Lydia was at a loss to decide the most fruitful one to choose first. As she considered this happy dilemma, her eye fell on the brightness of the new growth in her garden and that of her neighbours. A new season was beginning, new life breathing spring air, a whole new world emerging from the drab cocoon of an Oxford winter. And in that instant too, she saw herself closeted away in her room, immersed in past lives, insulated from the turn of the world. So instead of choosing a Dix or a Joslin, a James or a Martha, she packed up her papers, tidied her desk and elected to take a walk before the promise of the sunshine beyond her window was spent.

Out of her house and into the air, the day felt a good deal cooler than it had appeared from the warmth of her back room. She took the few steps along to Swan Street and across the narrow little bridge over Osney Stream. Then she followed the path as it ducked past the school and out to Ferry Hinksey Road. It was a well used route, but only by those who lived on the island; for the rest of

Oxford it served no purpose and was unknown territory. Straight away she was out of the city, skirting the playing fields and heading for Hinksey. Tongues of open countryside still run almost to the city walls, largely ignored and hidden behind the sprawl of development along its main roads. For those who know these places they provide an instant relief from the relentless noise and the commercial grind. Lydia's pace slowed as she walked, seeing children swinging, running, squealing at the age-old pleasures of a playground. Fathers kicked balls, mothers chatted with half an eye on yellow-booted infants toddling in puddles. Common enough sights, but Lydia saw them with the eye of the visitor in a strange land. She saw the buggies and the bikes with their stabilisers, the scarves and mittens, the glances she attracted from protective parents. She saw the steadier gaze and the pause in the chatter as a ruddy faced man, thin white hair and a beard that went to his waist, shirt-sleeved when he should not have been, came too close as he collected litter in a plastic bag. A man with history, a man with stories and unknown lives, with ideas and knowledge to be shared. But now a threat, an eccentric, a danger, the danger of difference. Lydia immediately had him down as a river dweller, somewhere down below the lock, smoke curling from a tin chimney on a narrow-boat festooned with flower pots and a washing line dangling across the stern. There was no menace in that gruff waterman, only the fear of a tabloid bogeyman.

She passed on to the soggy meadows, the path taking her under crackling power lines and up to the avenue of trees flanking the causeway to Hinksey. A veil of fresh green covered the hedgerow and in a break, framed by the pylons and the cables, she glimpsed the offices of Seacourt Tower to the north. No matter how many makeovers it had, it remained as unlovely as the day it was built. Had her tormented journal writer seen it that way, ever walked here and seen it brooding glumly over Botley? Or had it been no more than the building he worked in, the home of Pink2 and the office of conspiring colleagues intent on his destruction? Lydia allowed herself a smile at her own obsession. A walk in spring air, along an ancient track had brought her, for a few minutes at least, into the physical world, but how easily she slipped back to that other creation. As she walked on, she let the characters drift through her mind, seeing if they would settle to a pattern, find their places of their own accord. As they did so she saw clearly that no matter how special they had become to her, they were no different in their way than any other family over the generations. Each was unique yet shared so many common threads. When she'd discovered their lives, found S and her troubled husband and their untold story, when she had passed it all on to Dorothy, when both she and Dorothy were long gone, when all that had happened, the Joslins would sink back to being mere names and dates. There was no sense of depression in these thoughts, simply that she saw the saga for what it was, brief moments in the great sweep of time. She had her role to play, her own part in the Joslin story, and play it she would.

★

The usual combination of census returns, the indices of births, deaths and marriages, provided the answers she needed concerning Dix and Myers. To be completely sure she traced, for the third time, Isabella Dix back through her mother Prudence to John and Martha Jolly, hers and Papa's common forebear.

In 1861 Isabella and her sister Martha had shared the Dix household with their parents Prudence and James Dix. They still did so in 1871. Then Isabella married Papa Albert Joslin in 1874 and died a year later. Martha stayed with her parents at least until 1881 and probably until 1886 when she married Henry Myers at Coggeshall. What circumstance prompted Henry and Martha to call themselves Dix-Myers instead of plain Myers was lost in the five years that followed, but by 1891 they were recorded with the double-barrelled surname which had eluded Lydia for so long. Perhaps it was an accident of recording, a name spoken and written in the wrong column. Or perhaps Martha Dix, or more likely her father James, had sought to preserve the name despite having no sons to carry it. It could have been money, Martha from the relative wealth of the Dix farming dynasty, Henry Myers the Braintree shop assistant, a union sanctioned only on condition of an adjustment to his name. For whatever reason, Henry and James Dix-Myers carried both their parents' names. Their relationship to the Joslins, to Longlands, was complicated and Lydia settled on 'cousins' as being wide enough to cover the complexities of being Papa Albert's nephews by his first marriage as well as his second cousins by great grandfather John Jolly. Either tie would be enough to justify their presence at the family home in 1911, where nineteen year-old Alethia was no doubt already drawn to young James. But no marriage until 1922. War had indeed intervened. Even so, it was a long wait. Neither had Alethia married anyone else to 'fill the gap'. The question of what took them so long nagged at Lydia.

Henry was soon accounted for, once again courtesy of the war graves register. Paschendale 1916, rifleman Henry Dix-Myers died of wounds received. For James, Lydia could find no record beyond his medal card, the presence of which confirmed no more than his enlisting and that he had seen out the war in uniform. And if he had seen out the war, survived uninjured, why had he and Alethia not married until 1922? Did he take four years to recover from the scars? Or had he travelled abroad, seeking fortune and new worlds as an antidote to the horrors of Flanders? A search through passenger lists revealed nothing, hardly a Joslin amongst the travelling multitude bound for all parts of the Empire. Then it struck her. James might have married before 1922, despite the long-standing connection to Alethia. Sure enough, it looked as if he had: in 1919 to one Barbara Vaughan at Colchester. It might not be the James Dix-Myers that Lydia sought, but as there was but one of that name in the 1901 census, she was confident she had her man. But if James had married Barbara in 1919, what had become of her? Early death seemed to be a habit acquired by this family, and Barbara simply added to the list. Lydia found her entry in the summer of 1920 and duly noted the details. So, after a suitable period had elapsed, where else should James turn for solace than his childhood sweetheart Alethia? Not Alice, her twin, but Alethia. Then the subversive thought that maybe James could not tell them apart winked into Lydia's mind. She justified such subversion by telling herself that speculation was half the pleasure. Why would a man prefer one twin to another? Perhaps availability rather than romance provided the mundane answer. Of Alice she had no trace, perhaps she had disappeared from the family circle by the time that the widower James had felt the need of a new wife, and so saved him the problem of choice.

Lydia returned to the RAF album and the notes she'd made. Henry wrote to his parents and spoke of his sister V, who was surely Verity. His parents were now known to be James and Alethia so now she could look again for any records of the family, this time as Dix-Myers. Henry was born in the December quarter of 1922, as was Verity. Another set of twins, born to a mother who was herself twin. Of Bertie she could find no record. Again Lydia examined the album. Twins she had thought and twins Henry and Verity had been, and now that she knew it to be true, she could see how the young Alethia had turned out as a woman in her forties presiding over her brood. Surely Bertie was part of that brood, an integral part of the family, at least that is what the photographs said. But if it were true, then why did Henry not send his good wishes to B on his postcard home from the air training school as he had done for his sister V? No pictures of Bertie in uniform, or Verity for that matter. Had he served in the war, another casualty in a family of casualties? He was certainly older but not perhaps by much, and his image had been as lovingly placed and captioned as those of Henry and Verity. Could he possibly have been born before her marriage, conceived with someone other than James? If so then he would have been registered either as a Joslin or under the unknown father's name. Lydia checked through all her stray Joslin birth records for the first twenty years of the century. No Bertie or anything that might be Bertie. And if not Joslin or some variant, then finding him anywhere would be impossible.

So engrossed had she become in her searches and her puzzles that Dorothy was long overdue another letter. She had not even replied to the last from her, offering to contribute to the costs of certificates and, touchingly thought Lydia, the cost of all the phone calls. She supposed that the reference was to her 'computor' connection. At the end of April Lydia was able to tell Dorothy about Alethia and James and their family, explain how it all fitted in with the RAF album, how she knew nothing of Bertie, but that Henry had died in 1943, shot down while navigating a bomber over Germany. His body had been removed from its original burial place in 1945 and was now interred at Reichswald Forest War Cemetery, in the company of so many of his comrades. She could also tell her that a few months earlier Henry had married Kathleen Farrow, of whom Lydia had made no further enquiries. As far as she could tell, Henry had no children. Of Verity she could find no trace of a marriage or a death under Myers or Dix-Myers, even though she had looked right up to 1984. Another stray, another annoyingly loose end.

Dorothy's reply was almost instant, or at least, as near to instant as the Royal Mail allowed. She would be very pleased to see Lydia again in a couple of weeks and suggested that if the weather was suitable they might like to take a packed lunch and go to the gardens that Dorothy's mother had enjoyed visiting. Tantalisingly, she also said that she had found something else of her mother's and that Lydia might find it interesting. Where this might once have irritated Lydia, now she counted the positive and enjoyed the pleasure of anticipation. Whatever it was, it could hardly be that significant, it would not alter all that she knew, at best it might offer some new line of enquiry. Unless it was news of Bertie, and that was unlikely in the extreme.

By way of relief from failing to find the missing Dix-Myers, Lydia turned her attention to the last significant gaps in the family, Papa's grandchildren Albert and Harriet, only known surviving children of Albert Joslin and Beatrice Pelham. Lydia already knew the fate of their older sister Beatrice who died as a baby just a few weeks old in the winter of 1903. Mentally tossing the coin, Lydia surprised herself by choosing Harriet before Albert. First, she searched for an entry in the death registrations, searched until her eyes were sore from fifty years of entries flickering before them. Another half hour extended her search to sixty years and then on again to seventy, and with sleep calling her, Lydia finally called it a day at eighty-five. Either Harriet had been missed, married or emigrated, or she was that rarity amongst Joslins, long-lived.

In the next few evenings Lydia carried the search for Harriet through the marriages, and found only one that might fit. *Harriet M Jocelyn in 1937 in the district of Chelsea to a Mr Fuller*. It was without much conviction that she ordered a certificate. The spelling of the name was not the problem so much as that middle initial. The Harriet that she sought was Harriet Pelham Joslin. Lydia began to consider if there could possibly be some common factor to these 'missing' Joslin women, Alice, Verity and now Harriet. But on reflection it seemed a fanciful notion, finding a pattern where none existed.

Drawing a blank with Harriet, Lydia turned her attention to Albert and starting her quest in 1922, found almost instant success with a marriage in 1928 to Hannah Brightside that looked promising. Another two in 1929 and 1932 might also fit the bill, but she put these aside until she had the details for Albert and Hannah. A couple of days before she was to visit Worthing and find what treasure Dorothy had for her, the certificate arrived and confirmed her hopes. From all that it told her, she was happy to accept that this was a marriage for Papa's grandson. Finding any children of Albert and Hannah would wait until after she and Dorothy had shared a packed lunch.

*

From a bench below a chalky outcrop on Highdown, with the English Channel glittering in the distance, Dorothy and Lydia surveyed the landscape rolling away to the south, down to the sprawl of development that covers the coast in an almost unbroken band from Brighton to Littlehampton. The May sunshine bathed them in warmth and threatened to curl the corners of the ham sandwiches before they could be eaten. Dorothy's mother Fanny had chosen a good spot to be one of her favourites.

'It is lovely here, Dorothy. Did your mum get up here often?'

'No, I don't think so. We never had no car and there was no bus. When she was younger she'd cycle up here sometimes, I think. One of her friends used to come up with her, brought her up in the car in the last few years.'

'Did you come along as well?'

'Once or twice, but while mum was out it meant I could get a few things done.'

Lydia thought a moment about the cares of daughters for their mothers and, for all she knew, for their fathers too. She had been spared all that by her father's premature and sudden death and her mother's fierce independence, even to her last few months. True, she'd been the one who organised the home care, smoothed the transition and in secret had arranged her mother's affairs. But she had done none of the caring, none of the really hard dirty work, the grinding, day-in day-out commitment to care. Whereas Dorothy clearly had, finding her mother's absence a rare opportunity not for time for herself, but instead a chance to 'get a few things done'.

'Were you working then Dorothy, when your mother was ill?'

'Yes, I kept the job going, it was a matter of needing to really. There wasn't half the help in them days as there is now.'

'She must have been proud of you.'

'I don't know about that, but we got along alright. We was quite a team really. Funny, I just thought, that's what she used to say, 'We're a good team, you and I'. She'd say that a lot when I was young.'

'And now we're here in her spot. I expect she'd like that.'

'Probably.' Dorothy paused a moment, then leaning towards Lydia she said in a hushed tone, 'I'll tell you a little secret, if you like dear. I've never told anyone else before, but you'll be right with it.'

Lydia wondered what she could possibly be about to say, what secret of her mother's had she held all these years that Lydia could now be privileged to share.

'She's right here with us now.'

Lydia looked blankly, then around her, half expecting to see Fanny approaching them through the rose garden.

'I scattered her ashes here.'

'Oh' said Lydia with breathless relief, uncertain as to the right response to this revelation.

'I don't know as if I was meant to, if you are allowed to, but I did it anyway. I couldn't think what else to do and it didn't seem right to just have them thrown away. I just came up one day and did it when there was no one about.'

It didn't matter to Lydia one way or the other, it was the act of a loving daughter, probably the very last thing that she could have done for her mother, or at least for her mother's memory.

'I think you were right, Dorothy. And if you weren't supposed to, then it certainly doesn't matter now.'

They sat a while in silence, soaking up the sun and the soft murmurings of insects, the flittering of birds. Dorothy perhaps thought of her mother, while Lydia simply sank into tranquillity, glad for once to have her mind idling, untaxed by enquiry.

'Oh, Lydia I have that little discovery to share with you. I brought it with me, here have a look.' She withdrew a small envelope from her bag. 'It's not much, but it was in the kitchen drawer with some other bits and pieces.'

Lydia opened the envelope and examined the four photographs that it contained.

'Those two are snaps of me, I don't know why she kept them in particular.'

Lydia saw a young woman, in her twenties maybe, looking awkward and shy, her clothes both shapeless and ill-fitting. In each one Dorothy was half smiling and to Lydia's mind, probably asking her mother not to take the picture.

'Then there's those other two. You remember I said that I thought mum had a cousin or something come over once? I can't be sure but I think they was taken on that day, they were up here, I think. It's all changed now so you can't be sure.'

In the first, three women of varying ages sat on a bench in sunshine, at their feet two toddlers squatted, looking grimly at the camera. In the second there were only the younger and the older of the women, otherwise the scene was the same. The older woman, in her fifties perhaps, slim and poised in a dark coat and under a hat which might have been circa 1930; Fanny, Dorothy's mum, a little younger in a lighter half-length coat, hatless; the youngest of the trio and therefore probably the children's mother, still had the sparkle of youth about her, sitting in her floral print frock with its full skirt that shouted 1950's spread out on the bench.

Dorothy leant across and pointed to the figure missing in the second photograph. 'That's mum. I think she must've taken the other photo.'

'I wonder who took this one then?'

'There's nothing on them, but I thought they might be interesting.'

'Oh yes, they are, thank you. They were in a drawer you say?'

'Yes, you know how it is with kitchen drawers, they gets full of all kinds of stuff. I was looking for some drawing pins and see this envelope and as soon as I do, I knew what was in it right away, dear.'

Lydia wondered how long it had been since she had sorted out any of her own cupboards and drawers, how long it would yet be before she did. Forty years did not seem quite so long when looked at in this way. She held the photos beside each other and studied them. Something was familiar, but she was not sure what. She did not recognise the faces, the scene was foreign to her. Perhaps it was the period, perhaps it was the look which took her back to her own mother's family albums.

'Can I hang on to these for a while Dorothy? I'll let you have them back of course. I'll get copies done.'

'Yes dear, like I said, I was going to send them to you anyway.'

When they'd had their sit in the sunshine and the conversation began to flag, Lydia suggested they went down to the sea and walk along the promenade, just as generations of visitors had done. Dorothy was happy to do so, and show Lydia a little of the town that had been home all her life. She pointed out where she had worked all those years in the department store, and the landmark of the Dome cinema, where she and Frank, that had been his name, had done a little courting before he left for a new life 'down under'. At mid-afternoon they took tea in a café, which Dorothy announced on leaving had 'once been a nice place'. During their wanderings Lydia suggested to Dorothy that when she had done with the albums, found Dorothy's family as best she could, then perhaps Dorothy might like to visit some of the places connected to them, maybe even go across the Channel and visit the war graves. She was non-committal, grateful for the offer, but Lydia could tell that she had no appetite for such a project, and in that moment guessed also she was less interested in the detail of her family than Lydia was herself. Seeing Lydia, helping her, writing to her, was not all about Dorothy's family, it was also about pleasing this curiosity of a woman from Oxford who had popped so unexpectedly into her life.

⋆

In the following week Lydia did little with the Joslins, picking at this and that, but unable to settle to any concentrated effort. She had come so far, maybe to the point where all but the journal could be unravelled, and yet the urge had left her, temporarily at least. Behind it, she knew, was the knowledge that Dorothy did not really care about what she was doing. What had she expected, a bouquet and a fanfare? Dorothy was curious about her family and why would she not be, given her solitary upbringing? But the process was of only passing interest to her, she did not share in the pleasures of the chase, each new discovery was just another remote fact, connected in some way to her, but in what way was apparently immaterial.

This depression engulfed her until the Saturday after her lunch in the sunshine with Dorothy. Blazing June announced itself with a cold rain blowing down from the north, and the weekend held no attractions. None, that is, until a solitary letter plopped onto her doormat. The steady sloping handwriting was unfamiliar, the postmark smudged. It was typical of Lydia that she should try to work out who it might be from before taking the simple option of opening it, and she knew it. She slit the envelope neatly with a knife. As she read the single page her mouth opened a little more with every line.

The Old Rectory
Grantchester
Cambs

28th May

Dear Lydia

I hope you will not mind me writing to you, but I thought you would find it preferable to a phone call, or worse still, my turning up on your doorstep!

I shall be in Oxford on 16th June for a couple of nights and hope you will have a meal with me on that evening. And if you were interested I would be very pleased if you would be my guest at a conference on the 17th at Magdalen College. I think you would find it interesting, and if not the subject matter, then at least the occasion. I shall not be in any way offended if you are unable to accept. Please drop me a line or email me – kellaways55@googlemail.com.

How is the project going? Perhaps you have solved your puzzles, I know how deeply involved you were. I will be very interested to know how it all turned out.

Your friend from the Lakes
Stephen Kellaway

Lydia put the letter on her desk and sat staring out of the window for a few minutes, trying to gather her thoughts. Mixed up in them were the prospect of a meal with Stephen - someone she had already decided that she could never see or speak to again; going to a conference of all things; her limp lack of application with Joslins; and the energy she would need to dress herself up for the occasion. Her fingers twirled absentmindedly through her hair, grown longer than when she had last seen him, now tied back in a band for simple convenience. She would need to do something with her hair. She read the letter again, just to be sure exactly what it said, what additional meaning she might find hidden between the lines, but she found none that was anything but pure fancy. It was as straightforward as she would have expected from Stephen, had she expected anything at all. Her choices were abundantly clear. Either she could do nothing, pretend she'd not received the letter, or she could reply politely saying that she was busy or could not get the time off work. Or, just conceivably, she could accept, with all that would entail. Her instinct was to run and hide, but, in thinking about Stephen, their companionship as they walked round Loweswater came back to her, how they had paused a while here and there on their journey, taking in the landscape, each easy in the other's company. This would be something quite different, an intention, a plan, a decision, not the coincidence of a casual meeting, each far from home. Neither would it be the 'nearly' meeting outside the Randolph. Never one to act in haste, Lydia chose to do nothing. She would let the whole idea evolve, and see how it seemed when she woke tomorrow. She was quite sure it would be the first thought to come to her mind.

Despite her intention to forget the invitation for twenty-four hours, it did have one immediate effect - when her few household tasks had been done, she sat down to the Joslins with a fresh determination. She told herself that this was simply a new surge of energy, nothing to do with Stephen's letter, but a small part of her knew that if she should accept his offer, if she were to be asked how the project was going, then it would be satisfying to have something more than ham sandwiches with Dorothy to report. As usual at such points in her research, Lydia sifted through her notes, re-arranging them, refreshing her mind and re-making her list of outstanding questions. Still at the head of the list was Bertie Dix-Myers. She had looked in every place she could think of to find some trace of his existence, but all she had was what she had started with, his photos in the RAF album. She examined them again, minutely, looking for some missed clue, but she found none. Her notes confirmed that she had found no birth entry for him under Joslin or Myers or Dix-Myers. She had looked for Albert, Herbert and Hubert, for Bertram and Bertie, each with the same result.

Which meant either he was not registered, was missing from the index, or had been registered under another name. Unless of course he had been born abroad, in which case her search was certainly doomed to failure and she might as well not waste any more time on it. She had checked marriages until the end of the war and war graves too. Another possibility crept into her thoughts. She could have simply missed him, the depressing doubt that afflicts all such research. Had she really checked every page for every quarter for every year? Had she really thought to see if his name was added as an afterthought to the bottom of the typed lists? It was very easy to forget, and if she had, then there was no alternative but to start again, and while she was at it, she could see if Verity had fallen through the same crack. It was a daunting prospect. She thought of her little mistake in recording names from the graves around Cockermouth, how she might have not revisited them without Stephen's encouragement. Here he was encouraging her again.

At the very moment Lydia typed in '1922' to retrieve the first year's list of births she stopped. All this time she had seen Bertie through his mother's eyes, seen how she took care over his photographs, wrote the captions with the same love as for her twins. She had seen him as Alethia's son, whether by James or some previous liaison. Suppose he were not her son at all, but had come to take that place through love or circumstance? What if he were James' son but not hers? The fleeting pleasure of the insight was lost as she realised she'd never checked if James and Barbara Vaughan had a child. When had Barbara died? She looked it up in an instant. It was the June quarter of 1920, too soon after marriage for them to have had a child. A stupid assumption, of course they could have had a child, they could have had a child whose birth had led to Barbara's death. And so it was that she finally found Bertram A D Myers, registered in the same place and in the same quarter of the same year as his mother's death. Lydia took an educated guess that the 'D' in 'A D' would be Dix, and noted how the Dix and the Myers showed signs of separating again. The certificate would tell her if the 'A' was Albert, as she had a feeling it might be.

The first thoughts that entered Lydia's head as she blinked into Sunday morning were not of Stephen, nor his letter or anything about it. Her first thoughts were to question the wisdom of having drunk nearly a whole bottle of white burgundy the previous evening. She had intended only a glass or two, settled back in her chair and let her thoughts roam where they would while resisting any consideration of Stephen's letter. Resistance was futile and a third glass led to a fourth. Before she went to bed she already knew she would find an excuse to say yes to him, find some reason to justify such a course of action to herself. So later, as she sipped coffee propped up on her pillows, it was no surprise to find that the decision had been made, she would accept, and do her best to overcome the difficulties of time, of dress, and of confidence that would result.

9

The day they were to meet arrived far too quickly. It was on her before she had time to breathe. For two weeks, her life had seemed a whirlwind compared to its normal steady pace. With reluctance at first, then with a growing abandonment she'd shopped for clothes, renewed her supply of makeup, agonised over her hair, and finally selected some shoes. What she had spent on herself in the last two years she now splashed in a matter of days. While she was trying on a third dress in a shop that she felt far too old for, she noticed her underwear in the mirror. It was as grey and tired as her skin was pallid. In a couple of places the fabric was beginning to part company with the seams. It should be replaced. Not that she had even contemplated the notion that it might be seen be anyone else, seen by Stephen, no, it simply needed replacing. But to do so now, at this particular moment in her life, wasn't it just asking for trouble? Supposing that some development occurred to lead in that direction, the direction of trouble, wouldn't the quality of her bra provide the resolve that she might need? She sagged at the prospect. No, there would be no new bra to go with the new dress, what was hidden would stay hidden.

Now it came to preparing herself, she realised that there were some items that she had not considered. Her hands would have benefited from some attention and it would have helped if she'd had more recent practice in making her face look something other than a painted doll. With only an hour to the appointed time she decided to start again, this time using far less of everything. The result was not what she had hoped, but as she looked at her reflection she decided that it was passable and most certainly an improvement on the first attempt. She had finally settled on a loose fitting black dress with a modest neckline and sleeves just below the elbow. Lydia fervently hoped it would be appropriate to whatever the evening might hold. As a finishing touch she put on her one decent pair of earrings and necklace to match. They were hand-made, silver, and had been a present from Michael on their first wedding anniversary. She had often worn them in those far off days. As she fixed the clasp, Lydia realised they had become just objects, she could like them for what they were, their associations and meaning had died. The thought gave her a certain liberation.

Ready or not, she would have to do. It was a few minutes walk up into the centre of Oxford but it was raining, and she wished she'd been ready earlier. Too late to call a taxi, she set off through the puddles, her shabby winter coat completely at odds with the new finery beneath. She had sacrificed her usual bag for a smaller, dressier one that had lain unused at the bottom of her wardrobe for several years, a present from her brother and Joan if memory served her right. The long straps of the handles were too wide to sit well in the hand and yet were too short to be put over her shoulder. Once the evening was over it would return to the wardrobe to rest in peace for a few more years. As she neared St Giles, she was thankful her choice of shoes had leaned toward sensible rather than high fashion. Even so, they were tighter than she remembered them being in the shop. Approaching The Randolph it was impossible not to think of that moment when she had slunk into the shadows rather than risk speaking to the man she was about to meet inside. He could not possibly have guessed the irony in suggesting they meet there, where he was staying, before their meal. With as much poise as she could muster she ascended the steps, horribly aware that hers was not the million-dollar hair and the glittering beauty she had last seen with Stephen on those self same steps.

Loud young men in dinner jackets and willowy models sheathed in silk filled the foyer. Lydia stared about her, desperate to see a familiar face. She quickly slipped off her coat, partly to give herself something to do and partly to fold the offending garment over her arm.

'Hello, Lydia,' said a familiar voice behind her.

She turned and looked straight into the face of Gloria Fitzgerald.

'Blimey Lydia, look at you! You dark horse, you. Who's the lucky man? Are you at this bash tonight?'

Lydia was too shocked to speak, her mouth moved and a low noise emerged but it had no meaning.

'Come on, what's the deal?'

'I . . . I'm meeting someone, someone I know, someone I met, not a man.'

'Are you serious? You're meeting a woman dressed like that? Wow! this has to be seen.'

'No, no, it is a man, just not a man like that.'

'Yeah, right. Not a man that you get dressed up for, not a man you wear makeup for. For Christ's sake Lydia, give me some credit will you.'

'Ok, well, I just thought that in a place like this it would be better, you know, to dress up a bit.' Lydia was grasping for some reason to be there, some plausible excuse for the position in which she found herself.

'Wait a minute. You've got the day off tomorrow haven't you? You crafty . . . .'

Whatever Gloria was about to call her was cut short by Stephen Kellaway who had arrived at their side unnoticed.

'Hello Lydia, good to see you again,' and then without pause he turned and held out his hand to Gloria, 'Stephen Kellaway, pleased to meet you.'

'Oh and pleased to meet you too, Stephen Kellaway,' responded Gloria, pushing back her shoulders to ensure that her breasts held front and centre stage.

Lydia wished that she had never agreed to the idea, the meeting, the venue, any part of it. Her cheeks flamed and she yearned for the floor to open and swallow her, but no such miracle was forthcoming.

'Hello Stephen,' she said, with as much composure as she could gather, 'This is Gloria Fitzgerald, someone I work with.' Even in her confusion, she baulked at the word 'colleague'.

To Lydia's immense relief Stephen at once recognised the position and took immediate charge. Afterwards she wondered if he had watched her encounter with Gloria and summed it all up before he came across to them.

'Gloria, I don't wish to appear rude, but we really need to be getting along. You will excuse us won't you? Nice to have met you.' And with that he gently steered Lydia back towards the entrance, leaving an amazed and frustrated Gloria in their wake.

A taxi took them the short distance up the Woodstock Road to The Lemon Tree, recommended, Stephen had said, by a friend. He'd booked a table although on a Thursday night he need not have bothered, there were few diners, and while they sipped aperitifs, they had the little bar to themselves. It took Lydia a few minutes to recover herself from the embarrassments of The Randolph, and she groped for conversation before she recognised that it wasn't necessary. She let the silence grow until it was comfortable, relaxing into his company.

'Lydia, I think the first thing to say is thank you for coming. I did not really know the best way to get in touch and ask you.'

'It was lovely to get your letter, and kind of you to think of me. Do tell me what you think will be of interest to me at the college tomorrow.'

'Ah, the conference. Yes, I hope you enjoy it. It's put on by The Forensic Science Society, there are some interesting topics and good speakers. But like all these affairs, it's the coffee time conversations and lunchtime asides that make the day.'

'It sounds a little above my head, but if you think I'll enjoy it then I'll be glad to come and listen.'

'Good, though I have just realised that I have left the details, your pass and so on, back at the hotel. You must remind me to give them to you later.'

Lydia saw that she had only half remembered the easy smile, the economy with words, the lithe movement. Neither did she recall him looking as attractive, no, not so much attractive as distinguished, as he did now in his linen summer jacket, sage shirt open at the collar, slender hands holding a gin and tonic. 'Smart-casual' might have been coined for him, and yet there was a distinct touch of academia about him too.

'Stephen, I was wondering, just how did you find me? Did you get my address from the hotel?'

He looked at her quizzically for a brief moment, then smiled and shook his head a fraction. 'Nothing so clever, Lydia. I looked you up in the phone book.'

'The phone book?'

'Yes, well, the online version. You of all people should know there are very few 'Silverstreams' in Oxfordshire. Two in fact. One in Banbury I think, and you in Oxford.'

'Oh.' The phone book, yes, how blindingly obvious. And she was the one who secretly thought of herself as the great detective.

He was very keen to know how the Joslin saga was unfolding and once he had Lydia started, all her discoveries tumbled out over their meal. She picked up where they had left off in Cumbria, telling him all about Dorothy and her mother, how she had written to two hundred Joslins, identifying 'B' as Phoebe, Alethia and James, Albert and Hannah. Only at a couple of points did Stephen break her flow with a question, for the rest, he remembered enough of the story to pick it all up again as she went along.

'And just this week, after I heard from you, I had a very interesting excursion. You know, one of the real pleasures of all this is that it takes me down different paths, to places and events that I would know nothing about. And if I choose to linger a little in a place because it is interesting then I can, because there is no deadline, nothing depends on what I do.'

'A luxury, indeed, and the better to be enjoyed since you recognise it. So where did you go this week?'

'The thing is, I really wanted to have something to tell you, something more than a few more certificates ordered, something interesting. The whole thing had suddenly gone a little flat, I might have just given it all up, then your letter jerked me back to life and

I solved one problem easily enough when I saw my own stupid mistake. Then I had a brilliant stroke of luck.'

'Luck? Someone once said that the harder he worked, the luckier he got.'

'Well, I was looking for Bertie, the one who was Alethia's stepson, in the RAF and I'd looked before and there was nothing, and I was just following my nose through all sorts of different places and found all this information about prisoners of war. There's reams of it, some of the survivors still have reunions, they even invite their old guards from the camps. It seems extraordinary but apparently they do. Anyway, I started reading all about a camp called Stalag Luft 3, it was fascinating and horrible too, they just lined up a whole group of prisoners who had escaped and shot them. And among all the information was this little link to a site with lists of RAF POWs. And he was there, Bertie Dix-Myers was right there. He spent almost the whole war as a prisoner.'

Stephen smiled and studied her face, flushed with excitement even in re-telling the tale. He had been right to make contact with her again, despite his misgivings. Her brief note of acceptance had given nothing away, no clue as to her feelings, but the acceptance alone had surely said something. He realised she was looking at him with expectation of a reply. 'Yes, that's very good. I don't know where luck comes into it, though.'

'There's more! Stalag Luft 3 was the one where they dug the tunnels. *The Great Escape*. Tom, Dick and Harry they called them.' She saw that he was looking blank. 'It was a film, had Steve McQueen in it, it was very famous,' she implored.

'Oh, right, yes,' said Stephen, although he was thinking less about Steve McQueen and more about how wonderfully animated Lydia became, how passionate she could be once she warmed to her topic. Yet he could also see her fragility. Scarred, perhaps? Too often bruised by life? For the moment it did not matter.

'And so, Lydia, what's next? Where have you got to in this tale? I can see that Dorothy is the end of the road in one sense, but you still have the journal, and I'm guessing that is your real objective now.'

'Yes, it is. I didn't realise it for a long time, then when I saw that the albums would end up with Dorothy, one way or another, there was a moment when I didn't want to let them go. I couldn't let them go, not without understanding the journal.' Lydia hadn't put these thoughts into words before, not really been comfortable with such an admission, even to herself, but sitting with Stephen, lingering over the remains of an excellent meal in such sympathetic company, it all came into perspective, all made sense when she said it.

'It was the journal that made me think of you when this conference came up.' This was not entirely true, since he had been thinking of her quite often. 'You might bring it along with you, one of the speakers will be talking about his speciality. I think his presentation is called Documents – Inferences and Evidence. Even if it isn't immediately relevant I thought you would find it interesting and you never know what can come out of these things. It might even be fun.'

'It's a bit daunting, the idea of going to something like this.'

'They're just people, specialists I agree, but still just people. And nowhere near as . . .' he was going to say passionate but changed his mind, 'nowhere near as enthusiastic as you.'

Stephen had insisted she take a taxi home from the Randolph after they'd shared a final drink at the bar. Thankfully, the hotel had quietened, and better still, there was no sign of Gloria or her noisy companions. Time enough for that confrontation come Monday morning. He had given her the envelope with her pass and the conference programme, warning her that he would not be able to spend much time with her during the proceedings as he would be 'on duty'. She was surprised to find herself too excited to settle immediately to sleep, so she sat in her bed, letting images of the evening with Stephen flow through her mind. She allowed herself a smile at the thought that the state of her underwear had not come into question. He had been good company, not seeming to mind that she had talked far too much. Although, hadn't there been a moment, when she had looked at him and he was staring at her with, well, with an odd look in his eye, as if he wasn't really there at all? Maybe he had glazed over and hadn't noticed that she'd stopped talking. At length she took out the folder from its envelope to study the timetable for tomorrow. Her pass looked important enough, an identity badge wrapped in a plastic case and clipped to a ribbon to hang round her neck. 'Lydia Silverstream. Guest'. Precise and to the point. There she was too, on the list of forty or so delegates, where she could not help but notice that hers was the only name not followed by a series of initials.

Despite having lived in the city for so long, Lydia had never once ventured into any of the colleges, so she was interested to see that the precise venue was the Summer Common Room at Magdalen, which according to the little map was right in the heart of the ancient buildings of the college. The programme included a couple of coffee sessions, lunch at the college and a meal in the evening. Stephen hadn't said anything about that. Maybe it was always implied for such gatherings. The topics for the conference included '*Detecting DNA – Latest Developments*', '*Documents – Inferences and Evidence*' exactly as Stephen had recalled, '*Fire Scene Secrets*' and '*Evaluation and Interpretation of Evidence*', this last item of the day being presented by Sir Stephen Kellaway, FFSS. Lydia read it again. *Sir* Stephen? She couldn't grasp it for a moment. A small hole grew in her stomach and she had difficulty focusing on the paper in her hand. How could he not have told her, how could he let her get so out of her depth? Then, from being angry at the perceived deception, she became angry with herself for having been so stupid as to think she could move in his circles, go to his conference, chat over coffee with such men of science – 'the leaders in their fields' the programme said. She, Lydia Silverstream, 'guest', with her crushing ignorance, what made her think that she would have anything to share with these people, people with more letters after their names than she had in hers? Lydia clenched her hands so tightly that the programme tore as it scrunched in her fists.

Too agitated to stay in bed, she paced her tiny room for a minute or two, disoriented, dishevelled and disappointed. Slowly the turmoil subsided and she took herself down to the kitchen to make a hot drink. She needed something calming, something soothing, and the mechanical action of preparing it occupied a small part of her brain. The cup warmed her hands, soothed her senses. She found a blanket and took herself to her chair, tucking her legs underneath her. A dull depression seeped into her and began feeding on itself. Even to recognise her reaction as irrational was to underline her lack of confidence. The pleasures of the evening were mirages made from her own naivety, now exposed for what they were. If only she had stuck to her instincts, stayed hidden in the shadows and watched from a distance. Whichever way she turned her thoughts to find some virtue in them, there was another telling her there was no virtue to be found. Should she still go to this conference? If she did then surely it would only be because she lacked the nerve, the confidence, to stay away. But if she were to stay away, it would be proof indeed that she lacked the confidence to go. The image of her beleaguered journal writer, unable to select a pen from the two available, swam briefly before her. For an instant Lydia felt his dilemma, the paralysis of choice, before the shaft of insight closed.

*

'Ah, that. I thought perhaps you might have googled me,' was Stephen's slightly lame, apologetic reply.

He had found her standing, invisibly she hoped, beside an arch in the cloisters where they gave out onto the quad, where a few of the delegates had spilled out from the main building to enjoy the balmy summer day. He had been easy to avoid until then and she'd taken a seat at the very back of the auditorium for the first session of the day. If pressed, she would have admitted it had been interesting and, if she let her mind skip past the finer points of the technology and the science, she'd even enjoyed the chance to look into another world. Then, while the men, plus the solitary woman, of science talked their talk over coffee, Stephen had sought her out, only to be greeted a little coolly, he thought. Lydia was pale and her eyes were dark and sunken, all trace of the previous evening's zing quite gone. He'd enquired of her health, had she slept badly? 'Why didn't you tell me?' was all she'd said. When he had looked a little blankly, she showed him her crumpled programme of the day with her finger right by his name.

'Well, I didn't google you.' she said flatly.

'Perhaps it was a little vain of me,' he added, 'to think that you would be interested.' He was caught unawares by this turn of events, his title, like his academic honours, wasn't something that he often gave any thought to, nor expected others to. 'And it is this that has upset you? Do you somehow think that I am not the person that you thought I was? I have hidden nothing Lydia, I am who I am and I cannot help that.'

Direct and precise. Softly said, but nonetheless straight to the point. Such clarity of thought only served to reinforce Lydia's insecurities.

'In a way, I suppose. It made me think I didn't belong here, in your world,' which was as near to the truth as she felt able to venture.

They were moving into new territory, beyond the uncomplicated country walk, the pleasant meal. Something personal had appeared, and it had appeared at a most inconvenient time.

'Well, we can talk about my world another time perhaps, but for now we need to take our seats.' As they turned back towards the Common Room Lydia may have felt the slightest hint of his hand on her back, gently guiding her, or she may have imagined it.

The session on documents was presented by Felix Russell, a gawky young man in his late twenties. He appeared quite uncoordinated, as if his body had been assembled from various spare parts that had not become fully acquainted with each other. His clothes, a tweedy jacket over a check shirt and ill-knotted tie, belonged to an earlier generation. His lower half was hidden by the podium, but Lydia was sure that cord trousers and brogues would be close to the mark. As he finished each sentence his hand flew to his glasses to check that they were still securely placed across his nose. His delivery was poor, but he was listened to intently, and Lydia found his subject quite riveting, made all the more vivid for her by constant mental reference to her own document of mystery, her journal. He spoke of obtaining DNA from fingerprints on the paper; how the age and acid content of the paper affected the process; how the conditions of storage could cause minute changes in the chemistry; how the content and composition of the inks and graphite could determine the age of the writing. When he had finished with the chemistry he addressed the physical, and spoke of pressures and indentations, the slope of the writing. All these Lydia could comprehend with ease without need to understand the science. He turned to the typed, the photocopied and the computer printed, illustrating how, even here, special processes could reveal hidden snippets of knowledge. Next, he spoke of the words themselves, how it was only relatively recently that language experts had been asked to help forensic science by analysing the words beyond their obvious meanings to shed light on some other aspects of the writer. The first time such analysis had famously come to public attention had been the letters written by Peter Sutcliffe to the policeman leading the search for him. He talked about the choice of words and the combination of words and how they could help build a picture of the writer and how difficult it was for even a professional author to hide his 'writing profile', even when composing dialogue for one of his characters. He closed his presentation hinting at the shape of things to come, the power of computers in analysing both the chemistry and the language. The applause from his peers as he left the platform was more than polite, they had willed him to complete his task without mishap, and shared his relief at having done so.

Stephen had carefully ensured that Lydia was seated next to him for lunch at a table with a half a dozen others, including the awkward Felix, who was seated on her other side. Stephen introduced Lydia to him, adding that he thought they might have much to talk about.

'I really enjoyed your talk.'

'Thank you. I am not really very good at these things, public things.' His fingers flicked to his glasses.

'It doesn't matter, everybody seemed to think it was good.' He looked so uncomfortable, so much the fish-out-of-water, that Lydia found herself needing to encourage him, re-assure him of his right to be there.

'Professor Kellaway said that you had some writing, a document, that you wanted to talk about.'

Professor Kellaway. Another revelation, not that Lydia was too surprised. 'Ah, yes. I didn't know that he had mentioned it. It's not really that interesting. I mean it is for me, but probably not for you.'

'He suggested that there was something of a mystery involved.'

'To my way of looking at it, there are many odd, or at least unusual, things about it. It's a very long story, but I'll try and be brief. It's hand written, in a kind of old ledger. I think the ledger is much older than the writing. The entries start at the back and work forward. The writing is by one person, I'm sure, but in different inks and some pencil and the writing changes. It's in the form of a kind of journal, not exactly a diary. And the content is, well, a bit disturbing. I think the person who wrote it suffered some kind of breakdown. It ends abruptly, without any kind of resolution. No, that's not quite true, there is a resolution of a kind for the writer, but not for the reader. But then again I don't think it was written for a reader, I think it was only written for the writer.'

Lydia cut herself short, all too aware of how easily she could be carried away with the story. As she paused, she turned as if for validation to Stephen. He was looking at her as a father might look at a favourite daughter with a mix of affection and pride. Or was he looking at her as his pet project, his amateur protégé? The thought unsettled her.

'It does sound interesting, I'd certainly like to see it, do you have it with you?'

'Oh, no, I'm afraid not.' She had quite forgotten. It had been Stephen's suggestion of the previous evening, and had been lost in her private crisis. Now she saw that he had manipulated the meeting with Felix, designed it so that she could show him the journal, which he assumed she would have brought, just because he had suggested it. Why couldn't he have given her the reason for his suggestion, explained the circumstance, instead of arranging things to happen as if by chance? Besides which, she was suddenly unsure that she really wanted to share it with anyone. It was intensely private, never intended to be read by anyone, she alone held that privilege. If this Felix Russell, this expert in his field, were to see it and dismiss it as nonsense, where would that leave her? Uncertainty gnawed at her again and the idea of skipping the afternoon sessions crept into her mind.

Neither Felix Russell nor Lydia quite knew how to continue the conversation. Felix had done his bit, had easily complied with the great man's wishes, as he was duty bound to do, while Lydia had no inclination to reveal anything more. Stephen tried to include her in conversation with the expert on arson, but Lydia politely declined to be drawn. When the meal was finished, Felix offered her his hand for want of knowing any other way of bidding her goodbye and Stephen was immediately required elsewhere. If she wished she could just collect her coat, slip away and not a soul would notice.

The Botanic Gardens were busier than she thought they might be. It had been years since she was there on her only previous visit and that had been at night, when a son-et-lumiere had caught her attention and on a whim she had spent the evening wandering alone through the display. Now the voices around her were Japanese and American, interspersed with those of their Oxford guides. At the far corner of the gardens, close to the Cherwell, she found a spot beneath a great spread of branches and rested there in the warmth of the afternoon. Yesterday's rain had freshened the earth and the air was filled with the subtle scents of the garden. Light and shade played across the water, sparkling on its journey, soothing her troubled spirits, as the sight of moving water has done for so many. She would return to Magdalen in time for coffee and Stephen's presentation, she owed him that at least. But for an hour or so she would empty her mind, or at least let its jumbled contents settle a little. As the peace of the place enveloped her, a stray thought popped into her head: had they ever come here to walk and sit awhile by the river, the journal writer and his wife? If she looked hard enough through squinted eyes, would she catch some flicker of their presence? Instead of dismissing the idea as an idle waste, Lydia let herself drift with the notion. Hadn't he written of the river at one point? All along she had thought it was the Thames, what else would she think when it ran only yards from her home, but it might just as easily be the Cherwell or any other for that matter. As the minutes floated by, her passion re-asserted itself and she smiled at the thought of describing it so. She realised how directionless she had become when the drive to solve her puzzle waned, and welcomed the feeling of renewed vigour that its return brought her.

It was a refreshed and enlivened Lydia who congratulated Stephen on the excellence of his quite absorbing and wide-ranging review of forensic evidence. He couldn't help but notice the change in her, the colour in her cheeks, the life behind her eyes.

'I see you are feeling better.'

'Yes, thank you Stephen, I'm quite recovered. I'm sorry about this morning. And I didn't think you'd mind me missing the arson man.'

'Not at all, what did you do with yourself?'

'I had a very good hour in the Botanic Garden, have you been there?'

'No, but I know it's close by.'

'Perhaps I'll take you there one day,' Lydia said without thought or consideration.

'Good, yes, I'd like that. I take it we are friends again?'

'Yes, it was really so good of you to invite me today, but I won't be coming to the dinner tonight. I hope that's alright. I have things that I want to do.' Then, by way of confirming their friendship she added, 'And I will keep in touch, let you know how I'm getting on with the Joslins.'

Lydia took her time getting home, allowing herself a long detour through Rose Lane, along by Christ Church meadow to St. Aldates, then to Folly and the path by the river to Osney. All the while, her senses were alert for some feeling of place that she might find echoed in the journal. Despite being surrounded by the ghosts of millennia, none spoke to her. She paused a few moments by the

Pot Stream to read the inscription on Edgar Wilson's memorial, seeking some whispered insight from the drowned hero, but none came. It didn't deter or unsettle her, the whole weekend lay ahead, a weekend of her own pleasure, a weekend she was determined would be one of achievement and progress. She would re-read the journal, tease some new gem from its pages, follow Bertie where she could – ah! the phone book, thank you Stephen – and tackle the sandcastles album. And there were also those photographs that Dorothy had given her, they needed closer examination, some previously unseen connection might be gleaned from them.

To take advantage of the remains of the day, Lydia carefully arranged a table and comfortable chair in her patch of a garden. The evening would be long and warm and she would not need her computer for the task she had set herself. She poured a glass of Petit Chablis and put the bottle in a cooler, placed a pen, a pencil and a blue highlighter on the table, and settled herself with her carefully transcribed copy of the journal. Little new might be learned from the anger or the distress, nor the story such as it was; what she was looking for was any fact that might easily have been overlooked, overshadowed by the power of the emotion. Facts which, when drawn together, might offer some additional insight to the circumstances of the writer or even the object of his distress.

The dusk had begun to envelop her by the time she had carefully read every word again, trying without success to ignore the anguish, trying to see only the unconsidered trifles buried in the words. She'd used her highlight pen in twenty or so places on the manuscript to remind her of the fragments that she had found. None of them came as a surprise, there was no shock of discovery, rather, that taken as a whole, they could amount to a little more than the sum of the fragments. She carefully wrote out a summary of her findings in the last light of the day.

S: A teacher, aged 31 in summer 1983, when her godmother/cousin/aunt(?) Phoebe Joslin died in Cockermouth. Described as short haired, sharp featured with wide mouth. Enjoys gardening (rose bushes) on a small plot. Attends conferences/training in summer holidays. French holiday with writer.

Writer: Advertising copywriter(?), 8 years with company(Pink2?) in 1983 so started in 1975. Drives to work (in Botley?). Has female GP(?).

They: Have friends H & J. Had a child who died at (or near) birth. Live near a river which they could 'walk right into'.

As she wrote the details, Lydia felt sure that she was on firm ground with these facts, paltry as they were. She knew in themselves they would not lead her to the writer, but she also knew they could prevent her heading down a blind alley in her quest. Another small detail, not a fact, but perhaps interesting, caught her eye. At the end of both of the last two entries the writer had used the words 'Mr Punch'. Lydia could not guess at their significance, although clearly they had some special meaning for the author. Her sense of place told her that these were people living in a town of some size, even though some rural outposts would have shops and rivers that you could 'walk right into'. If he did work in Botley, as she surmised, then the obvious town was Oxford, with Abingdon a close second. Consideration might be given to Kidlington, even Woodstock or Witney. But all this was more than twenty, nearer thirty, years ago, and as she well knew, things have a habit of changing.

Putting her papers to one side, Lydia poured the last of the bottle and lit a large candle, lemon scented supposedly to repel insects. The steady glow of the flame in the still air wrapped the deepening night around her like a blanket. For a little while longer, the sun's heat, stored in the bricks of her house, radiated back on her to keep the chill at bay. Every time she had read the journal, she felt a fraction closer to the lives it encompassed, the world they inhabited. Familiarity dulled the shock of the insight to another's mind, to the innermost secrets entrusted to a neglected notebook. But they were still shocking, still they said that he planned to eliminate his wife. Lydia baulked at thinking of 'kill', even though she knew that was what it might mean. 'Kill' might simply be her obvious interpretation of the words, 'eliminate' might be closer to the reality, he may simply have had a plan by which he could leave her, or make her leave him. And yet, those words about '*casting a leaf to the forest floor to be lost amongst all the other leaves*', what other meaning could be contained there? But she ran ahead of herself again, there was no solution to be found simply by re-reading the journal, nor even by forensic examination, despite what Felix Russell might have said. Or whatever help Stephen might wish to offer. She let him drift back into her thoughts with a degree of pleasure, despite her erratic behaviour towards him. They had parted amicably enough, no doors were closed and they certainly knew a little more about each other, even if it was not what might have been anticipated twenty-four hours previously. She would continue with her own mixture of method and feeling until either she found answers or all avenues had been explored. When she found the connection, and she was very sure that she would, found who they might be, then there was the chance of an answer.

★

Mr Punch. It was that character's name which came first into Lydia's head when she woke in the morning. He must surely be Judy's murderous husband. Murderous? Even in her waking moment had she seen the simple connection, the simple reason that entries thirty and thirty-one ended with that particular name? It seemed tenuous, and yet somehow fitted with the fractured mind of the man who'd written it. And now that she came to think about it, did Mr Punch kill Judy, or was it the crocodile? And the more she thought about it the more she realised that although Punch and Judy were a part of the language, instantly recognisable, she really couldn't remember anything about the story.

By lunchtime, still in her pyjamas and dressing gown, Lydia had read all that she could find about *Punchinello* and his murderous exploits. First the baby, beaten to death when left in his care, then Judy for discovering the crime. Then came the assaults on the policeman, deceiving the hangman, brushes with the crocodile, and at each new twist, each victory over his enemies, the star turn cries 'that's the way to do it!' Little wonder that today's Punch and Judy had been reduced to anodyne blandness. Such scenes of domestic violence would never do for today's fresh-faced innocents.

But even in her cynicism, she had to concede it was probably right. She had never suffered anything more than indifference from Michael before their divorce, but she read enough and knew enough to know that many wives suffered far worse than a blow with Mr Punch's slapstick.

Lydia read the passages from the journal again, to see if the famous catch-phrase might be substituted for 'Mr Punch'. *'So long as I can hang on to that sequence and repeat it faultlessly that will be the way to do it. Mr Punch I think.'* and *'This I think is the world without her even though she sleeps a sleep through this last night. Check mate in the game. Mr Punch.'* As soon as she did so, it was obvious that there was no need for substitution, the writer had not written 'Mr Punch' as some code with some deep meaning. He was almost quoting from the script, and simply attributing the quote. A seriousness settled over her as this discovery sunk in. Remove the comic clothing, remove crocodiles and sausages, remove the hunch back and the hook nose, and you were left with a dark core of violence, murder and deception.

The sobering thought of such crimes came even closer to home when Lydia remembered that her writer had something else in common with the evil puppet. A dead child. Quickly she turned through the pages to the passage. It was fresh in her mind from last night but she wanted the exact wording. '. . .*that tiny scrap of a person, that dead, dead baby lay for a few minutes in his Perspex crib, for all the world peacefully asleep as any other baby on the ward except that he wasn't breathing.'* It was with some relief that Lydia could detect no hint of malice in the words, no suggestion that the death might have been anything but a private tragedy. On the contrary, there was something tender and caring in the 'tiny scrap of a person' phrase. Whatever crimes he had considered, planned, even committed, he had not killed his son.

10

It was the prospect of a fresh challenge, rather than the potentially tedious business of filling out the details of lives she thought she already knew, that prompted Lydia to reach for her 'sandcastles' album. It was either that or hunt for a marriage for Bertie or look for Albert and Hannah's children, neither of which she much relished. It had been a while since she had held the book, longer since she had so diligently made her notes on the names and the places. Cheap board with a dimpled surface bound the black card pages where stick-on corners held the precious records of family life in their places. The captions were carefully written in white pencil or crayon under each snapshot until near the end, by which time the faces were so familiar that a simple page heading had been considered sufficient. Slowly she leafed through, re-acquainting herself with the 1950s, with Fred, Susan and Paul, Beryl and Archie, and of course with 'self', the one seeming constant in every album. Fred and 'self' were certainly husband and wife, Susan and Paul their children. They holidayed in Margate and Hastings, Devon and the Dales. So, Lydia guessed, most likely the album covered four years, four summer holidays with a few other snaps in between. The shiny Humber with the white-walled tyres appeared for the third holiday, the summer in Devon at Pickwell Manor.

Then there were Beryl and Archie, 'the Arncliffes' according to a Margate caption, their regular holiday companions with their two children Linda and Stephen. Pretty much of an age with Susan and

Paul, which was only to be expected. Archie, like Fred, smoked a pipe, whether on the beach in a deck chair or picnicking in the Dales. How long since Lydia had seen anyone smoke a pipe? A centuries old tradition had apparently vanished in less than a generation. Fred and Archie both looked so much older than fathers of young children did today, but then again, they had lived through different times, had more reason to have aged. And Lydia's mind being the way it was, she fell to wondering what these two daddies had done in the war, and whether later, she would need to answer that question.

The summer holidays gave up nothing of their secrets, no matter how hard Lydia looked at them, no matter how often she examined the faces or the backgrounds with her magnifying glass. She turned her attention to the scattering of photos that interspersed the holidays. One of 'self' and Fred simply captioned 'London', a busy street with a trolleybus in the background, not a scene that Lydia recognised. But a trolleybus, that might at least date the snap as being no later than a certain year, another straw to be clutched at should she need to. There was Susan, for it was surely her, aged about four or five, half hidden by fluttering pigeons in Trafalgar Square. Here was Fred in gardening mode, posed with his foot on a spade on what looked like an allotment, the ever present pipe gripped in his teeth. Next to him, 'self' stood by the railings on some promenade, headscarf flapping in the breeze, with the town pier in the background. Without the repitition of the faces, they would be no more than a random selection of snapshots. There on the last page was 'self' again, sitting on a plaid picnic rug with tasselled edges, looking up at the camera. Her two children had their backs to the lens, while a fourth figure sat in a folding chair, the face in shadow under a broad-brimmed hat. A hat from another era, thought Lydia, but a favourite hat, or perhaps an only hat. With a sudden surge of recognition, Lydia grabbed the magnifying glass and looked again. No, more than that, it was a familiar hat! This was a hat she'd seen before in another photograph. The RAF album? She looked again at 'self' and the skirt spread out on the blanket, saw the floral pattern that had cried out 1950s when she had seen it before in Dorothy's kitchen drawer photographs. She scrabbled for the envelope and slid out the battered prints; same dress, same 'self', same hat on the same figure of the older woman. A stiffened straw hat with a broad ribbon around the crown, a best hat, a hat to wear when visiting, an old hat bought in better days. But most importantly to Lydia, it was a hat to link Dorothy and the sandcastles, a link absolutely confirmed by the face and bold print dress of 'self'.

Dorothy's recollection was of 'cousins', and why should they not be cousins, whether first or second or any number she chose, it did not matter. But Lydia felt there was more to it than that, for while the sandcastles 'self' might be a cousin, then so too might the figure in the hat, for why else would she be both picnicking on a plaid rug and in the gardens at Highdown with Dorothy and her mother? Frustratingly, there was no caption to the picture, not even a title for the page, which seemed to be a collection of odd snaps, maybe not even in time with the holidays, just left-overs that could fill the last page of the album. Did 'self' think that anyone looking would be bound to know who all these people were? Of course she would never have anticipated a stranger poring over them, ignorant of any aspect of their lives. But Lydia realised she might not be completely ignorant, she may know all about their parents or their grandparents or even their great grandparents. These people, this 'self', this Fred, these children, they would have Joslin blood in their veins and if not Joslin then Dix or Myers, possibly all three if they ran true to the pattern of the generations.

All of which brought her back to the task of researching the births, marriages and deaths to fill out the details of Bertie Dix-Myers and find possible children for Albert and Hannah Joslin. There remained a possibility that the sandcastles family belonged to one of those missing girls, to Verity, Harriet or Alice, and the thought did not sit well. Lydia had spent many hours searching and researching for each of them and found trace of neither death nor marriage. Sifting through those same hundreds of index pages yet again was a dismal prospect, one she would only contemplate if all else failed. Surely there was some further insight to be gained from the album, something of which later she might think 'oh, yes, now I see it, if only I had realised.' It was tempting to sit longer, to turn and re-turn the pages, but Lydia knew she would be better off coming to it later, with a fresh mind. If there were some further gem it might be she'd already seen it, already logged it in the subconscious where a night's sleep might reveal its place in the scheme of things. And besides, her weekend was all but done and none of her domestic needs had been attended to - the fridge was nearly as empty as her knicker drawer. If ever there was a day for clean underwear it was surely tomorrow, for tomorrow was her birthday. There would be a card and a little present from her colleagues, she would buy some cakes to be handed round, but above all there would be a grilling from Gloria about Stephen.

Lydia arrived early in her office, intending to avoid a reception committee, but even so, she was not the first. No sooner was she at her desk than Gloria strolled over with exaggerated casualness and very deliberately perched on the corner, her raised eyebrows asking the questions unanswered since Thursday night at the Randolph.

'Well?'

'Well what, Gloria?'

'You know jolly well what.'

'I haven't bought the cakes yet, I'll get them at lunchtime.' Lydia had not exactly rehearsed the conversation, but she had armed herself with a few mischievous ideas.

'Cakes?! Oh, all right, yes, happy birthday Lydia. And what did mister Stephen Kellaway give you? Something nice to put a smile on your face?'

The temptation to correct her, to say 'oh, you mean *Sir* Stephen Kellaway,' was almost irresistable, but Lydia let the moment pass, after all, who was she to start flaunting his title. The thought produced a smile that Gloria took to be the answer she was looking for.

'Ah! I knew it.' Gloria was triumphant. 'Come on then, tell all. Where have you been hiding him?'

'Just a friend, Gloria. He was visiting Oxford and we met up. We had a meal, spent some time together on Friday and that was it.' Yes, thought Lydia, that was it. When it was all pared down to the facts, that was it.

Not that Gloria would take that as an answer. She needed the when and the how and the where, his whole life story. Lydia also stripped these things, as much as she knew of them, down to their bare bones. And in doing so she realised how little she really knew of the man, maybe she should have googled him after all. She didn't even know if he was married.

'You don't know? If you don't know, didn't ask, and he didn't say, then he's married.' Something warmer in her tone, something confiding, gave Lydia the impression of having been admitted to membership of Gloria's club. 'If you didn't ask then you know he is. They're always married if they don't say, trust me, Lydia, they're always married.' There was a resignation, a weariness, in her voice that spoke of a Gloria who Lydia had not seen before, would have doubted even existed.

'Yes, maybe.' She might have added 'but it doesn't matter', but she had no wish to be drawn deeper into the discussion. Even if Lydia could have ordered her own confused thoughts about Stephen into something that she understood, she was not ready to discuss them. She was, after all, a mere novice in the sisterhood of single women and had been admitted on false papers.

*

For a few days Lydia waited in vain for some inspiration to strike regarding the sandcastles album. She told herself it was the right way, her way, to do things, even though she knew it was also an excuse to defer the resumption of the methodical enquiry into Bertie Myers and Albert and Hannah Joslin. They most probably held the key to progress, but they were her last unexplored lines and if they were exhausted without resolution she wasn't quite sure how she would continue. Having come so far, and she was sure, got so close, conceding defeat would be a huge anticlimax. True, she would still be able to give Dorothy her family, give her names and dates to go with photographs, but in her own eyes it would leave some business forever unfinished.

Albert and Hannah would provide the stiffer challenge, so it was for that reason Lydia chose to start with them. Albert Pelham Joslin, 'Papa' Joslin's grandson who had squatted at his father's feet on that baking summer day in 1911, married Hannah Brightside at Westminster in June 1928 at the age of twenty-five years. Hannah was nearly a year his senior. Such a healthy, well fed, middle-class couple in their prime would surely have produced children quickly and in numbers. Isolating those children from the great mass of other Joslins was the problem. At least the name was not Williams, had it been that common then her search would have ended before it had begun. Even so, the first results threw up no less than eighty-two Joslin babies for only 1929 to 1931. Somewhere in Essex would have helped narrow it down to twenty-five, but apart from the family roots and Albert's birth there was no reason to do so. Hannah was born and married in London, and their babies could have been born anywhere, even abroad, beyond the reach of her search. But Albert had declared himself to be an 'exchange dealer' at his marriage, and where more likely than London would he carry on such a profession. Lydia examined each page of the index with great care, conscious of her previous errors and oversights. She was diligent in checking all the Joslins and the variations that she knew, then added another, 'Josling', when she found a Dianna of that name in June 1929.

The first to be found was Ethel Beatrice in the December quarter of 1929, registered in Wandsworth, mother's maiden name Brightside. A certificate later would confirm the father, but Lydia had no doubt at all it would be Albert. An hour later and she had Violet Hannah, September 1934, also Wandsworth. Rose Elizabeth followed in the same place, June 1936. Lydia took her search on to 1950 without finding another Joslin baby born to a Brightside mother. The results were satisfying. To have found a boy child would have been slightly more encouraging, but she was content with the three girls - assuming that they had survived. For every birth there is the inevitability of a balancing death, and Lydia's next task was to see about killing off this happy south London family.

According to the absence of their names from the register, all three girls had survived those dangerous early years, but then they would have been confronted by war. Perhaps they had been evacuated, as tens of thousands of others had been, only to be recalled by their parents as the greatest dangers were perceived to have passed. Working through the war years Lydia found no mention of the girls or their mother, but slightly to her surprise found an Albert in the same district, with a death entry for the September quarter of 1944. She'd been looking for the children, not the parents. A casualty of war, or something more natural? A certificate would provide the answer and tell if this was her Albert, but in the meantime she wondered just how many Albert Joslins might have been in Wandsworth during that time. Certainly there were unlikely to be more than one who was an exchange dealer with a wife named Hannah. This dead Albert might have been simply a stray, a soldier on leave perhaps, run down by a lorry. Lydia smiled at her own fancies, far less likely than the chance that this was indeed her Albert. She pictured a solidly middle class family, father working somewhere in the city, mother not working, but doing her bit for the war effort, three house-trained girls, the eldest, at fifteen, still at school but without the modern 'teenage' label to live up to. Such a family, comfortably off and conscious of their place in the world, would probably have had a telephone.

Something had nagged at her ever since her day with Stephen. She had forgotten the telephone directories, as she most often did, despite her success with Pink2. They were a fairly recent addition to her armoury of research tools and cumbersome to use, but they could be extremely helpful, if only to turn the possible into the probable. Outside of London, there seemed little logic to the way towns were grouped together in the various volumes. Even with the right volume, the images of many pages had to be viewed before the correct one could be established. With patience and a little trial and error, her possible Albert became a probable with the discovery of *'Joslin, A. P, 16 Ansell Road S W 17 . . . STReatham 3507'* in the 1942 directory. To cross check and improve the probability, Lydia then looked up Ansell Road to establish it was in Tooting. Then it was a short step to confirm that Tooting was part of the Wandsworth registration district. So, her Wandsworth family were really a Tooting family, or at least, her *Joslin, A.P.* was a Tooting man. She was confident she'd find Hannah, Ethel, Violet and Rose there too. But they would wait their turn for her searches until the facts were confirmed by their birth certificates.

Turning her attention back to the troublesome Bertie, Alethia's stepson, the POW from Stalag Luft 3, Lydia found the information she sought almost immediately. In 1947 Bertie had married Helen Fox at Amersham, Bucks. Finding anything else proved to be more difficult. No children that she could see, no entry in any likely telephone directory, nothing to show a trace until a possible death in 1971 of a Bertram D Myers at Chesham, also in Bucks.

All of which left Lydia hanging on news of the Joslins from Tooting. Dorothy was overdue a letter to keep her up to date with news of her family, and the time had stretched out since Stephen's visit to Oxford. Brought up to write a thank-you letter for every present received, Lydia's guilt at not having written to Stephen grew with every passing day. An email would suffice, it did not have to say very much, but the longer it went on the harder the words were to find. If only she had dashed off a quick note the day after, instead of leaving it, but more than a week later a quick note would not do. A letter would demand even more of her, so she settled on a postcard, which by its public nature and restricted size would excuse her from anything but the briefest message. She could even leave out the apology that had been forming in her head and concentrate on the 'thank you' instead.

She chose a card with Magdalen Tower viewed from the bridge and wrote '*A really good day, thank you for inviting me for a glimpse of your world.*' And signed it simply with her name. She thought the reference to 'your world' would remind him of their abbreviated conversation about titles, and thought too that Stephen would know that she'd remembered it. No sooner had she written his address on the card than she was struck forcibly by the fact that she knew his home address. He had written it on the letter he had sent her, it was not a university address, a 'department of' address, it was his home and she was about to send him a card. What married man would do so, however innocent the friendship, when the receipt of mail might need explanation? Lydia tried hard to see this message dropping onto her front door-mat when she was a wife, but the distance was too great, the possibility too remote. In the space that she had left above her name, Lydia carefully inserted '*Joslins and sandcastles going well*'. It would keep her pledge to tell him of progress, leave it open for him to enquire further, and, she was almost ashamed to admit, would certainly intrigue a third party.

Her letter to Dorothy required less thought: a simple statement of progress and of how helpful the kitchen drawer photos had been; a hint of what might yet be discovered; an updated box chart of Papa Joslin's offspring showing Dorothy's three newly acquired second cousins; and a brief description of her visit to the Botanic Garden. No doubt there would be a reply from Worthing in a day or so. As she thought of that seaside town and her walk with Dorothy along the promenade, another picture came to mind, that picture of 'self', the one by the sea with the pier in the background. Might that be Worthing? Before she sealed the letter Lydia carefully removed the photo from its album, quickly scanned and copied it, then slipped it in with the letter, adding a PS to explain its presence. Apart from the location, it might just jog another of Dorothy's memories.

As she had the album in her hand, it seemed the right moment to spend a little time with it again. The balmy days of the start of the month had been overtaken by a cooler, wetter spell, so rather than sit outside in the evening air as she would have preferred, she had to be satisfied with her chair and the remainder of last night's Chablis. Slowly she turned the pages, trying to empty her mind of all knowledge, to see the images for the first time, waiting for some detail, some incongruity to make itself apparent. No matter how important the pictures had been to the people in them, no matter what memories were brought to mind when 'self' - it was probably 'self' and not Fred – lingered over them, they were simply a collection of family photos. People played cricket on beaches, had picnics, lots of picnics, sat in deckchairs, paddled in the sea, built sandcastles decorated with paper flags, licked ice creams. Nothing in there like some of Lydia's own childhood when her father had required her to pose with her brother in various staged scenes of make believe. There had been a spell when her brother had demanded that she be his victim in whatever game he was playing, whether it was cowboys and indians or knights and dragons. Just once it would have been good to have been the rescued princess, but Brian always cast her as the slain baddie. If her father was around during one of these times he would invariably have them re-enact a scene he thought suitable for a photograph, even if it meant Lydia had to be re-tied to a tree. Sometimes he would devise a tableau for the characters of the day and add some embellishment of his own like a lasso or a mask. No sign of such photographs here, but then Lydia's mother never put them in her albums either.

There was the stray at the end of the album, the one she had copied and sent to Dorothy, that one had been more contrived than most. 'Self' had been deliberately placed right there, half profile, looking past the camera to some unseen point. But even if it were Worthing or some other identifiable place, Lydia could not see there was more to be made of it. As she turned the pages again and took another sip of wine, a second picture took her attention. At face value it was unremarkable and easily overlooked amongst all the other snaps. The two girls, Susan and Linda, uncaptioned but certainly them, sitting on a dry stone wall somewhere in the Dales. They sat either side of a signpost, the old-fashioned country type, with arms that ended in pointing fingers to indicate the direction. The girls were looking at the camera but each was also pointing at the other. Susan, on the left pointed right at Linda, while Linda on the right pointed left at Susan. Lydia could not imagine any reason for such positions to occur naturally, they had certainly been asked to sit and point, but for what purpose? Whatever it was, they were happy to take their places, for the usual scowls were replaced with broad grins. They shared the joke, understood why they were sat there. Now they just needed to share the joke with Lydia.

Maybe it involved the places pointed to, that the signpost was wrong and the correct directions were exactly opposite. Under her magnifying glass Lydia could just make out the places indicated. Above Susan was 'Arncliffe' and above Linda was what appeared to be 'Ingleby'. Lydia was about to find them in her gazetteer when she saw the joke. The joke was the names themselves. Susan, beneath the sign showing Arncliffe, pointed at her friend whose name was Linda Arncliffe. Linda sat beneath the name Ingleby, pointing at her friend Susan. And if the joke were to have any meaning at all then Susan must be Susan Ingleby. No wonder the families stopped at the sign, arranged their children and snapped the event. Lydia was away and running with the scene, tasting the packed lunch with spam and salad-cream sandwiches, listening to the laughter as they arranged each other beneath the signpost, half a dozen photos no doubt. Only one made it to the album, the best one of course. The Arncliffes would have put their own version of it into their album with no caption either, the same joke needing no explanation for them either. That was if she really had the joke. Lydia was so pleased with herself that she did not dare spoil it by allowing more than a flicker of doubt to creep in.

Where there was Susan Ingleby there also was her father, Fred, and her brother Paul, and the as yet unnamed 'self'. But she would be found soon enough, her children were aged about seven and six on the Dales holiday and that appeared to be 1960 give or take a year or so. She would start with Susan, find the likely births from 1950 onwards, move on to Paul, and with their mother's name find Fred's marriage to her. Simple stuff, the kind of thing she had done a thousand times. Unless they were not Inglebys, but like Bertie Myers, playing ducks and drakes with their name, sometimes double barrelled and sometimes not. Back at her desk, it took a few moments to discover there were but three Susan Inglebys registered between 1949 and 1954. Hardly daring to look, Lydia checked each of the mother's maiden names, willing the word Joslin or, if pushed, then Myers or Dix to appear. The second of the three was so exactly what she hoped for that she could scarcely believe it. '*Ingleby, Susan D, September quarter 1952, Aylesbury, mother's maiden name Joslin*'. Not only that but there was that 'D' again, a 'D' that to Lydia said 'Dix'.

Paul Ingleby was easier still, just two entries to check and the first gave the same mother's name as for Susan. And Paul was also Paul D. D for Dix, it was more probable by the minute. Instead of Aylesbury, he was registered in Oxford. Finally she was home, the connections were all becoming apparent, the Inglebys were Oxford, the very reason she was sat there now looking at their births was Oxford. Lydia hugged the pleasure to herself, even thought of opening another bottle of wine to celebrate. But it grew late and as the euphoria of the moment passed she was overcome by a wave of tiredness. Mrs 'Self' Ingleby could keep her secrets for one more day.

★

As predicted, Dorothy's answering letter arrived in a couple of days, along with a message from Stephen. He replied in the same vein, a postcard with a picture of St John's College, Cambridge. '*It was just a glimpse, if you would like a longer look, come over and tell all about Joslins and sandcastles. Stephen. PS I have plenty of room.*' Coded words, just as hers had been, as if to say 'two can play at that game.' Behind the cipher were answers to questions she didn't realise she'd asked, hadn't even framed in her mind. But, the answer to one that she had: Stephen had no wife at home. Now it was clearly up to her to take him up on the offer or let the matter lie. It would wait until she knew what to do, but the invitation pleased her.

Dorothy's letter held nothing between the lines, simply a note to say the photograph held no meaning for her and nothing further had come to light. She wished Lydia would think about visiting her again, she would be pleased to have her stay over. Two invitations in one day, next thing she knew she'd be out partying with Gloria.

Lydia replied immediately.

Dear Dorothy

Thank you for your kind invitation, I will take you up on it one day, but I am not sure when, perhaps later in the summer.

You will be interested to know that in the short time since I last wrote there has been progress with your second cousin Ethel Beatrice Joslin. She married Frederick Ingleby in 1951 at Chelsea and they had two children (as far as I know), Susan and Paul who are technically your 'second cousins once removed'. I found something about Ethel's father and it seems that he was killed by a V1 in June 1944 while he was on ARP duty in south London and Ethel died in 1972. I have not yet tracked down anything about the other two girls, Ethel's sisters Violet and Rose. With Susan and Paul the family is almost up to date, although I am waiting for quite a few birth and death certificates to be absolutely sure. You will see that I have enclosed yet another version of the little diagram of your family.

Hope this finds you well and enjoying the warm weather. Maybe we can go back to your mother's place at Highdown next time I see you.

Kind regards

Lydia

⋆

The first of the new batch of certificates arrived at the beginning of July, confirming all that Lydia had expected about the Joslin girls, Ethel's marriage, and their father's death. The informant to the registrar was not his wife Hannah, but a police constable, suggesting that Hannah and her daughters were not living in the area when Albert was killed. Lydia wondered if they might have been staying out of London, out of harm's way, in Essex perhaps, with the children's grandparents. How would they have heard the news of their father's death? Who at that time would have known their whereabouts? A neighbour maybe, a neighbour who opened her door when the police called at the house in Ansell Road to give Hannah the news. A neighbour who said no, Mrs Joslin was away with the girls at Mr Joslin's parents in Essex and how sorry she was to hear of poor Mr Joslin, such a nice man. Yes, it would have been something like that, no screaming or hysterics, it was one bomb amongst a thousand bombs, one death amongst a thousand deaths. The first bomb of the Doodlebug Summer, special in its own peculiar way, but for Albert it could have been any bomb.

The surprise came a day or so later with Susan and Paul's details. They had been registered as Susan Dorcas and Paul Donald. So much for her Dix idea. Lydia had been so sure it would be Dix, that some undetected connection would have led to that name re-appearing. But it was not so, she must have spent so long chasing the name that she was ready to assign it to any stray 'D' that appeared. But Dorcas? Where did that come from? No Joslin bore that name as far as she knew and surely it wasn't fashionable in 1952. She began to rehearse the steps she would take to check back through the family in search of a Dorcas, before she stopped herself. What did it matter, beyond her own curiosity? For an instant a great depression welled inside her again. What did any of it matter beyond her own curiosity? She fought down the feeling before it had a chance to take hold. It was, yes she could say it to herself, her passion, her interest. In some way it defined her. And there was Dorothy, kind, gentle, slightly other-world Dorothy, who knew something of her own family because of Lydia. There was also Stephen, for the moment Lydia could not quite grasp how he fitted in to her reasoning, but without her passion she would never have met him, and after all, it was he who had first described it so. Which reminded her about his still unanswered invitation. The reply had taken shape in her head, and the answer was going to be 'yes', but first she would do as he had thought she might, she would google him.

To her complete astonishment, Lydia found she would have to sift through more than a thousand entries if she were to read everything on offer regarding Sir Stephen Kellaway. By excluding certain words associated with other Stephen Kellaways, like 'athletics', 'aerial' and 'lettings', she could dispose or more than half. There seemed little alternative to simply wading through them. Such a well-documented man would surely have had a few biographical notes written about him. There was more than enough about his career, papers he had published, committees he had chaired, his honours and awards, but she could find nothing about the man himself. What she was looking for, as she recognised after a while, was something to tell her about his private life, or to be more precise, whether he was or had been married. She could ask him, but the asking would also be asking 'are you available?' and the question would suggest she was interested. In her mind's eye it was not that she was interested, rather that she did not want any surprises if she were to become interested. Gloria's cautionary words came back to her, 'if you don't ask and they don't say, then they're married.' She was probably right more often than not, but he had freely given his address and phone number, he could be the exception that proved the rule.

With no additional information of any use, Lydia decided on a tentative acceptance, something she could withdraw from easily enough if she later chose. A private note rather than a public postcard was called for and she would keep the tone light. Continuing with the post rather than using email retained a certain distance that she wanted to preserve, at least for the present. After a few minutes thought, she settled on '*to avoid further surprises I took your google advice, but it didn't tell me anything I didn't know.*' It was asking without asking, and sat comfortably enough in the middle of her brief acceptance. She also suggested a couple of possible dates.

As soon as she had posted it, she regretted the words. Stephen would see exactly what they meant and why she had asked in that way. If only she'd had the courage to have come straight out with it and simply asked him. And what did it matter anyway, she was hardly involved with him, she was not contemplating an affair with him. She hadn't contemplated an affair with anybody, ever, not while she was married and certainly not in the immediate aftermath. There had been one or two invitations, more hints and suggestions really, in the months after the divorce, all from the husbands of her few friends from the world of coupledom. As that world had receded and with it the friends, so too had the suggestions. As the months and years had passed she'd found her own level, contented herself with her own company, and found that answering to no one was compensation enough for the absence of a man in her life. Lydia could remember quite vividly thinking as a child that when she was grown up she would be able to eat a whole tin of peaches whenever she wished. On odd occasions her single status had allowed her to do exactly that.

*

As the film reader whirred its way through the months Lydia paused its progress every few seconds to check the date. She was looking for what she hoped would be a very specific day. According to his death certificate, Paul Donald Ingleby drowned on August 27th 1967 and his death registered on 2nd of October 'after coroner's inquest'. It had been a surprise to find the entry for Paul, the first of the Ingleby deaths, before those of his parents and with no sign of anything for Susan. But there was no denying it, she had all three unfolded on the table beside her in the library while she searched the micro-film for some mention of the affair in the newspaper archive. If he died on the 27th then any report would likely be in the *Oxford Times* for Friday 1st. She stopped at the 8th September and slowly wound back. There it was on page 4, '*Boy 12 Feared Drowned. The search for Paul Ingleby, who disappeared last Sunday while playing near the river at Iffley, was officially called off on Wednesday. A police spokesman said that a watch would be kept on the river down to Henley but that the formal search had been abandoned. Paul was last seen with his sister Susan (14) near the boat slide at Iffley. An extensive search was mounted immediately but nothing has been found. Police and river authorities again warned parents of the dangers that the river presented.*' A sad little addition to the long list of those claimed by the Thames.

Lydia scrolled on to October looking for a report of the inquest. Friday 6th October would be favourite and sure enough, a few moments scanning the pages brought her to it. '*Misadventure Verdict. The Oxford coroner on Monday returned a verdict of misadventure following the death of 12-year old Paul Ingleby. The court heard evidence that Paul, a good swimmer, had gone missing at Iffley following an argument with his sister Susan (14). Despite an extensive search his body was not found until 20th September when it was recovered from the Thames near Sutton*

Courtenay. In announcing the verdict, the coroner stated that Paul's sister Susan should not feel any responsibility for her brother's death as she had done all that she could by promptly raising the alarm when he had disappeared. He was entirely satisfied that the disagreement with her brother over the need to return home played no part in the tragedy. The coroner also warned that it was unsafe to swim in the river where unseen currents could present a danger to the strongest of swimmers.'

What a scar to bear through life, thought Lydia. What a burden to carry, the tears of your parents and your own guilt, no matter how misplaced. She could see the teenage Susan, running screaming to the nearest person, gasping her story then watching and waiting helplessly. Her father and mother, panicked and distraught, torn between comforting their daughter and weeping for their son. Long days with any realistic hope quickly diminished until weeks later a policeman calls and suggests they sit down and they know that the news they have waited for has finally arrived. The grim day is brought back to life and Susan heaves great inconsolable sobs into her pillow, while her parents hold each other and wonder at the meaning of anything. Lydia felt the prick of a tear in her eye as she read again the official record that she held in her hand. All these certificates, be they death or otherwise, these anonymous records, they all held stories of joy and tears, smiles and anguish in other lives.

Had that family, Fred and Ethel, the teenage Susan, had they ever recovered? Or had the trauma gnawed at them like the cancer that took first Ethel three years later and Fred three years after that? Maybe that was all the cancer needed, a trigger to begin its insidious progress. On August 27th 1967 Susan had woken in her fourteen year old world, pop-music on the radio, family around her, unknowing of what the days and weeks ahead held for her. Unknowing that by nightfall her brother would be drowned, that before she would be eighteen her mother would be gone and by twenty she would be reporting her father's death. What of her after that, what would she carry through her life from these losses?

Lydia looked again at the entries on Fred Ingleby's death certificate. There was Susan, '*S.D.Ingleby – Daughter*', neatly typed in the box provided for the informant. Lydia paused and looked long and hard again. Perhaps it was the simple juxtaposition of the initials, perhaps it was the time spent feeling for her young life, but whatever it was Lydia saw them properly for the first time. Susan Dorcas Ingleby. SDI. She knew exactly what happened to Susan. She'd grown up to become a teacher, to marry a man like Mr Punch, she'd grown up to have baby who died after a few brief hours. In that box of albums there could only be one SDI, one SDI who featured in both the journal and sandcastles. And knowing who she was, knowing her life, meant she knew who the journal writer was, who it was who wrote of Mr Punch and hiding a body where it would never be found - *'like a leaf on the forest floor'*.

11

Quite what she expected to find at Stephen's house in Grantchester, Lydia was not entirely sure. She had a picture half formed in her mind from the address, The Old Rectory, and she knew something of it from the satellite image Google Earth provided for her, but the feel of the place eluded her. She would discover soon enough but it was not only the physical she couldn't quite grasp, it was also Stephen. She could not see how or why he was ready to make her even the tiniest space in his life. These questions were born in part from her fragile self-confidence, but also from serious and, to her own satisfaction at least, objective thought on the subject. Admittedly, these thoughts had troubled her more after she'd written to accept his invitation than before, but as Gloria had said in her no-nonsense way, what was there to lose, she would get a nice weekend, some good food and a few drinks. To this list of potential benefits, Gloria had added the possibility of Stephen being good in bed, although she had put it more bluntly than that. Where once Lydia would have done her utmost to conceal any hint of her life outside of the office, those few words that she and Gloria had exchanged about married men had begun a subtle change between them. For years Lydia had seen nothing but the shallowness of the younger woman's view of life, her brashness, her apparently single-minded pursuit of sex and pleasure. More recently, she been surprised to discover beneath all the dross was someone who had deeper feelings and a previously unseen generosity of spirit.

Taking something of Gloria's simpler approach but without, she hoped, too much of the selfish aspect, Lydia anticipated the weekend with the pleasure of new discoveries. Discoveries which she would accept for whatever they might turn out to be. She had decided there would be no shocks, no unwelcome surprises, no introspection as to her right to be there, whatever the weekend had in store she would take it all in her stride. If Stephen were to turn out to be married or divorced or even homosexual, she'd discounted each possibility; if the house was a bachelor's grubby mess or the height of chic, she would still find her space in it; if it was cold with noisy plumbing or over heated with a log fire, she would adjust accordingly.

To underline her openness to any eventuality, she had shopped for what she hoped were the smart-casual clothes to suit any course the weekend might take. After agonising over the choice, she had finally selected a dress in graphite grey, shot through with a hint of sparkle in a silk fabric that slipped through the fingers like water. It was probably the most expensive dress she had ever bought and she earnestly hoped it would be suitable for a cocktail party or the finest of restaurants. To this she'd added sensible black trousers for any occasion and two tailored blouses, crushed raspberry and navy blue. To complete her weekend ensemble she bought flat shoes for a walk round the village and a pair with a little more heel to go with the sparkling dress. After a slight hesitation, this shopping had also included new underwear, justified by need but decided by the moment.

It was late in the morning when the little red Nisan crunched to a halt on the gravel of The Old Rectory drive. Barely had she opened the door to stretch out her legs before Stephen emerged from the side of the house, sun hat in hand, the same easy flowing stride that she'd first noted at Loweswater.

'Lydia, I am so glad that you've made it.' One arm round her back, a gentle pressure from his hand between her shoulder blades, a touch of cheeks that she might have made into a kiss if her name had been Gloria.

'Thank you. I'm very glad to be here.' She stood back half a step and took in the house before her and was immediately reminded of the photograph of the old Joslin house, Longlands. Rectories were built for big families and this was no exception. Perhaps older than Longlands by a century or so and stone rather than brick, but the same solidity, the same weight, the same statement of importance. The Old Rectory still made that statement with an ease and assurance that the aspiring classes who had built Longlands never quite mastered. Two storeys with a crenellated roof line, an elegant square of a house. Stephen led her not through the front door, but round to the side from which he had emerged. The gravel drive, the neat lawns and pruned shrubs already indicated she would not be entering a bachelor's mess. He took her in through French windows to a comfortable sitting room, the kind you would want to find in an expensive country hotel, but rarely do.

'Let me take you up to your room and show you where things are. While you're doing that I'll see about some drinks.'

Her room was large and bright, a soft stream of air gently billowing net curtains across the open window. Beyond was a croquet lawn, gravel paths, currant bushes in their cages, a few fruit trees sheltered by the deep orange of an old brick wall. To one side were flourishing vegetable beds, to the other a little-used tennis court. It was, thought Lydia, exactly what she might have expected, exactly what might have intimidated her not long ago.

She turned from the window to see Stephen still standing by the doorway and almost involuntarily her eye moved to the bed beside him. A great heavy double bed, which, like the rest of the furniture in the room, spoke more of arts-and-crafts than high street superstore. He followed her gaze. 'Don't worry, it has a good new mattress. I'm told that it's extremely comfortable.' The question of who had told him hung briefly in the air, but they both chose to ignore it. 'I'll go and get those drinks. When you are ready just come back down the way we came in. Oh, there's a bathroom opposite, no en-suite here, I'm afraid.' And with that he was gone to the drinks. Not asked what she might like to drink, noted Lydia, but an assumption made that she would like what he would prepare for her.

As soon as he was gone, she tried the bed. A firm modern mattress met her bounce. She stretched out on the covers and every aspect of it met with her approval, especially the size. The house could so easily have been cold and impersonal, but it was not, it was much more a home than she had expected, despite its apparently solitary inhabitant. She guessed that it might be home to more than just Stephen and that a female hand had left its mark.

'I thought we might both enjoy a glass of this on a hot summer's day. We had some at the Lemon Tree.' Stephen drew the bottle of Prosecco from the ice bucket. Lydia nodded in appreciation. For a few minutes they sat in smiling silence in the shade of the awning, sipping the wine, absorbing the place and the moment.

'How's the googling?'

'Oh, very informative, very educational, very useful if you want to know about Sir Stephen Kellaway, forensic archaeologist, author of papers, man of science, advisor to government and prized committee member.'

'But?'

'But, as I think you well know, not much use for anything else.' Far more easily than she had imagined, Lydia had asked all the unasked questions in one simple statement.

'I can tell you whatever you wish to know, unless it is too private, in which case it might wait until . . .' the pause was not made for effect, whatever he had been going to say, he altered to 'until another time.'

'Yes, of course.' He really was the easiest of men to be with. Lydia had not even finished her glass and she felt a light headedness and a dryness of mouth that required another sip.

'Well, Lydia, the essential facts. I am not married, but I was. Elspeth, my wife, died twelve years ago. I have a daughter Jacqueline who is in her thirties, and we get along very well. She works in London but I see her quite often, and there are no grandchildren. It was Jacqueline who commented on the quality of the mattress. Oh, and I'm a little older than you. Sixty-three. One sister, Felicity, who I mentioned once before. Happy childhood, minor public school then Cambridge.' He paused a moment, surprised at how quickly he had summarised his life, then added with a smile, 'I expect you know the rest.'

She had sought answers and now she had them, sparse as they were. To Lydia he seemed glad to have the awkward business of the day completed, as if he had rehearsed his answer in readiness for the question and was relieved to have the exam over.

'I'm sorry about your wife,' Lydia said, looking straight into his eyes, searching for some hint as to his feelings for Elspeth, 'but glad about your daughter.'

'It's not fresh any more, it was another life.' It was not so much the door slammed on further enquiry, but for once he did not leave it open.

For a while they watched the bubbles rise in their glasses, and let the soft hum of an English summer enfold their thoughts.

'And you Lydia, tell me about you.'

Tell him about her? There was nothing to tell, she hadn't given a single thought to the idea that he would have any interest in her. He was the enigma requiring a solution, not she.

'Me? Nothing to tell really, beyond what you know. I'm very ordinary.' Then she realised stupidly what he meant. 'Ah, yes, well, I was also married, but Michael is alive and well as far as I know. We were divorced about ten or eleven years ago. No drama, more a withering on the vine until we just went our separate ways when he found someone else. As you just said, it was another life. And no children.'

'And you've been alone since then.' It should have been a question but Stephen made a statement of it, more as if he turned it over in his mind and spoke the thought aloud.

Lydia answered anyway. 'Yes, and for the most part, not unhappy about that.'

Then they spoke of living single lives, spoke in the way that old friends comfortably do, even though they spoke of things old friends would already know. Stephen talked of the gardener from the village, Roger, who came in a couple of days a week in the season and made sure that he had all the produce from the garden that he needed and took the rest for himself and his family. He told her about Mrs Webb who kept the house clean and tidy and cooked him a meal or two each week and made sure the fridge was cleaned out when it needed to be, just as she had for years since soon after his daughter Jacqueline had been born. She came and stayed with him once a week, sometimes for a few days at a time, which in itself told Lydia all that anyone could want to know about father and daughter.

In return Lydia had little to offer him, a potted history of life since divorce took no more than a few sentences. She had no son to match his daughter, a house that, for all it was often neglected, could never justify hired help, and a garden that hardly deserved the same name as the grounds she now sat in. But as much as she did say, she said without apology. In contrast to that day at Magdalen, she did not feel out of place in these grand and unfamiliar surroundings, no demons of doubt circled to pounce. She offered no false token of resistance as Stephen refilled her glass and then his own to empty the bottle. When he suggested they bring out the lunch that the loyal Mrs Webb had prepared for them, Lydia went with him to the kitchen as if she had done it may times before.

While they broke bread still warm from the oven and washed down smoked salmon with a fresh bottle, they spoke more of children and the lack of them, and how each of them could imagine the other's feelings. They talked of nieces and nephews and how they could become surrogate children. Mention of Stephen's niece Fiona inevitably brought Phoebe Joslin to Lydia's mind and Phoebe brought memories of Loweswater and Cockermouth for them both to share again.

'And did you bring your Joslin treasures with you?'

Until the moment of her arrival Lydia had been bursting to tell him the news of her great discoveries, but in the pleasure of seeing him, the warmth of the summer garden, the bubbles in the creamy wine, the Joslins and their affairs had slipped from her mind. 'Oh, yes, I did. I have everything in one of my cases.'

'I wondered if two cases might be a little much for a single night,' he smiled at her.

'Stephen, I know who the journal writer is, I know who his wife is. I think that I know everyone in the albums.'

'That's wonderful! Not just wonderful but amazing too, you have put so much into it. Does Dorothy, was it Dorothy, does she know all this?'

'No, I haven't told her but I'm going to see her in September. There's one thing I don't know, I don't know what happened to Susan, she is the SDI in the journal, the writer's wife. The story just stops, I can find no trace of anything.' Then in a moment of confidence only partly supplied by the Prosecco, she added, 'Maybe you can see where I've missed something or where I should go next. Maybe you can see the answer, maybe it is staring me in the face all the time.'

He looked at her for a moment before answering, recognising the honour that she was offering him, giving up sole ownership of her precious project. 'Are you sure? You know I am interested to look, but to contribute something at this stage when you have come so far? Thank you, of course I'll help. Well, that does rather assume that I have some help to give. So tell me, who is this journal writer and how did you find him.'

'He is, or was, Andrew Stephen Myers. And here's the thing, Susan, his wife who is a child in sandcastles, is . . .'

'Sandcastles?' he interrupted her.

'That's what I call the album with all the holiday pictures, sandcastles. There's that one, the oldest one which is Longlands, and the RAF album. The empty one I called the VE Day album. But Susan was a Joslin, or rather her mother was, and Andrew was a Myers or a Dix Myers, and they were related. To be precise, they were fourth cousins twice removed,' she concluded triumphantly

'All right, I can see it's somehow important, but you may have lost me somewhere. What does that mean, fourth cousin twice removed?'

'Well, it means that Susan's five times great grandfather, or five-g grandfather, who was John Jolly, was also Andrew's three times great grandfather.'

'Right.' Stephen paused before adding, 'And the significance of that is?'

'First it is unusual, but second it explains how the RAF album and the other two could have come to be together. Andrew would have had the RAF album from his family and Susan would have had the others from hers.'

'I think you'd better tell me the whole thing.'

'Shall I get the albums and my notes?'

'No, just take me on from where we were in Oxford.'

So as the afternoon drifted lazily on, Lydia told Stephen how she had found that Susan was an Ingleby from the photo of the two girls under the road sign. From there she had found the family, found her mother was Ethel Joslin, and that Susan was Papa's great great granddaughter, and how Susan had married Andrew in Abingdon in 1976. Stephen let her run on through the discoveries, the certificates, the births and the deaths. He learnt how Andrew was the elusive Bertie's son and Lydia guessed he might have been born in Rhodesia or South Africa, which was why she couldn't find any trace of him until he popped up on Bertie's death registration with an address in South Africa in 1971. Then in 1975 when his mother died he appeared again, only by that time he was living in Chesham, at the same address as his mother. It all tumbled out as she laid each new revelation before him to be wondered at. Try as he might, he still couldn't quite share her enthusiasm, her passion for the subject, but he enjoyed seeing the life and excitement it brought to her face. She was so animated that he stopped trying to take in all the details of her discoveries and settled for catching the gist while enjoying her pleasure. Even when she came to an abrupt halt, saying that was as far as she could go, she knew who they were, she knew so much about them, but could find no trace of either of them dead or alive in the years after the journal, even then Lydia spoke with an intensity that Stephen found quite captivating.

'And what have you brought with you?'

'Nearly everything. The albums and the journal obviously, and all the notes I have made, all the certificates and my laptop. You can look at the Joslin family tree on that.'

'Well, I think if you show me what you have, then allow me a while to read it all and try and understand it, then it is possible some new avenue might suggest itself.'

Stephen brought the second suitcase down from Lydia's room and together they arranged its contents in his study. She explained each of her treasures, showed him how she'd filed the certificates, explained how the Joslin family could be viewed and how their sometimes confusing relationships came about by the marriage of cousins. Finally Lydia presented him with the precious journal, both the original which she now kept in a plastic document bag, and her transcript.

'Ah, the journal itself,' he said with not entirely false deference. 'Funny to think that I now have it in my hand. Remember talking about it as we walked in Loweswater?'

'Yes I do.' Lydia let the scene take shape in her mind again, just as she had several times before. 'Where do you want to start?'

'Lydia, if it is alright with you, I'll roughly follow your course, spend time with the albums, look at your notes about them, see how you've fitted the family together, then read the journal. I want to have some sense of the people that is beyond the facts you've discovered and see if I find a similar picture is formed.'

He seemed to have no doubt as to how to go about the task, a new and interesting case, but a procedure he was familiar with. And he seemed ready to undertake it without her. Lydia imagined how he might have overseen some junior's investigations when the conclusions were open to question, how he would have taken all the papers, shut himself away until the job was done.

'Shall I leave you to it? It might take you quite a while.'

'Is that alright? Not the best of hosts perhaps, to leave you to your own devices. I thought you would want . . .' His voice trailed off and Lydia saw uncertainty in him for the first time.

'I can amuse myself. I'm practised at it, remember? I'll do a little exploring if that's ok.'

'Good, yes, please do. Oh and I had planned that we would eat out tonight, there is a taxi from the village booked for seven thirty. A place in Cambridge.'

'That will be lovely, thank you. I'll leave you to it.'

'I'll come and find you if I'm stuck,' he called after her, delighted she'd instantly understood his need to look at her puzzle in his own way, how easy it was for her to simply let him do so.

The heat of the day had abated as Lydia strolled round the grounds. They stretched further than she had realised, and all was tidiness and order. Beyond the little orchard and the roses clambering over the brick behind it, lay a paddock, occupied by a solitary horse that came to investigate her but quickly lost interest. Had Jacqueline had a pony she wondered, maybe Elspeth had ridden? Was it Elspeth's framed picture on Stephen's desk? Surely it must be, a golden haired young woman with a pageboy cut last fashionable in the seventies, posed in a black and white studio portrait. Another life, yes, but the echoes remained. After a while she took herself back to the seats under the awning and retrieved the bottle from the ice bucket. It was still cool enough although the ice was long gone. She was greatly tempted to explore the rest of the house, to see who else was important enough for Stephen to have their photographs displayed, but she contented herself with sitting in the peace of the garden. She should be feeling like a fish out of water, should be tempted to run home to West Street. Instead she felt as relaxed as she had anywhere since, well, she was not sure since when. Maybe since a day in the Lakes.

*

When Lydia woke she was unsure for a few moments if she were awake or still dreaming. Nothing around her was familiar, in fact it hardly seemed real at all. She was in someone else's room, the morning sun angled in through white net curtains stirring softly across an open window. She felt sure that she would recognize the scene beyond the window and yet she could not quite say what it would be. The room was silent and beyond the room, the house was silent.

As the world solidified, recollection flooded in, and she stretched out in the bed, hugging the pleasure of the moment to herself. Scenes from the previous day flickered through her head, bubbles streaming in her glass as they sat in the shade, the scents of the garden wafting around them, Stephen working quietly away at her papers as she opened his study door to check on progress, the swish of gravel as the taxi took them to dinner. The restaurant was not intimidating, as she had feared it might be, but informal and quite unpretentious. They'd passed two untroubled and pleasurable hours there, lingering over their meal, then over coffee until the car returned to carry them back to Grantchester. After the rare indulgence of a brandy, shared under the last strands of light in the night sky, they had said their goodnights and exchanged an awkward kiss, unpractised as they were in such familiarity. Stephen had looked right into her and repeated his goodnight.

Lydia lay perfectly still in her bed, letting the moments from yesterday flow round her without question or reservation until she was happy she had them properly arranged, that no sudden recall would unsettle her day. Then she showered and dressed, ready for whatever Sunday might have to add to her memories.

The house remained silent as she entered the kitchen, but she was not first there, the aroma of fresh coffee greeted her and a clean mug was waiting ready for her by the pot. She helped herself, then went to Stephen's study, pushed open the door and found him exactly where she had the evening before, with her Joslin papers spread across his desk. She noticed too that Elspeth's photograph had been pushed back to make room for a reference book.

'Good morning, Lydia. How was the bed?'

'Very comfortable, you can tell your daughter that she had it right. Have you been up long looking at my puzzle?'

'Maybe an hour or so. I hadn't realised the journal was so long, I was just finishing it again. I tried reading the original, but that would've taken all day, so I've dipped into it, looked at the way each entry was written to get the sense of it, then read your transcript. It's very powerful. It's raw and disturbing, the word subversive comes to my mind, but I don't quite know why. I understand how you've got hooked on it.'

'The big question is whether you have any ideas.'

Stephen paused a moment and looked out at the summer morning before answering. 'Maybe, but I have a few notes of my own and a question or two first. I'll finish this off quickly, then we can have some breakfast.'

They settled on juice, toast and more coffee and took themselves round to the sunny side of the house by the rose garden. Stephen brought his page of notes, the file of certificates and a paper copy of the Joslin family tree from Lydia's laptop.

'You had some questions?'

'I haven't been through every name and date to check if they are right and anyway, I'm guessing it would mean taking each reference and re-doing the search. Is that right?'

'Yes.'

'And tell me if I am correct also when I say your premise is that the family you have established, all the generations, all the detail, that family is the one in the albums for sure because it is the one that fits best.'

'No, not quite. I think it is the family in the albums because it fits exactly where it is possible to measure that fit, and because I think the probability is very high that it's the family and that the probability is extremely low that there'd be another family that could fit any better. Nothing in the family, the certificates, the references, contradicts the albums. Nothing in the albums contradicts the family.'

'And the family proves the albums are linked?'

'Yes, plus the other things, like Dorothy having a photo of Phoebe with her mother, and Phoebe in the sandcastles album. And although it isn't proof, there is the simple fact that they were all together in one box.'

'Which could have been pure coincidence.' Stephen's tone was that of the fair inquisitor, not the dismissive prosecutor.

'It could, and I treated it as such to begin with. I started from that point.' Lydia took another sip of coffee, desperate to know where he was leading, but willing to be patient.

Stephen nodded to himself and gazed into the middle distance for a few moments. 'And if they had been in the same box but tied together by a ribbon with a neat bow then you would probably have made the opposite decision and assumed that they were linked right from the start.'

'I suppose so.'

'For what it is worth, I think you've bound them together with a very pretty ribbon and tied a very neat bow in it. If it was submitted as a thesis, I think you would get a first class degree. I am sure you are right.'

'Thank you, kind sir,' she said, making a mock bow. 'And the journal, what do you make of that?'

'I wasn't really prepared for it. I know you had told me about it, but it has to be seen and read. Oh, and now I understand about the little fragments of paper falling out of it. I don't know what a psychologist would say about it, it could be a very interesting study.'

'Have you any ideas where I should go with it now? Or should I just drop it, case unsolved.'

'No, I think there are things that you could do.'

'Really?' Lydia could hardly wait.

'But before I say anything, my ideas are just suggestions, I don't know if they are right, I'm not saying they are right and you are wrong.'

'I wouldn't have asked you if I wasn't ready to listen.'

'Alright then,' he smiled at her. 'I think you'll like this. Option one. Andrew, desperate and disturbed, does somehow do away with Susan, he has a master plan, the perfect crime. In which case you have already solved the puzzle, no body, no death to record, maybe a missing person record filed somewhere, but nothing for anybody to care about. And Andrew? Well, he just disappears. All part of the plan, people do it all the time, just look at the streets of London or any big city and you'll see them, nobody knows or cares who they are or what they are. So, frustrating as it is for you, that's the answer, you've found it. And it has the virtue of fitting with all the known facts and with the things that he hints at in his journal. More than hints at, almost openly declares.'

Lydia was crestfallen. 'So you're saying that I can't find the answer because what I've discovered is actually true and therefore no answer can be found?'

'If we accept, if you accept, option one.'

'Go on.'

'Option two. Susan survives Andrew's intention or his attempt and they are still out there somewhere living as man and wife. Ex-directory, unregistered to vote, emigrated to Canada, whatever you like, but essentially nothing happened. That too fits with everything you have found. You yourself have said it has seemed easier to find the facts about people long dead than it is about the living'

'True, but I'm beginning to feel a little bit stupid.'

'Don't. You are not, I haven't finished.'

'There is, I think, one small problem with both of these possibilities. I don't know if you will agree. You touched on it yourself a long time ago but in all your work I think it has been overlooked. The problem is simple: how did these albums and the journal come to be a job-lot in a house clearance sale just a year or so ago, twenty or more years after the supposed events.'

Lydia thought for a moment before answering slowly. 'It fits with option two if they have recently died or emigrated or moved house or whatever else might have happened to them.'

'Yes, it could, but not with option one. For if that were to hold true then who would have held them all this time. The obvious answer is a son or daughter or some other relative, but what relative? As far as you know their one son died in infancy and they neither of them had anyone else, as you have demonstrated to your own satisfaction at least. And, since I trust your research, to mine too.'

'So the auction sale is significant. Yes, I see that. Somehow it has always been so, but I lost sight of it.'

'These are just ideas, Lydia. More coffee?'

While Stephen attended to a fresh brew, she took herself round the path through the rose garden, then along behind the courgettes and tomatoes to the little orchard. Her head swam with possibilities and probabilities that she couldn't grasp. The idea that if she was right then by definition she could never prove it, was hard to take in. If ever there was a fool's errand then this has surely been it. She glanced up across the manicured lawn and saw Stephen looking directly at her. For a few seconds before she rejoined him on the terrace, they both stood still and looked at each other's figures in the landscape, and each saw how well the other fitted.

'Stephen, I understand what you have said, but at another level I don't really know what to make of it. I thought you said there were things that I might do.'

'There is more, and this is more difficult. Option three. When you look at the whole story as you have done, and rightly done, you had no other way of looking at it, when you look through the lens of the journal there is an obvious logic to the lack of any information about Susan's death. After all, his plan worked, as in option one. Option one takes what Andrew has written as true and as possible. We are taking it not quite at face value because he doesn't actually say 'kill' or 'murder', but the inference is clear. He says many other things too, not least about Susan, and we have an insight into how she felt about him. Naturally we think he is unbalanced and his view is distorted, as well it might be, but if we are to take a part of what he says as true, then why not all of it? And if not true, then at least true from his point of view. After all, he had no motive for deliberate deception, even though he may have been deceiving himself.'

'Ok, but how does it help? I went through it several times and tried to extract every possible fact. I even made a list of facts, most of which are untested because I can't find anything about them from the records.'

'A question first. Susan and Andrew were related, fourth cousins you said?'

'Yes and no, fourth cousins but twice removed.' From Stephen's expression she saw a fresh explanation was required. 'The generations in each side of the family got out of synch, so although they were of similar age, Susan had more generations back to their common ancestor, John Jolly, than Andrew does. If Alethia had been Andrew's grandmother instead of his step-grandmother they would have been once removed.' Stephen looked even more puzzled, so Lydia added, 'Forget that last bit, it doesn't matter.'

'Good,' he said and they both laughed.

'The question is, do you think they knew they were related?'

Lydia thought for a moment before answering. 'I have no way of knowing. If I had to guess I would say probably not. Why?'

'It might not be anything. I was trying to imagine what it would feel like to meet and marry someone and then find out you were already related. I couldn't really get any sense of it. You hear of men marrying their long-lost sisters, but that's not the same thing at all.'

'Do you think he might have mentioned it in his journal if he had known?'

'Yes, you're right, he might have done. And going much further back there was a lot of intermarriage within the family?'

'I haven't gone that far with it, but for sure the Joslins, the Jollys and the Dixes were linked one way and another in the 1800s, so probably before that too. Land-owning farmers wanting to keep the property in the family, looking for alliances that would protect their investments. But that's no more than guessing.'

'Educated guessing, though. Next question. You looked for a record of Susan's death from what you estimate to be the date of the last entry in the journal up to when?'

'I'd have to check, but around 1995 I think.'

'Alright, so point number one would be to look right up to the present day, because if you found it then you would know that he did not kill her, maybe didn't even try to kill her when he said.'

'Ok, yes, a good point. I can do that easily enough.'

'And while you're at it, did you ever look for a marriage for Susan over that period?'

'A marriage? No, it didn't occur to me.' Then, as she looked at him calmly sitting there giving his considered judgement on her private project, for a brief moment she felt like his student in a tutorial. A pet student certainly, but a student none the less, and for an instant she was back at the lunch in Magdalen College, with

Stephen the lauded master disappointed at his protégé. The old uncertainties, kept at bay since her arrival, threatened to surface again.

Unknowingly, Stephen came to her rescue. 'No, and in your place it would not have occurred to me. Let me tell you the idea that is option three. It struck me that your Susan had been particularly unfortunate.'

'In what way unfortunate?'

'I say that to put the kindest possible interpretation on the misfortune to have seen her brother drown, watched her father die of cancer and seen her new-born son suddenly succumb to what we would call today 'sudden infant death syndrome'. And to top it off, she had a husband who appeared to be planning to kill her. Even if she did not know it.'

'I hadn't thought of it that way,' she said flatly. Lydia hadn't thought of it in any way, the deaths of the male members of Susan's family had been just deaths, like all the others she had tracked and carefully recorded. But she did not see quite where Stephen was leading. 'So how is this option three?'

'It goes back to the journal and taking what Andrew has to say about her as true. The business of the affair with another man while she was away on a course, the idea that she was trying to somehow poison him, and the constant theme that she was trying to mentally destabilise him. We see him as a troubled man, driven almost literally to his wits' end and we imagine a loving and long-suffering wife, the potential victim of his paranoia. What if he wasn't paranoid, what if she was having an affair, what if she was slowly poisoning him, what if she encouraged his paranoia, who is the victim then?'

'Go back a minute, back to her brother and father. Misfortune is one thing but you are saying something else.'

'Her brother died of drowning as we know, but I would love to see the post mortem report. He was in the river a good while before he was found and it would be interesting to see if there were any head injuries too. They would easily have been overlooked or explained as having been sustained after he went in the water. Her father died of cancer but there is a suggestion from the death certificate that he also had an excess of dimorphone. I was looking it up when you came in this morning. It's a kind of morphine. So one could imagine that someone might have helped him along to spare him pain. It has always happened, people have always done it, even doctors. It's known, it's accepted, but it is rarely spoken of. Although less so these days, after the Shipman murders.'

Lydia was reeling. All this seemed a leap too far, a step into pure conjecture. She wanted to counter the idea but couldn't find the right words to object.

Stephen saw her frowning disbelief and continued, 'Lydia this is just an idea, but it comes from you, it is about probabilities. Let's go on to her son, Simon. He died aged two days of what the doctor has recorded as 'respiratory failure from unknown causes'. This is in 1978 when cot death, as it was called then, would have been recorded just like that. It is only more recently that it's been more deeply investigated and given a syndrome. Cot death was just one of those awful things that happened sometimes.' He paused a fraction before adding, 'Like drowning and like helping someone on their way. And the common factor here is Susan.'

Lydia held up a hand to stop him. 'Yes, but why would she do these things? This is still a huge jump.'

'Before I answer that, and you're right, motive is important, let me ask this. Suppose you found a death entry for Andrew and you found it was something like, I don't know, let's say an overdose of whatever drug he was on. What are the chances she would have the four significant males in her life die in these particular circumstances?'

'I don't know, but I can guess that it would be pretty rare. But that doesn't prove anything.'

'No, and if I can turn that round on you, your whole construction does not prove anything, but you think, and I think, that it is highly likely, highly probable. And option three has a little way to go yet, so bear with me. Remember the auction? Suppose it were Susan who was the survivor, then she would be the one who has held the albums all this time, and it could be Susan who has recently died or emigrated and had her house cleared. It is all just a possible option. But one I thought you could investigate. Actually,' he looked straight at her, 'I thought it might be an option that would really appeal to you.'

★

Sleep came in snatches for Lydia that Sunday night, back in her suddenly cramped little bed. Her whole house seemed to have shrunk, she was the Gulliver in the Lilliputian world of Osney, her garden a mere window box, her bedroom a broom cupboard. The journey home had been grindingly slow, her own fault for leaving much later than intended. But her mind raced on despite her tiredness, the possibilities and probabilities of Susan and Andrew throwing up first one solution and then another before they melted away to be replaced by a third and a fourth. Mixed in with that blighted relationship were thoughts of Stephen, thoughts of his world and whether she would have any place in it, would want any place in it. They had parted with affection, exchanged a single kiss to the cheek that lasted a fraction of a second longer than it might have done, the same small pressure in the small of her back as they embraced. Had she returned it with a squeeze of his hand? She might have done, she was not sure. And all the while she knew she must sleep because she must work tomorrow and the more she worried about that, the less she could sleep, the eternal catch-22 for insomniacs. Like investigating the perfect murder, so perfect that it cannot be found so cannot be investigated. She could see the logic, understand the conundrum, see that it could not be solved, but her mind refused to accept it, still searched for answers. An idea winked into her head, an idea about the journal, the journal and perfection, and it seemed important, but its importance evaporated as she reached to grasp it and the idea was gone, overlaid with the notion of Susan's re-marriage. She knew she would have to fill the gaps Stephen had found in her searches, see if there was some record waiting where she hadn't looked, an answer that would tie a loose string, but she did not want to find it. She wanted to be right, even though it was the ultimate dead end, and she wanted to be wrong so that her puzzle might be solved. Tonight it had been easy to excuse herself through tiredness, but she would have to do it, and soon.

★

Inevitably, Gloria was by her side the moment she stepped into her office. Lydia had not steeled herself for the encounter, not prepared any smart lines to rebut the enquiry that was sure to come. Yes, thank you, she'd had a very good weekend, and no, she looked so awful because she had slept so badly.

'And did you . . .' Gloria left the question unasked, without her usual direct and graphic phrasing.

Lydia smiled at her, wondering what possible understanding Gloria would have of the way she and Stephen had spent their time. 'No, we didn't.'

'Oh, well maybe next time. There will be a next time, won't there?'

'Yes, I think so. We'll see.'

'So he's not married then?'

'Was married. His wife died quite a few years ago. One grownup daughter.'

'Rich?'

Of course he was rich, rich beyond anything that she or Gloria might ever aspire to without a lottery win, but it hadn't crossed Lydia's mind the whole time she had been with him. 'Probably. I mean yes, what you and I would call rich.'

'You're a lucky cow then, Lydia,' Gloria said without a trace of envy, said as a statement of fact. 'Don't let him get away. And if he does, then give him my number.'

Lydia wanted to say that she couldn't imagine anything less likely than Stephen and Gloria getting together, but instead she said 'I don't think he's your type,' adding to herself, 'and oh Gloria, you're certainly not his.'

'You never know, do you? Anyway, you know me, they're all my type. Especially if they're still breathing.' She laughed at her own weakness and Lydia laughed with her. Straight-to-the-point

Gloria, no messing with compatibility or the love thing, no thought of age or romance. If the sex and money boxes were ticked, that was good enough for her. And yet that very willingness to settle for anything was probably what kept everything beyond her reach.

For the next few evenings Lydia found reasons to be busy, too busy to sit at her computer and revisit the searches for her problem pair. There were the usual household jobs and she stretched these to their limits. Then there were bills to be paid and a birthday card for her sister-in-law Joan, for whom she deliberately chose something quite unsuitably risqué. She started a note to Stephen to thank him for the weekend and spent a whole evening composing it with exactly the right amount of warmth, spontaneity and sincerity, before throwing it in the bin and scribbling 'Great weekend, thank you' on a postcard from the Botanic Garden. Neither of them had mentioned it, but she knew that he liked their use of the old-fashioned post.

Not that she let these distractions keep her from thinking. On the contrary, she had Stephen's page of notes and his third option was ever-present in her mind. She let the concept mature a little, let herself grow accustomed to the possibilities it presented, turning it one way and another to be sure that should it be true, she would be ready for that truth. Slowly she began to accept it as a genuine possibility, but Susan's motives remained a stumbling block. She stopped being cross that Stephen could have so quickly analysed the complexities of the situation and by the end of the week was ready to start looking. She dived straight in with a search for the deaths of every Susan Myers listed from 1983 to the present day. Not a single entry satisfied a birth date of 1952. Following Stephen's suggestion, she turned her attention to marriages. Eight theoretical possibilities suggested themselves, but none that showed a middle initial of D, and none in Oxford or the surrounding districts. It would take time and money to check each one and Lydia's instinct told her they would be irrelevant to her quest. Her original search might have been flawed but it looked as though there was nothing to find after all. The 'perfect crime' of option one began to look favourite again. Why did that make her think of the journal? She had not read it again since Stephen suggested a different slant to the story it told, maybe with that eye she would find some nuance, some answer to the nag in her head. Perhaps one more read through might just be what was needed, even though she almost knew it by heart. She would abandon her fruitless searching and sit with it one more time.

Half way through the pages for the second time, Lydia put the old ledger down and contemplated her empty wine glass. It was Friday and another would not hurt. She had read enough, there was nothing more to be gained from the pages, neither in her typed copy nor the original scrawl. It was what it was, a record of sorts of one man's pain driving him towards the impossibly perfect crime, whether in deed or purely in thought might never be known. There was no such thing, of course, everyone knew that, there was always a mistake, something was always overlooked. What had Andrew overlooked? He had been so careful not to commit anything specific to his journal, destroying each copy of the plan he wrote out to be sure that he could remember it. Lydia laughed out loud when the realisation struck her. The journal itself was the mistake. The perfect crime demanded that he should have destroyed the journal. As long as it existed there was a chance that someone, as she herself had done, would be able to point a finger at Andrew and demand an explanation. In all that time since he wrote it anybody could have seen it, even Susan could have seen it. That stopped Lydia short in her tracks. Susan could have seen it. What if she had, what would she have done with that knowledge? Confronted him, accused him, flown into a rage, left him, divorced him? Stephen's option three suddenly came alive. If she had seen the journal, she could have had a motive. Now Lydia turned the search on its head and began looking for Andrew's death. She had looked before, right up to 1995 and found nothing. Now she checked again as far as the searches allowed - and still she found nothing, no Andrew S Myers with a birth date anything like 1949, a date she had calculated from their marriage certificate. It was late, she was tired, and the prospect of another couple of hours of frustration was too daunting. She would sleep on her 'imperfect crime' theory and see how it looked in the morning.

Some dream, some subconscious process of the night gave her unexpected direction the moment she woke. Even though it was early, a quick check beyond her window confirmed the glorious summer would hold for another day. She dressed and coffeed herself quickly to be sure not to lose the moment, not to doubt her intention. She would walk by the river down as far as Iffley and see if some fragment of Susan or the rest of the Inglebys remained. It had no logic, no possibility of yielding any fact or adding any knowledge, but it would take her to a place where she knew Susan would once have been. Like her trip all that time ago to the Lakes and to Longlands, it would take Lydia closer to the heart of the matter.

It was too early for anybody but joggers and the occasional dog walker to be about on the towpath, which was a quiet place at the best of times. The river's summer traffic of cruisers and narrowboats had not begun to stir as she followed the path to Grandpont and the busyness of Folly where the punts and skiffs were being made ready for the day's tourists. Down past Christ Church meadow on the opposite bank to where she had walked from her conference day with Stephen, on through the illusion of open country even though she was still in the city, one of Oxford's great charms. Past Donnington she took a detour along Weirs Lane and then left along the footpath by the houseboats near the weir pool. An odd way to live, Lydia had always thought, squashed into tiny quarters, half connected to the world and half removed.

At Iffley she stopped to sit awhile and let the sights and sounds wash over her. The place was deserted save for the lock keeper pottering about his business. The Thames was at its summer low, but beyond the lock the steady flow of water over the weir was unabated. A few yards from where she sat was the boat slide. Where had Paul Ingleby entered the water? Where was sister Susan when he did so? A little down from the slide was a footbridge. Under it a tongue of the river lapped dark and secluded. Lydia half closed her eyes, listening for the shouts, the demand that he should come home with her, his plea for a little longer with the water, she walking away telling him she would go without him, then turning and calling him, telling him to stop fooling about. He gives no answer and her voice rises, angry that he will not comply, anxious that he might have come to harm. She runs to where she last saw him. Louder she calls, screaming his name and all the while the rush of water and the steep banks conceal the sound. Yes, this was the spot, this was the story from the newspaper, this was the story that the family heard, that the inquest heard, this was the way that Paul Ingleby died. Until Stephen had sown the seed of doubt with his third option. It was the same story, everything was the same, it was still all true, everything in exactly the same place and in exactly the same order. It just needed the addition of a sudden flash of anger, a shove, a missed footing, a head that cracked on an unseen stone beneath the water. Little things, tiny differences that change the world.

Stirring from her reverie, Lydia walked on, across the weir and up the path into the village. Before setting out she had reminded herself of the address. The Ingleby house, where Fred and Ethel had died, the house Susan had run back to without her brother. Now she walked round the streets until she came to it, a narrow Edwardian house, a straight path from the front door to the road, a narrow strip of lawn, brown in the August sun. The house was mute, no sign of life from within, no secrets given away. Lydia walked on and then, at a suitable distance, turned and retraced her steps to hesitate once again as she passed the old Ingleby home. Had Susan lived there after her father's death, inherited it all? Most probably. Independent, young, carefree - the world would have been her oyster, she could have lived any life she wanted. Lydia looked up at the windows of the front bedroom, curtains drawn closed. It would have been her parent's bedroom, it would have been where Fred died, peacefully for sure with the morphine numbing his senses, floating him away down the stream. Susan, attentive as ever, held his hand, told him everything would be fine, he just needed to rest, to sleep, she would get the doctor round in a little while, there was nothing to worry about. Is the pain bad again? Let me get your medicine, it's not quite time but it won't matter, there, it will work in a minute.

Little differences, that was all it took. Get me a drink, Susan. Get me to the toilet, Susan. Sit here, Susan. Where's your brother, Susan, where's my Paul?

Two letters were waiting on her doormat when she returned, both junk mail she guessed, and she put them aside while making a belated breakfast. Orange juice, toast and coffee would remind her of last weekend, the comfort and pleasure of breakfast with Stephen on the terrace. She wondered what he might be doing today, right now, while she spread her toast. Then she remembered that his daughter would be with him, waking in the same bed she had woken in, watching the same net curtain dance in the same breeze at the same window. With a start she realised Jacqueline was not much younger than she was. To distract herself from this train of thought she turned to her post. One junk, one not. The one that was not was from National Savings, who wrote to her every now and again regarding her long ago purchased Premium Bonds. They had never won anything and she did not expect them to have done so this time. She had written to tell them when she reverted to her maiden name but the letters still came addressed to Mrs L Fordham. Lydia looked at the envelope for a few moments, then cast the letter aside and went to her computer. If she had reverted to her maiden name then so would Susan, independent, carefree, world-is-my-oyster Susan. Come to that, she might never have been Mrs Andrew Myers at all. She had been a teacher, hadn't she, and there was many a teacher who stayed as Miss something to the children in her class rather than confuse them with a change to Mrs something-else. And even after years of marriage, her husband had initially identified her by her unmarried initials, SDI. Even before she had the first results on her screen, Lydia knew that Susan Dorcas Ingleby had never taken her husband's name.

Lydia was so excited at the discovery she was tempted to call Stephen immediately, to share the excitement with him. She was at the point of dialling when she remembered Jacqueline and thought better of it. Even so, she had to tell him right away, and another postcard just would not do. She emailed him a simple message *'SDI married James Victor Watson, Oxford, June quarter 1992. Hooray! L.'* When he would read it she did not know, but she had sent it as soon as she had discovered the truth, and in that way shared the moment with him. Waiting to check the certificate was not needed, even though through good habit she ordered a copy. Next, she would see if there was a death entry for Susan or James Watson, then check the telephone directory.

In her excitement she quite forgot that if Susan had married James Watson in 1992 then her husband Andrew had not killed her in 1984.

12

Finding Susan's marriage immediately opened the door to the bare details of what remained of her life. She had died in 2006, eleven years after her husband James. In the week while Lydia waited for the certificates and the vital information they might reveal, she revisited the newspaper archive at the local studies centre near the Westgate. She could see no reference to the marriage, even though she diligently checked through the announcement columns for April, May and June 1992. Susan's passing was similarly unremarked by the press. The death of James Watson, however, had attracted a couple of fascinating column inches on March 17th 1995.

'Sudden Death of Local Builder – James Watson (74), former head of the Oxford building company Watson Homes, died suddenly at his home in Cumnor on Tuesday night from what is believed to have been a heart attack. His wife Susan (42) was with him. Mr Watson started his company immediately after WWII and prospered during the post-war building boom. He retired and sold the company soon after marrying in 1992. Funeral arrangements will be announced following a post mortem.'

As she read this, Stephen's words came back to her – 'particularly unfortunate' he had said, but Lydia wondered if she may also have been particularly fortunate. Most likely she would have been left a wealthy woman.

Ten days passed before the two death certificates arrived. A quick cross reference to medical terminology confirmed the initial report about James Watson had been correct, '*myocardial infarction*' was indeed a heart attack. The informant to the registrar was predictable, and to Lydia's way of thinking, depressingly so, '*Susan D. Ingleby (wife)*'. At least the third death she had registered and the fourth at which she'd been present, not counting her own on 3rd July 2006, when she suffered a stroke and died in the same house as her husband. It was just a mile or so away from where Lydia sat, she could drive there in a few minutes, walk it in half an hour, but she felt no urge to do so; no trace of the Watsons would remain, there would be no echo for even the most sensitive of ears to hear. All that was left of them now were the records she held in her hand, with all their tantalising ambiguity right there on the page. She was almost convinced of Stephen's third option and could not help but see a final irony that Susan, who seemed to have remained an Ingleby all her life, had her death recorded as a Watson, the one moment when she had no say in the matter.

The days dragged by and she was at the point of giving up the requested marriage certificate as lost when the envelope with the green address window fluttered onto her doormat. Carefully she slit it open and unfolded the document. There she was, still Ingleby of course, aged thirty-nine years with an address in Summertown, marrying seventy-two year old James Victor Watson at the Oxford registry office on 2nd May. Susan had given her marital status as 'widow'. Andrew was dead. Not missing, not buried anonymously somewhere, not a leaf on the forest floor, but officially dead. And if he were officially dead, then where was the record of that death? There must be one, for if not then Susan would hardly so publicly declare herself to be a widow. It did not make much sense.

By the evening Lydia had made herself a list of reasons why she could find no record of Andrew or his death. Top of that list was 'missed it!' which she heavily underlined and left there, even though she checked the index twice more to be sure she had not. Then came 'abroad', 'lost at sea' – although she was not sure about that one, 'not registered', and finally 'transcription error' meaning that the index she was using was incomplete or wrong. She saw a long path ahead of her, trying to discover one simple thing that should have been so easy, and she grew suddenly weary at the prospect. To compound her problem, Lydia realised that finding the word 'widow' did not mean that Andrew was dead at all. It simply meant that Susan could justify her marriage without the possible inconvenience of a divorce. For some reason she may have been in a hurry to marry James; maybe she had presented herself as single and did not have time to make it so, maybe she needed to seize the moment, maybe James was ill already. There had been a time when Lydia would have thought nothing but good of Susan, ill of Andrew, but now she could not find a charitable motive for any of her actions. With no proof at all, she had her condemned as a bigamist marrying an older man for his money, and far worse besides.

An urgent need to talk to Stephen swept through her. They had used the post but lately had taken to emailing in a business like way, without any of the coded fun of their postcards. They had not spoken since the weekend at Grantchester, neither of them finding the right moment to make that closer contact. She had his number right from the start, it was there on his first letter to her where he'd given her every possible means of reply. The regular but unpredictable presence of Jacqueline at The Old Rectory had made her pause before, and it did so again. As she popped open her email the little symbol beside his name in her list of contacts blinked green. He was at his computer right now. Quickly she typed 'Can I call you?' and clicked send before she thought better of it. Two minutes later her phone rang.

'That was a nice surprise, so I thought I'd give you one.'

'Hello, Stephen, yes, thank you. I wasn't sure about just calling.'

'Please do, anytime,' then a slight pause before he added, 'I'm usually here on my own, and if I'm not then it doesn't matter.' He had understood her hesitation. 'It must be something important. The unfortunate Susan?'

'Yes. Susan. I sent you the other things about her death, but I got her marriage details today.'

'Informative?'

'You could say that. When she married James Watson she was a widow. Or at least, she said she was a widow.'

'Ah.'

'But I've double and treble checked and I can't find anything about Andrew dying. I've written out a few ideas, but wanted to talk them through.'

She rehearsed her list with him and they discussed all the possibilities. Stephen added one small refinement, suggesting that Andrew might not be dead, but only 'officially' dead having been missing for a certain length of time, but he was not sure how the process worked. He thought probably that even then there would need to be some indication the missing person had died. And he was fairly sure a death certificate would have been issued. From the problem of Andrew, the conversation turned to Susan.

'I have to admit, she does look more unfortunate at every turn,' Lydia conceded.

'Statistically I suspect that she may have been uniquely unfortunate. Which makes me think you might look at it the way that you started out, the way that you showed me, look at the probabilities. So make a judgement as to which of all the reasons you cannot find Andrew is the most likely, then take that and see what you can do about it. Or just take the one that you can do something about and then find it or eliminate it. It's a bit thin, but all I can think of.'

'I suppose so, I would guess that the most likely thing is that the index is wrong in some way, the record is there, but I just can't see it.'

'There is one other possibility, but I haven't liked to suggest it.'

'Suggest away, I'm almost past caring.'

'Alright, but if you don't like it then say so. I know quite a few people, that is, have contacts with people who might be in a better position to find out things.' He tried to be as tentative and vague as he could, acutely aware how protective Lydia still was about her Joslins. He had been invited into that world once but had no intention of presuming the invitation was still open.

Lydia was wary of his idea. 'The police, you mean?'

'Not exactly, maybe someone who knows someone at the Home Office. But I won't if you think not, entirely up to you.'

'I'll think about it,' then quickly as an afterthought, 'Thank you, I should have said. Ok, why not.'

'You could think of it as just another resource that you're tapping in to.'

'I could.'

*

Suddenly the summer was gone. The rain swept in from the sea in torrents along Marine Parade and hurled itself at the windows of the café on Worthing Pier. Dorothy and Lydia had decided to venture out for lunch despite the forecast of 'blustery showers', but now they looked out at a bleak white-capped Channel crashing up the shingle, only to draw back, clawing the pebbles down again by the ton, and they thought it might have been better to have stayed indoors.

'You're not walking so well, Dorothy.'

'No, dear, old age catching up with me.'

'Have you seen the doctor about it?' Lydia asked, although it was no surprise to hear that Dorothy had not. 'They can do some great things these days, even getting a hip replaced is commonplace. It could change your life.'

'Maybe one day, we'll see how it goes. But you look well, dear.'

'I am well, I am very well.'

The small talk continued, about everything and nothing, Lydia keen to tell of her discoveries yet unsure of how they would be received. She had brought all the albums with her and left them at Dorothy's. It was the day that she had originally hoped for and then come to resist, as the end of her journey down the Joslin line had approached. Now she had arrived at her destination, or as good as, so far as Dorothy was concerned, and she had few regrets. The albums had run their course, there was nothing more to be gained from them, no purpose in her keeping them. The same was true of the journal, but she had not brought it with her, there might yet be a reason to refer to it. She was not sure if she would ever give it to Dorothy, she had no real claim on it and would never make any sense of it. Lydia could easily have written to her, simply sent her the family details as she knew them and left Dorothy to draw her own conclusions if she wished. For all she'd been supportive, encouraging Lydia to find more at each step, Lydia was not even sure Dorothy had looked at the diagrams she had sent her, or understood them if she had. Besides, there was the problem of Susan, Dorothy's second cousin by one remove, and Susan's story was not quite concluded. She felt the need to prepare Dorothy for what might emerge.

'Dorothy, remember when you said to me that you didn't want me to look into anything concerning your father, that you thought it was better to leave things as they were?'

Dorothy looked up quickly from her cheese omelette. Was she anxious for knowledge or anxious to remain innocent? Lydia could not tell.

'Yes, I remember. I thought a lot about that afterwards, thought whether I would want to know. I hadn't had to think about it for years. None of it makes any difference, does it? Nothing would change, whether we know or not, and the truth might be worse than not knowing. Who knows the truth after all these years?' Dorothy caught something in Lydia's expression, 'No, dear, I don't mean what you have done, all these names and dates, all that's amazing, I mean who knows the truth, there are so many versions of the truth don't you think?'

What a curious wisdom she had, thought Lydia, this unworldly old lady, living out her spinster life in her mother's house. She wondered where the knowledge, the insight into worldly affairs had come from. There were indeed many versions of the truth, but, as Lydia realised, all too often her own hobby, her passion for finding solutions, demanded there be only one.

'No, no, Dorothy, I haven't looked at your father at all, not once. I only know what you've told me.'

'Good. Now I know that, I'm relieved. I thought you might be about to tell me something.'

'There are some other things though, some things that I'm still not really sure about, and one thing that I am pretty sure of. Not so much a discovery, more a conclusion. It doesn't change anything, doesn't alter a single thing. But in a way I find it a little bit sad.'

'What's that, dear?'

'You don't have to remember all the stuff I've sent you, but remember that Albert Joslin is your great grandfather? He's the one in that first big picture, the one of the family in the blazing hot summer of 1911, the one that started all this off. He's got all his family around him, I've always called him 'Papa' because that is how his daughter Alethia identified him in the caption.'

'Yes, I think I know who you mean. I've looked at the copy you sent me several times. My grandfather Joseph is in that picture too.'

'Yes he is. Well, of all that family, Albert, his five children and all his grandchildren and great grandchildren, I think you may be the last Joslin. That is, the last Joslin with Papa's blood in your veins.'

Dorothy looked out through the rain spattered window, along the length of the parade as it appeared and disappeared in the squalls. She looked for a long time, no expression apparent on her face, before she said half to herself, half to Lydia, 'I don't feel sad, I don't think you should. It's just life, it's no sadder than my mother not having any grandchildren. I always thought I was the end of the line anyway. Like you, you're the end of your line, aren't you?'

'Well, I have my brother, he has children.'

'Not yours though.'

When they had splashed their way back to Dorothy's home, hung their wet things in the little bathroom at the back and steamed a little in front of the electric fire, Dorothy remembered Lydia had said there were other things to tell her about.

'It's about your second cousin Susan and her husband Andrew. He was a relative too, but more distant. I found out that he wrote the diary I mentioned once and it has some strange things in it. And from that we found some other things about Susan which are also a bit strange. Or they might be.'

'We? Who's we?' Dorothy instantly rounded on the inconsistency.

'I have a friend who's been really helpful when I've been stuck trying to sort it all out.'

'Oh, I thought it was just you and me who knew about all this.' Almost imperceptibly Dorothy had stiffened, her tone a fraction cooler towards Lydia than a moment before. It had never occurred to Lydia that Dorothy would mind about Stephen or anybody else knowing about her family. She felt a rush of guilt as if she had broken some great confidence.

'Dorothy, I'm so sorry, I didn't think, I mean all these names and dates, they're just that really, just names and dates, they're open to anyone, there are millions and millions of them and millions of people all over the world looking at them.'

'I expect there are, but you've put them all together to make my family. I don't suppose it makes any difference. It was a bit of a surprise to think that there was someone else looking at all this, someone I didn't know, a stranger. I thought it was just you.'

'I should have told you, I'm sorry,' then almost to her surprise she heard herself saying, 'He's a lovely man, and he's very discreet. There's no one else.' Lydia crossed her fingers in the habit from childhood, in case she was not telling the truth. Jacqueline might know, someone in some department might know if Stephen had needed to explain himself when he'd made his private enquiries. All this time she had thought it was her project, her enquiry, that Dorothy was not really engaged. In fact, Lydia had come to think of the Joslins as being her family more than Dorothy's, and now here was Dorothy laying claim to them, protecting their privacy.

'What's his name, dear?' Dorothy had forgiven her.

'Stephen.'

'And you trust him. I can see that.'

Lydia nodded.

'And you and this Stephen have discovered some strange things. What kind of strange things?'

'Well, that's just it Dorothy, I don't know yet if they are strange. What I wanted to ask you was whether you would want to know anything anyway. A bit like knowing, or not knowing, about your father.'

'Something bad, is it?'

'It might be.'

'Isn't there enough bad in the world already, dear?'

Suddenly Lydia felt as if she were seeking permission to make her enquiries, which was not the way she'd meant things to go. She had no intention of giving Dorothy a veto, not now, not anytime. She shifted tack a little.

'Probably, but we won't be adding to it. It's either there or it isn't. I just wanted to know if I should tell you anything that might come out. In case you didn't want to know.'

'I'll think about it, dear.'

⋆

Whenever Lydia had visited Dorothy, the return to her home always gave her a fresh eye for its shortcomings. Always she saw the parallels between the house in Orke Road with its mish-mash of dated contents and her own shabby belongings. Nor was the likeness confined to the objects, for it was all too easy to imagine herself in Dorothy's place in thirty years or so. They were not the same, far from it, but they could end up the same way. It was unsettling, and compounded by the unsatisfactory nature of this last visit. Dorothy had caught her unawares with her sensitivities to Stephen's involvement, but that horse was running now, and there was no stopping it. The trouble was too, that Lydia could half understand how she felt, and the guilt she'd experienced had not entirely dissipated. Somehow, she had been cast as the outsider taking advantage of a helpless woman, exploiting her family for her own selfish reasons. Lydia could not get out of her head that there might be a germ of truth in it. But she had handed Dorothy the albums, kept her promise on that, even though she still had the copies she had made of some of the photographs. The promised Joslin report would take all her notes, her research and the family tree and combine it all into one document. When it was complete she would neatly bind it and send it to Dorothy. The greater part of it could be done right now, but until the final chapter could be written Lydia held back from thinking about it. Meanwhile the cardboard box that had lived beside her desk for so long was gone. Only the journal remained with her and this she kept safely in its plastic folder in the bottom drawer of her desk.

Probabilities, Stephen had said, and he was right, it was how she had worked on the Joslin puzzle right from the beginning, how she always worked in the absence of hard facts, whether on her own family with its apparently easily traced surname, or anyone else's. If Andrew were dead, still a big 'if' in Lydia's mind, and if he'd been registered properly, and in the county, then a simple error or omission was the most likely reason for his absence from the index. A first step to verifying this would be to check the physical index held at the registry office. If he were not there then Lydia didn't know which way she would turn next. At the back of her mind she hung on to the idea that he was not dead, that Susan had chosen to be a widow out of convenience, he had simply disappeared and his wife had not tried, or been able, to find him.

No matter how hard she tried, Lydia could find no way into the events that had taken place after the last entry in the journal. There were plenty of clues to Andrew's state of mind, clues to his intentions, clues that he was taking some form of medication, knowingly or otherwise, but the image of that final scene would not coalesce. Lydia pulled out the sheets of her typed version of the journal and turned to the thirty-first and last entry with its familiar final words.

'I am at once calm and excited, nervous and elated. [It] just occurs to me as I write those words that it may simply be a migraine in waiting. Or the [vicious indigestion] that wrecks my snatches of sleep. All is ready and I have everything in [perfection] in my head. Rehearsed and rehearsed until I know it in my sleep, can walk with my eyes tight shut. This book has done its job, been the space needed. It seems certain that this will be the last entry, something I did not realise until I wrote it out now. Maybe a new book will be needed another day. Tomorrow is another world a new world a better world. Or it is oblivion. Which would be its own peculiar blessing. But

action will cause reaction and something will happen. The leaf will be cast to the forest floor where it will lie anonymously turning to mould. Though a million feet were to walk right by it, none would pause to remark its presence. Even I would not be able to detect it. The future at once looks crystal clear and impenetrable. The calmness of the centre has flowed out to envelop me and all around is light and clarity but the horizon remains black and infinite. This I think is the world without her even though she sleeps a sleep through this last night. Check mate in the game. Mr Punch.'

Whatever Andrew had in mind for Susan, his own future was uncertain. '*A better world or oblivion,*' he had written. Better if he removed her from his world, oblivion if he failed? He sees a world without her, even though she is still sleeping in tonight's world. With diamond clarity a stark thought came blindingly to Lydia, something that had never caught her eye, for all the times that she had read it. What if the leaf cast to the forest floor were not Susan, but Andrew? This last entry, perhaps more before it, was a suicide note. How could she not have considered that? Like Stephen's unexpected third option that had so surprised her, this shift in the reading made her sag as if she had been physically winded. Recovering herself, she read again through the last half dozen entries. A plan to be rid of Susan, yes, but the means might as easily be self-destruction as murder. She had been so set on Andrew the tormented killer, the desperate, unbalanced man consumed with an unrequited love, so set on that, she had seen no other picture. Then Stephen, taking facts and statistics and yes, her own theory of probabilities, had sown the seeds of that other way, the too-often-unfortunate Susan, and she had needed little persuasion to take that up. Now the truth seemed obvious, he had tried to kill himself in such a way as to never be found. If the attempt had failed then he had simply disappeared, become one of those who live a half-life on the edge of society, unnoticed by anyone, a leaf on the forest floor. It all fitted perfectly and Lydia glowed in the rush of achievement, the familiar surge of pleasure which came with a puzzle solved.

She turned again to Susan's second marriage and her declared status. If Andrew had succeeded in ending his life but failed to conceal the fact, then Susan would have been a widow plain and simple. If he had succeeded on both counts then she would have been a widow by default and Lydia was not at all sure how such things were recorded. No doubt a legal process would have been gone through and some record would exist somewhere, but she had no idea where. If the plan had failed completely then Susan was a widow of convenience, and who could blame her for that? Andrew might be alive still, rotting in a psychiatric ward somewhere, although Lydia knew that to be unlikely. More chance that he was grubbing along in the gutters, being 'cared for in the community'. She might even have seen him that very day, the dishevelled figure shuffling anxiously to and fro along Paradise Street by the Castle Mill stream where the flotsam and jetsam of the Thames gathers by the old weir. He'd stared right at her, fiercely clutching the plastic bag with his few possessions tightly to him, then let out a stream of foul abuse that may have been aimed at her, but may just as easily have been meant for some person not present.

The elation of her new discovery was tempered by the realisation that it might take her further from an answer rather than closer to it. She had a chance of finding Andrew if he were dead but almost none if he were alive but lost. A few minutes earlier she had been on the verge of calling Stephen to share her new insight, but now it seemed less like something to celebrate, more a fresh hurdle, and possibly a final insurmountable one. His 'someone-who-knew-someone' might have come up with something helpful, but if that were the case Lydia was sure that he would have mailed or called her, and he had done neither. For a while she sat and let the whole saga play out in her head, letting the generations slip by in snatches of light here and there. A photograph, a newspaper report, a change of address, the births and deaths, the spreading family year by year seeping away from their once solid roots in Essex, all this and more she had come to know. Perhaps now she was seeking the unknowable, the unguessable, and as Dorothy had said, maybe it was better left in the past. Was it some kind of justice she was seeking, and if so then, for whom? For Andrew, for Susan? Perhaps even for Dorothy, the last of Papa's Joslins.

⋆

'I feel so stupid.'

'Again?' Stephen gently chided her. 'That's getting to be a habit. What have you done now?'

'More what I hadn't done.'

After seriously considering closing the Joslin book once and for all, Lydia had decided that so long as Stephen's discreet enquiries were continuing, she might as well take his advice and tackle the most obvious possibility, an error in the index. So she'd made an appointment at the registry office and taken the day off work to sit with the original index, all the way from 1984 through to 1992. She had looked at every entry, taking care to make no mistakes, no omissions in the mind-numbing task. At each entry which could possibly be Andrew Stephen Myers, regardless of the actual name or the way it was spelt, she logged a record on her laptop of all the details and what reason had made her add them to the list. Then she rated it with a score out of ten as to how strongly she felt it might be her man. Each entry she deemed worthy of obtaining a copy of the original was going to cost money, and while she was prepared to spend a little, she was not prepared to spend a lot. When she completed the list, she would look at those with the highest ratings and prioritise those for whom she would obtain certificates. What she would most liked to have done was search through the registers themselves, page by page, but this was not allowed to her.

The little side room she'd been allocated was stiflingly hot with a window that wouldn't open and a radiator with a broken thermostat. It was hard to concentrate as she searched line by line through each year. More than once she caught herself drifting off on some tangent while her fingers continued to slide the ruler down the column of names, and she had to return to the start of the page. Only the occasional excitement of an addition to her list, the rating of how likely it might be, relieved the monotony. By mid-afternoon she had twenty-seven names on her list, even thinking to include a Mylar and an Andic Meers. She had given none a higher rating than six. Susan had declared herself a widow on 2nd May 1992 and Lydia was just finishing the 1991 index and was not encouraged by the results so far. Tired, hot and dehydrated, she started on 1992 and even then almost missed it. Andrea S Muers. Wrong sex, wrong name, but as she typed it out, she saw that it would be the one. Two little typos, that was all it had taken. Perhaps the clerk who had made them was as tired and hot as she was. She rated Andrea Muers as a ten, then although tempted to do otherwise, carried on to the end of the index. She did not add further to her list.

Stephen laughed, not unkindly, but as one sharing a joke. 'The thing is that you found him, so why stupid?'

'I could have found him earlier, without all that fuss, if I had tried out a few more imaginative search combinations.'

'And now you have found him, what do you have?'

'I got the copy certificate there and then, I have it in my hand now. It was just the index that was wrong, he's Andrew Stephen Myers on the register. He died in hospital on 4th April 1992 from something to do with his liver and maybe pneumonia and something else called GCS3, whatever that might be. I'm sure you'll not be surprised to learn that Susan registered his death.'

'Interesting.'

'Maybe, but it looks like the end of the line, we know all the answers we will ever know. I don't think we can lay this one at her door.'

'I like the 'we', thank you. I heard back from that friend who can find things. There was nothing on Andrew Myers after 1983. At least, that was the last national insurance contribution recorded. But I didn't tell you that.'

Lydia didn't quite know how to respond, so she just said 'Oh.'

'There is one other thing that might be interesting, might help when you think about these things. I spoke to a friend of mine at college, a man who knows about statistics, and asked what the chances were of Susan being so unfortunate. He had no idea, but he did think the whole thing was a great exercise for his students to come up with some ideas on how to calculate it.'

She was on the verge of telling him about her inspired new reading of the journal, but stopped herself. She had been reluctantly forced to discard the idea as soon as she discovered Andrew had not died until eight years after the last journal entry. It had come as a blow, so soon after formulating what seemed like the perfect theory. But 'Susan the serial killer' now seemed just as unlikely. 'You still think that your option three is the answer, don't you?'

'I honestly don't know. But if you send me a copy of that certificate I'll show it to a doctor friend of mine and do a little digging. Are you still alright about that, Lydia?'

'I think so. I mentioned that Dorothy's not very keen, didn't I?'

13

'Oh, right.' Her brother Brian was surprised and Lydia thought there might have been a touch of relief in his voice when she told him that she would not be seeing him over the Christmas holiday.

'But if you like I can come over on the Sunday before, I can see you then. I'll bring the girls' presents over.'

'Yes, I'm sure that'll be fine. I'll have to check with Joan, but it'll be ok. So you're going away?'

'Yes, a place near Cambridge, just for a night or two.' Lydia knew she couldn't get away with saying nothing but wanted to say as little as possible. Anyone on the outside would read far more into her spending time with Stephen at Christmas than they should. But Brian's curiosity, being that of a man, ran no deeper and additional details were not needed. When she had told Gloria, to pre-empt the inevitable question, Gloria opened her eyes wide and said 'go get him, girl', which was far from Lydia's intentions but further still from what Gloria might once have said. It seemed to Lydia that just as she had found a different side to Gloria, so Gloria in turn had seen something more in Lydia than the staid, go nowhere, do nothing, boring colleague. After all their years of working together they had stopped baiting each other.

The invitation to Grantchester had been hesitantly made and even more hesitantly accepted. He had suggested a night or two and hinted that Christmas day might be good as he would be on his own after breakfast. Jacqueline would stay Christmas Eve and thought she might then go to see friends in Ely. It struck Lydia that such an arrangement would be at the very least unusual; surely a daughter who spent as much time as she did in her father's house would be there on Christmas Day. She guessed that if she should decline the invitation then Jacqueline would find a way to return later in the day and resume her place at the table. She'd protested that Stephen should really be visiting her, it was her turn, but even as she was saying the words, she knew it would not work at the house in West Street. At Osney he would be a fish out of water and she would be too nervous, too anxious that he was suitably amused and occupied to take any pleasure in his visit. The confines of the house would throw them too physically close together, with no means of escape should they want one. He would have made the best of it, raised no complaint, been the perfect guest, but Lydia had seen how he lived, how he enjoyed his spaces. After accepting, when she was honest with herself, she knew she would prefer to spend a couple of days in Cambridgeshire than with her brother in Banbury or even her own home in Osney. A single night's stay hardly qualified her to feel at home in The Old Rectory, but Stephen's house had welcomed her more than any other home she could remember.

For two months Lydia had put off writing to Dorothy with her final word on the Joslins. Even with the details of Andrew's death she had been unwilling to close the book, but whatever remained to be discovered or conjectured, it would not change the family history as far as Dorothy was concerned. Her ideas, her theories would not feature in the document she would prepare, it would be strictly the facts as she had uncovered them through all the births, marriages and deaths, all the war records she could find, and the census entries that she'd accumulated. It would be something that Dorothy could pore over if she wished, something, that if she had a keen eye for coincidence or probability, she could wonder about, just as Lydia had wondered for so long. With the holiday approaching she was determined to finish it and have it neatly bound by way of being a Christmas present. She had already decided that she would put a copy of the 1911 Longlands photograph of 'Papa' and his family on the cover. Ten days before Christmas she completed it and was able to write to Dorothy.

My dear Dorothy

I hope you will be pleased to see that I have finally produced your family's history. I have even managed to tidy up a couple of the loose ends. It has given me so much pleasure to discover it all and to be able to re-unite the albums with the family, there is no one else to whom they should now belong. If when you read it through you find anything that you don't follow then please let me know and I will explain. All the certificates are in a section at the back. I know you said about sending money once it was complete but I hope you will not. Think of it as my hobby, and as hobbies go, it is not an expensive one. And it does take me to places where I might not otherwise go, and to meet people that I would certainly not otherwise meet.

I know we will stay in touch, but I just want to say that I have also enjoyed meeting you and becoming friends. You have always made me so welcome and encouraged me to carry on. I will come and see you again when the spring is here and we can take a trip out together, perhaps to Highdown if the weather suits us.

I am off to see Stephen for a couple of days over Christmas, which will be a nice break and I am looking forward to it.

I hope you have a very Happy Christmas.

Your friend

Lydia

As she signed her letter, Lydia wondered what Dorothy would be doing for Christmas and imagined it would be the same as any other year, and probably much the same as any other day. For a fanciful moment she thought of Dorothy at Grantchester, enjoying the nearest thing she would ever have to a family Christmas. She would find Stephen most likeable and the last vestiges of concern about him sharing her family secrets would disappear, she'd be warm and comfortable and well fed. With that last thought Lydia realised that it was the hand of charity, not friendship, which she mentally offered to Dorothy, seasonal charity because she was sorry for her solitude, sorry for her condition, when it was plain to anyone that Dorothy was not sorry for herself in the slightest. The pleasure she supposed Dorothy would find was actually her own anticipated pleasure.

Lydia's next problem was the present she should buy for Stephen. She always found her brother difficult enough, but Stephen was an entirely new challenge. As far as presents were concerned, he was a completely unknown quantity. Clearly he had everything that a man of his age and position could want, not that she really knew anything of his possessions beyond what she had seen around his house, and it occurred to her that none of these had been particularly personal. They were just objects without any obvious sentimental value. She suspected most had been in their places since Elspeth had died, dusted dutifully each week by Mrs Webb and then replaced. They were where they were by default, they had their places and they stayed in them, not by design but through inertia. Despite that, the house had not frozen at the moment of her death, it had remained a living thing. It was the house that Stephen and Elspeth had made their home, where they had raised Jacqueline, and she and her father still gave it life.

A book was the obvious fallback, as it is so often for those who have everything they want, but Lydia was not even sure of his taste in reading. In fact, beyond her own observations, she had little idea what his taste in anything might be apart from food and wine. Except for the one thing she knew for sure: he liked the Lake District. With this sudden inspiration in mind, Lydia searched the miles of shelves in Oxford's bookshops for something suitable. She found plenty of volumes on the Lakes, but nothing that took her fancy. One helpful assistant suggested something by Alfred Wainwright would be most suitable and showed her a facsimile edition of one of his famous handbooks. Lydia was tempted but decided that it would be exactly the book that Stephen would already have, and no doubt in the original. Then, as he swung his computer screen round to show Lydia some of the huge choice open to her, a single word caught her eye: 'Loweswater'. The book in question was *Excursion to Loweswater: A Lakeland Visit 1865*. Immediately she enquired about it, the title alone suggesting it was exactly what she wanted, personal and thoughtful but without the slightest risk of it being inappropriate or unwanted. He could value the gift for what it was and still leave it unread if he chose too. The helpful assistant found her a copy. Only as it was handed to her did she notice that one of the authors was named Lydia, which gave her an additional sense of satisfaction.

⋆

Christmas Day, like the ones before it, dawned dull, damp and chilly, a stale day, a groundhog day, a day for staying indoors. So deserted were the roads that Lydia wondered if she alone was happy to rise early and head away from the clammy Thames. It had been tempting to leave even earlier but she wasn't expected until mid-day, and she had no intention of arriving at The Old Rectory before then. She guessed how the movements of the day would have been carefully choreographed, with Jacqueline slipping away mid-morning to ensure that she and Lydia did not overlap. One day they might, but today was not that day, and she had no desire to risk the unexpected.

Arriving on the stroke of twelve, she was glad to have the murky journey behind her, gladder still of the warm embrace from Stephen. The attractions of the house were not dimmed by the season, it still sat comfortably in its grounds, the bare trees still dense enough that it was still screened from the lane. In the sitting room a log fire blazed up the chimney, inviting Lydia to warm her hands to the flames, even though they were not cold. Around the room were arranged dozens of cards, but a Christmas tree was not evident. Lydia had not been bothered to put out her own few cards, they had stayed in a small pile on her kitchen table and, like Stephen, there was no tree. She'd never had one since sharing a life with Michael, and now couldn't quite remember why they had ever bothered. Most likely because it was what you did, what the neighbours expected to see. Stephen offered her a sherry, and they stood either side of the fire sipping their glasses, speaking of small things until they settled into silence. Her mind went back to the first time they had shared a drink in the sunshine at the Kirkstile Inn, and how neither of them had found it necessary to fill gaps in conversation.

The thought of Loweswater brought Lydia to the gift she had for Stephen and she wondered what the right moment might be to give it to him. After a minute or so longer looking into the flames, she saw no reason not to take that little initiative.

'Stephen, I have a small present for you.' She reached into her bag for the book, which she had paid careful attention to wrapping, even adding a stick-on silver bow and a card.

'And I have one for you, if you'll wait a moment please.' He was back from his study in a few seconds.

They smiled when they saw that they were obviously about to exchange books, his also neatly wrapped and ribboned. Their smiles turned to laughs when they found that they had both chosen *Excursion to Loweswater*.

'I'd half thought of buying it for myself when I found it,' he said, 'but I'm glad that I didn't. Thank you.'

'And thank you too, Stephen, it's perfect for me.'

Coming together easily in a gentle embrace, they exchanged their first kiss worthy of the name while the wood crackled in the grate.

'We've shifted Christmas by a day. I had my Christmas lunch yesterday, Mrs Webb came in and got it going then Jacqueline and I finished it off. We generally do that, only this year we did it a day early. So today is the twenty-sixth as far as food is concerned, it's cold leftovers.'

They helped themselves to what Jacqueline had set out for them in the kitchen before she had disappeared to Ely, then ate in the dining room where a second fire burned. In time, their conversation turned to the Joslins, to Dorothy, and to the binder that Lydia had sent to her.

'You felt it was time.' Again, Stephen made an observation where another might have asked a question.

'Yes, I did. I'd been putting it off, half thinking that there might be something that you would find, but then I realised whatever there was didn't alter what I would give to Dorothy. I didn't tell you before, but I think I found out what GCS means, and once I knew that, I knew I wouldn't be adding anything to the history for her. Even then I took a while to get it done, then along came Christmas and it seemed a good time.'

'What did you make of GCS?'

'It wasn't difficult really. I think it's the Glasgow Coma Scale and is used to describe how deep a patient's coma is.' Stephen was nodding in agreement. 'But I expect you knew that.'

'Not really, I'd seen it somewhere before, but I wasn't sure until my medical friend explained it.'

'I can't make up my mind if it is a good way to go or a terrible way to go. It could be either, I suppose. But you said that you had some news, a discovery.' Lydia had wanted to know the details when Stephen mentioned a discovery, all the more so because he had been non-specific, almost casual in telling her. In the busyness of the season, the work on Dorothy's report, its importance had been lost.

'A discovery. Yes, but before I tell you, there are a couple of things.' He paused a moment and looked past her out to the grey stillness of the day. 'I have to say this, although I know I don't need to,' his eyes returned to hers, 'I hope you don't mind. You can never tell anyone about it. It's not secret, it's just that you, that is we, shouldn't know.'

Lydia's mind raced ahead over the most improbable ideas, but she held her impatience in check. 'Go on, and the other thing?'

'It doesn't change anything, it's not an answer, just another fact, another set of facts.'

'Stephen, just tell me, please,' she implored.

'Andrew Myers died after being in a coma for eight years. At his death he was assessed on the scale as being at level three, the deepest level.'

'Eight years?' Lydia quickly did the calculation. 'You mean he was in a coma since 1984?'

'Yes.'

As she struggled to appreciate the significance of what he was saying, another question formed itself, a question she was wary of asking, a question that even in the asking she understood why she would not be able to tell anyone the answer. 'How do you know this?'

'I have seen his medical records.'

'But you can't do that, it's private,' she exclaimed, 'You can't just look at people's records. Can you?'

'You can, if you have good reason and if you do so anonymously and you know how to. And as for privacy, it doesn't really arise. Andrew's dead.'

Lydia was even more mystified.

'Let me explain. I have slightly cheated. I have seen his medical record, but I have not seen his name. The doctors are all there, the dates, the drugs, the doses, everything, but not his name. It is all anonymous.'

'Then how on earth do you know it's Andrew Myers?'

'Because you told me when he died and the cause of death, it's there on the certificate you sent me. That's how I know whose record I was looking at.'

'Stephen, you'll have to explain more, I still don't follow.'

'There are not many people who die in the way that Andrew Myers died. So, I suggested, without actually saying so, that a post graduate student was thinking of preparing a paper on the incidence of coma deaths and wanted some background medical information. I proposed a period from 1990 to 1999 and signed off the request in the usual way. It took a long time to come through, but I received the documents a few weeks ago, when I spoke to you. Some poor soul had found all the records of all the people who died in such circumstances, copied them and then laboriously removed all reference to the patients' names with a black marker. It makes it all anonymous, all ready for a research worker to use for whatever purpose they have in mind.'

Lydia was astonished. 'You said 'in the usual way', what did you mean, does this happen often?'

'All the time, not by me, but the drug companies, government departments, and of course, the universities.'

'You did it through the university?'

'In a way, that's why I said I cheated a little. Not really my department, but there is some overlap with medicine.'

'I don't know what to say. Will it be a problem? Will someone ask about the paper?'

'No, but I will salve my conscience by giving it all to just such a student who was looking for a research model for a funding proposal. In fact I already have.'

Lydia had been so taken up by the process, the revelation so shocking and amazing he could just call for information and have it delivered to his doorstep, that she almost overlooked the information itself. 'So, you just matched Andrew's death to an anonymous medical record, as easy as that.' It was her turn to make a statement that needed no confirmation, then after a moment's thought she added, 'Did it take long?'

Stephen smiled. 'Probabilities, Lydia. How many records do you think there were? Let me tell you. There were one hundred and twenty seven for the ten years. And in 1992 only six, one of which was in Oxford. So, no, it did not take long, only a few minutes.'

'You said that it didn't change anything.'

'Well, you may think it does, but in essence it remains that Andrew Myers died on the date you found, in the way that is recorded, his wife re-married and properly referred to herself as a widow.'

'There's a 'but' in here somewhere,' Lydia said cautiously.

'No there isn't. More of an 'and' than a 'but'. We now know he was in a coma for eight years having been admitted with liver failure. And we now know that was caused by a mixture of alcohol and Veratin poisoning. Apparently that was an anti-depressant drug, amitriptyline. The version that Andrew was taking was called Veratin.'

'Alcohol poisoning? And this drug? That means an overdose, does it?'

'Yes, but I'd guess that the mixture of the two was probably a factor as well.'

Lydia tried to take in what he was saying, trying to divine some extra meaning, some new alternative to the events she had played through her mind so often. It came back to her idea of suicide, the idea that she had grasped so quickly only to discard on finding the date of Andrew's death.

'I did have another thought, I was going to tell you, then when I found his death it seemed irrelevant. Now I wonder about it again.' Stephen waited for her to tell him. 'The last time I read his journal I thought I saw the very opposite of what I'd seen all along. I thought I saw a suicide note. The overdose, then the coma, it seems possible again now.'

Silence settled round them again as the day beyond the windows began to fade into misty gloom. The house lay still, no board creaked, no clock ticked, no tap dripped.

'You may be right,' Stephen said quietly, then almost apologetically added, 'There's one last thing, one detail more to add to the picture. As I have said, Andrew finally died from pneumonia. The extra detail is that he died ten days after all treatment was stopped.' He let this fact sink in for a moment. 'They stopped treating him, stopped keeping him alive. The signature on the consent form was S. D. Ingleby.'

★

A little before five the telephone rang. Lydia could only hear one side of the conversation, but it could only be Jacqueline. Yes, everything was fine, yes, a good lunch, very pleasant, yes, yes, no, you stay and enjoy yourself, we're fine. Yes, I will, and you. The choreography in action: she had said she would call and see how things were then come back if he wanted her to, if Lydia should not have arrived for some reason, if her father was in need of excuse or escape. But he had no need of rescue, 'we're fine' he'd said. And so we are, thought Lydia.

When she had hung up her few clothes, she stayed a while in her room staring out into the darkness. Across the bottom of the garden, where she knew the paddock began, the mist had closed in and hung in a damp shroud, dimly reflecting back the light from the house. Save for that faint illumination there was nothing but her reflection and that of the room around her. It struck her again how still the house was, even though she knew it to be alive with glowing fires, mince pies warming in the kitchen, a glass of wine and Stephen's good company waiting for her downstairs. And she wondered if this stillness, this comfortable quiet, was a reflection of the man who lived here, or whether he had taken on the persona of the house.

When she returned to the sitting room, she found Stephen had started reading her present.

'Any good?' she asked.

'Hopeless,' he replied without looking up at her.

She sat opposite him and took up her copy of *Excursion to Loweswater*, but left it unopened on her lap. Instead she stared into the fire, letting the flames mesmerise her. The Joslins, the Myers and the Inglebys, all seemed to swirl and dance in time with the flickering fire. She could feel them slipping away from her, waiting only for the last puzzle piece to be put in place. For no apparent reason, Dorothy floated back into her mind, sitting at home alone, Lydia presumed, with a magazine or even with the her family history and the albums spread out beside her. What had become of Susan's property, who had she left it to? If there were no will, Dorothy might have a claim to the estate, a claim that could now be supported by a wealth of evidence. The thought pleased Lydia so much so that she said it out loud and looked up to see that Stephen had stopped reading and was also gazing into the fire.

'I thought you were reading.'

'I was, then I saw that you were deep in thought. It's a great thing about an open fire isn't it?'

'A great thing.'

'What did you say about a claim?'

'I was thinking that if Susan left no will, then Dorothy might have a claim on the estate.'

'She might. Will you tell her?'

'Probably not. No, I don't think so.' Lydia hesitated a moment before asking, 'What do you think about the suicide idea, you didn't say?' Stephen's expression gave her the answer. 'You don't like it.'

'You know his journal better than I do and if you see it there, then it has to be possible, but that would make . . . ah, I knew there was something else I meant to tell you. My statistical friend, I mentioned him I think. He set his students the problem of Susan's chances of such great, er . . . misfortune. Well, he was very pleased with what they came up with in the way of how to calculate such a thing. The general consensus was that the number lay somewhere between winning the lottery and winning the lottery three times. That was without Andrew's particularly unfortunate end factored in. In short, the answer was likely to be one in many millions, billions perhaps.'

'Against that you might ask, what are the chances that Susan could have had a hand in the death of her brother, father, son and two husbands, and never been suspected?'

'True.'

'And suicide, you said you didn't like it?'

'Well, let's suppose that you are right, Andrew's carefully rehearsed plan, his perfect method of being rid of Susan, was to kill himself in some fantastically cunning way. If we accept that, then we have to admit that downing a bottle of scotch with a handful of his medication was not the most original idea in the world. But only you and I might see that, at the time it may have been what people thought. So, no, personally I don't think he tried to kill himself, at least not by the method that eventually did for him.'

'When you put it like that, I have to agree, but I don't really want to.'

'You might still be right, he might have tried suicide, or taken a drink too much in desperation when the careful plan he had nurtured for so long had failed.'

'Either way it would mean that Susan had not killed him.'

'Ironically enough, in a way she definitely did. She signed the paper that led to his certain death. It wasn't murder, no one would even call it killing, but however you look at it she had a hand in his death. And if I were to let my imagination run on a little further, then who is to say that she did not give him a little push towards an overdose, a push towards mixing it with alcohol. Who is to say that she didn't give him a big push in a moment of spite, a flash of anger at his state of mind, his clawing dependency on her. It still might not be murder, might not even be manslaughter. But these are just my imaginings.'

Lydia thought back to her walk to Iffley, how she had caught echoes of the Inglebys, and now here was Stephen, of all people, catching echoes of his own. Not only that, but they resonated with hers, the flash of anger, the push into the water, the extra dose to speed the way, he saw them as his imaginings, she as the flickers of another time in the corner of her eye. There was the baby Simon, struggling briefly as his mother kept the breath from his lungs to silence his cries. No harm meant, just a moment to change a life, a moment to take a life, then a suitable pause, a few minutes to be sure that he was quiet before a call to the nurse, the frantic action to revive the child, the curtains drawn round her, she distraught and all the while knowing the script, remembering how it all played out with her brother Paul. What tripped the switch again with Andrew, what demand did he make, what action was misplaced just enough to tip the balance? Have another drink Andrew, don't forget your pills Andrew, I read your journal Andrew, can you hear me Andrew, be careful what you wish for Andrew, just one more Andrew, go to sleep Andrew, you'll feel better in a while. How easily he slips away, how easily her father slipped away, gently down the stream with no fuss, no complaint. But with the aid of science Andrew hung on somehow, hung on to a gossamer thread of life for eight years until she was finally persuaded that the kindest thing, the very best thing, the loving thing, was to let him go, let him quietly slide the last inch down into the abyss.

A log shifting in the fire sent up a shower of sparks and broke her reverie. Stephen had resumed his reading but looked up at her, a cloud of concern across his face.

'Are you alright?' He leaned forward in his chair, poised to comfort her. 'Lydia, you look upset, almost tearful.'

'No, I'm fine. Just sorting out a few things, seeing if there is some truth in this sad story. One thing, when you said Susan was unfortunate, you used that word in a certain way, but whatever truths lie hidden under the facts, she really was unfortunate. More than that, she was positively blighted.'

'Go on.'

'On the one hand, she may have been completely innocent in all these deaths in her life, and that would make her really unfortunate, a string of tragedies that would have had the most depressing repetition about them. She would truly have suffered greatly and no less so for the familiarity of losing someone close. Her whole life punctuated at regular intervals with tragic loss and intense sadness. Imagine her grief at each loss, with a residue from each one gradually accumulating within her.' Lydia caught herself short, realising how thoughtless her words might sound. 'Oh, I didn't mean to . . .' she stumbled.

He understood her sudden faltering. 'Thank you, but it's fine, not a problem. You are thinking of Elspeth, which is kind and considerate. I stopped grieving a long time ago, only smiles left now. You were saying about a tragic life.'

Lydia gathered her thoughts again. 'Yes, well, at the other extreme, the same events, but she somehow played a crucial, even malignant, part. And triggered by what? Some mental disorder, some traumatic childhood experience? And between the two extremes, a mix of both. A fatal accident to her brother that scars her for life, a beloved father helped out of his pain, the unexplained and awful loss of her only child, a husband who almost kills himself but instead places the responsibility upon her to make the final cut. Then at last she finds comfort with an older man only for him to be taken suddenly from her too. Whichever way you look at it she was more than unlucky.'

'Yes,' Stephen nodded, 'and so there you have at least one truth, a life beset with regular tragedy.'

'Something we could agree on,' Lydia said, 'even though you still think the worst, don't you?'

'I could say that you want to see the best. But we see the same things, just through different eyes. Perhaps I've grown too cynical, seen too many things.'

'And I am too innocent, too willing to see the best?'

'As for innocence, I doubt it, but willing to see the best, yes. And don't forget that there is another huge difference.'

'Oh?'

'Well, you are a woman and I am not,' he paused a moment and looked right into her. 'I think that gives us a different eye, regardless of anything else. We start from quite different places.'

Lydia considered this for a moment, the process made a fraction more difficult by the particular shade of grey in Stephen's eyes. 'So you are ready to see Susan the impulsive killer, while I see Andrew the psychopath?'

'Something like that. Don't we naturally take the part of our own sex, all else being equal?'

The Old Rectory sat still in its garden and the garden sat still in the village. Beyond the mists in the paddock the world turned silently round them. Stephen brought in a few more logs and banked up the fire one last time for the evening. He and Lydia sat either side of the flickering light in warmth and comfort, while the tiny bubbles in their glasses traced waving trails to the surface. Lydia let herself sink into the pleasure of the moment, feeling the anxieties of other lives in other times drain away from her. At the back of the fire, behind the flames, patches of soot glowed orange in the heat, criss-crossing patterns that she could make nothing of and felt no urge to do so.

'I had so wanted to find the truth, the absolute truth,' she said quietly, almost to herself.

'And now?' Stephen gently prompted.

'Now I see only many shades of truth, and my truth, the one I choose to be the truth, is as true as any other.'

*

The traffic on the Botley Road had only just started to build towards its Saturday peak as Lydia navigated the blue Nissan through the teeming rain into the city by St Giles and then up the Banbury Road towards Bodicote. Running against what traffic there was, it would take her no more than twenty-five minutes. She had timed it the previous evening when she'd been to look at something that had caught her eye in the catalogue. There had been hardly anyone there, the cold and the wet keeping all but the most avid bargain hunter safely at home on a Friday night. The car-booters and the dealers would be wary of picking up stock when few customers would be tempted out to buy it on a dank Sunday morning in January. All of which suited her extremely well, as it would reduce the competition for all but the pricier lots. Her own targets were hopefully not in that category. The first was a box of coins and tokens, all worn and quite unexceptional, nothing a collector would find any interest in. What had attracted her was the catalogue description, which stated 'assorted coins and medals'. When she had rummaged through it she had unearthed two medals, both without their ribbons, both scratched and tarnished, but crucially both were inscribed with the recipient's name. One was a WWI medal, the 1914 Star, the other given in recognition of some civic service in Birmingham in 1870. The second item that had brought her out on such a foul morning, she'd come across quite by accident. Paintings would not usually interest her, but something about the face of the young girl portrayed rather amateurishly on a little unframed watercolour, caught her attention. It was signed by an illegible hand but on the back was the faded pencil inscription 'Miss Sophia Smithers August 1842'. Both lots were in the catalogue with estimates of ten pounds against them and Lydia had high hopes of acquiring at least one.

Lydia's Report for Dorothy

For Dorothy Joslin.

This is the information regarding your family history. These things can be quite difficult to follow if you are not familiar with the terminology that is often used and it is easy to get lost in the different generations, so I have set this out in what I hope are easy to follow sections which correspond to a particular family. The first one covers 'Papa' and 'Mama's' family, which are your great grandparents and their children, including your grandfather Joseph.

All the birth, marriage and death certificates are in a section at the back, plus copies of a few other records like the census sheets. The census information has been included in the report where it concerns your own ancestors but I have not completed all the details for everyone else. The census details are noted with the year and the word 'cen' after it, so where you see '1881cen' that means the 1881 census and so on. Also at the back is a diagram showing all the family that have been found. It is too big to fit on a single sheet so I have taped them together so that you can fold it out to have a view of them all.

You will see that there are a few other notes included about some of the people mentioned, and these are where I have drawn on some other sources, or where there are still some questions unanswered. You will be able to work out who most of the people are in the albums, but just as a marker for you I have noted a few of the photographs against the people in the report, especially the one which started the whole process, the 1911 Longlands family. I thought it was the best one to go on the front of this so I hope you like it.

Albert Joslin (your great grandfather) and his family

Birth Date: 17 Mar 1851
Birth Place: Bocking End
Death Date: 29 May 1923
Death Place: Bocking End
Occupation: Wine Trader/Dealer

This is 'Papa' in the 1911 Longlands photo, your great grandfather. The old house still stands, but has been much changed and added to. It is currently a care home for the elderly.

1871cen Chelmsford, age 20, where he lives with his uncle Joseph.
1881cen Bocking end age 30 with his wife Pitternelle(23) and son Albert (2).
1891cen Bocking End, age 38, a wine dealer, with wife Pitternel (33) born London, son Albert(12) born Coggeshall, daughter Isabella(9), son Joseph(7) both born Bocking. Also resident Albert's mother Loveday Joslin (64) and Adelle Speen, domestic servant.
1901cen Bocking End, age 48, a wine and spirit merchant, with wife Pitternel(43), son Joseph(17) and daughters Isabella(19), Alice(8) and Aletha(8). Also resident Alice Speen 16 yo domestic servant. Note that son Albert has left home.

Spouse: Pitternell White
Birth Date: Mar 1858
Birth Place: Holborn, London
Death Date: 4 Jun 1931
Death Place: Bocking
This is 'Mama' in the 1911 Longlands Photo, your great grandmother. In various records she is shown as Pitternel, Pitternell and Pitternelle.

Marriage Date: 2 May 1878
Marriage Place: Coggeshall
Other wife: Isabella Dix
Children:

1 Albert Joslin

Birth Date:	3 Mar 1879
Birth Place:	Coggeshall
Death Date:	3 Jan 1961
Death Place:	Bocking
Occupation:	Ag. Dealer

1901cen Lodging in Colchester, unmarried age 22, an agricultural dealer. (Note - recorded as Jocelyn).

This is the Albert, your great uncle, sitting next to 'Mama' in the Longlands 1911 photo.

Spouse: Beatrice Pelham

Birth Date:	1882
Birth Place:	Saffron Walden
Death Date:	9 Jun 1963
Death Place:	Braintree

Beatrice is seated on the left of the middle row of figures in the Longlands 1911 photograph.

Marriage Date:	3 Feb 1902
Marriage Place:	Bocking, Essex
Children:	Beatrice Pelham
	Albert Pelham
	Harriet Pelham

2 Isabella Joslin

Birth Date:	14 Sep 1881
Birth Place:	Bocking
Death Date:	9 Nov 1948
Death Place:	Colchester

Isabella, your great aunt, is seated next to her father in the Longlands 1911 photograph.

Spouse: Francis Marshall
Birth Date: 1876
Birth Place: Coggeshall
Death Date: 1916
Death Place: France
Occupation: 1902-4 Insurance Agent (from children's birth certificates)
Marriage Date: 1901
Marriage Place: Bocking
Children: Phoebe 'Bee' Isabella
Albert William Francis

3 Joseph Joslin

Birth Date: 2 Mar 1883
Birth Place: Bocking
Death Date: 9 May 1915
Death Place: Near Ypres, France

Your grandfather Joseph died without having ever seen his daughter Fanny (your mother), possibly without even knowing that he was a father. In the 1911 Longlands photograph he is seated and on the far right of the row.

Spouse: Fanny Holland
Birth Date: 1886
Birth Place: Colchester
Death Date: 9 Oct 1922
Death Place: Bocking
Marriage Date: 15 Aug 1914
Marriage Place: Colchester
Children: Fanny

4 Alice Joslin

Birth Date: 2 Sep 1892
Birth Place: Bocking

Death Date: 31 Oct 1914
Death Place: At sea off Whitby
Burial Place: Never recovered
Occupation: Volunteer nurse

Recorded as killed when the hospital ship Rohilla was wrecked 1914. She was serving as a nurse. In the 1911 Longlands photograph she is standing next to her sister Alethia, third from the left in the back row.

5 Alethia Joslin

Birth Date: 2 Sep 1892
Birth Place: Bocking
Death Date: 10 Jul 1970
Death Place: Braintree

Alethia is also variously recorded as Aletha and Alethea.

Alethia is the original elusive 'self' of the 1911 Longlands photograph. She is standing second from the left, next to a visitor, Mr Melville. She and Alice are your great aunts.

Spouse: James Dix Myers
Birth Date: 4 Jul 1892
Birth Place: Braintree
Death Date: 2 May 1968
Death Place: Braintree
Spouse Father: Henry Myers (1856-1928)
Spouse Mother: Martha Dix (1858-1929)

James is standing in the back row, second from the right next to his brother Henry in the Longlands 1911 photograph.

According to the postcard sent by their son Henry from training camp in October 1942, James and Alethia were living at 27 Grenville Road, Braintree, Essex.

Marriage Date: 8 Mar 1922
Marriage Place: Chelmsford

Children: Henry Dix
Verity Dix

Albert Joslin (your great uncle) and his family

Birth Date: 3 Mar 1879
Birth Place: Coggeshall
Death Date: 3 Jan 1961
Death Place: Bocking
Occupation: Ag. Dealer

Notes: 1901cen Lodging in Colchester, unmarried age 22, an agricultural dealer. (Note - recorded as Jocelyn).

This is the Albert sitting to the right of 'Mama' as you look at the Longlands 1911 photo.

Spouse: Beatrice Pelham
Birth Date: 1882
Birth Place: Saffron Walden
Death Date: 9 Jun 1963
Death Place: Braintree

Beatrice is seated on the left of the middle row of figures in the Longlands 1911 photograph.

Marriage Date: 3 Feb 1902
Marriage Place: Bocking, Essex
Children:

1 Beatrice Pelham Joslin

Birth Date: 2 Dec 1902
Birth Place: Bocking End
Christen Date: 8 Jan 1903
Christen Place: Bocking
Death Date: 10 Jan 1903
Death Place: Bocking End

2 Albert Pelham Joslin

Birth Date:	6 Aug 1903
Birth Place:	Braintree, Essex
Death Date:	1944
Death Place:	Tooting, London
Occupation:	Commodities Dealer

1942 Telephone directory gives address of Joslin A P as 16 Ansell Road SW17.

Note, died as a result of a VI bomb, one of the first to land on London.

This is the Albert who is sitting cross legged on the grass second from the right in the Longlands 1911 photograph.

Spouse:	Hannah Brightside
Birth Date:	18 Sep 1902
Birth Place:	St Marylebone
Death Date:	Sep 1949
Death Place:	London
Marriage Date:	19 Jun 1928
Marriage Place:	Westminster
Children:	Ethel Beatrice
	Violet Hannah
	Rose Elizabeth

3 Harriet Pelham Joslin

Birth Date:	7 Jul 1905
Birth Place:	Bocking
Death Date:	4 Apr 1997
Death Place:	Maldon, Essex

Dorothy, this is the Harriet in the 1911 Longlands photograph. The only record I can find that fits the facts is a death record for Harriet Joslin in 1997. She died a spinster in a care home in Maldon.

Francis Marshall (who married your great aunt Isabella) and their family

Birth Date: 1876
Birth Place: Coggeshall
Death Date: 1916
Death Place: France
Occupation: 1902-4 Insurance Agent (from children's birth certificates)

Spouse: Isabella Joslin (your great aunt)
Birth Date: 14 Sep 1881
Birth Place: Bocking
Death Date: 9 Nov 1948
Death Place: Colchester
Spouse Father: Albert Joslin (1851-1923)
Spouse Mother: Pitternell White (1858-1931)
Isabella is seated next to her father in the Longlands 1911 photograph.

Marriage Date: 1901
Marriage Place: Bocking
Children:

1 Phoebe 'Bee' Isabella Marshall

Birth Date: 29 May 1902
Birth Place: Coggershall
Death Date: About 17 Jul 1983
Death Place: Bride's Cottage, Bridekirk Cockermouth
Burial Date: Jul 1983
Burial Place: Bridekirk, Cumbria

Phoebe was the first of the family that I was able to identify with any certainty. It was Phoebe's grave that I found in Bridekirk churchyard. Phoebe visited your mother together with Ethel Ingleby (Joslin) and Ethel's children Susan and Paul.

Phoebe is in the Longlands 1911 photograph as 'Bee'

1.2 Albert William Francis Marshall

Birth Date: 11 Nov 1904
Birth Place: Braintree
Death Date: 1939
Death Place: France

Albert is in the Longlands 1911 photograph and is captioned as 'Albert M'.

Joseph Joslin (your grandfather) and his family

Birth Date: 2 Mar 1883
Birth Place: Bocking
Death Date: 9 May 1915
Death Place: Near Ypres, France

Joseph died without having ever seen his daughter Fanny, possibly without even knowing that he was a father. In the 1911 Longlands photograph he is seated and on the far right of the row.

Spouse: Fanny Holland
Birth Date: 1886
Birth Place: Colchester
Death Date: 9 Oct 1922
Death Place: Bocking

The photo of Fanny in Longlands album matches your photo from your mother's papers. The rest of the information you already have so I have not repeated anything but the bare facts here.

Marriage Date: 15 Aug 1914
Marriage Place: Colchester
Children: Fanny

1 Fanny Joslin (your mother)

Birth Date: 19 Apr 1915
Birth Place: Colchester
Death Date: 1963
Death Place: Brighton
Spouse: Byron Weston
Occupation: RN
Reported to have died at sea.

Children: Dorothy

James Dix Myers (who married your great aunt Alethia) and their family

Birth Date: 4 Jul 1892
Birth Place: Braintree
Death Date: 2 May 1968
Death Place: Braintree

James is standing in the back row, second from the right next to his brother Henry in the Longlands 1911 photograph. According to the postcard sent by their son Henry from training camp in October 1942, James and Alethia were living at 27 Grenville Road, Braintree, Essex.

Spouse: Alethia Joslin (your great aunt)
Birth Date: 2 Sep 1892
Birth Place: Bocking
Death Date: 10 Jul 1970
Death Place: Braintree
Spouse Father: Albert Joslin (1851-1923)
Spouse Mother: Pitternell White (1858-1931)
Other Spouse: Barbara Vaughan

Note. Alethia is also variously recorded as Aletha and Alethea. Alethia is the original elusive 'self' of the 1911 Longlands photograph. She is

standing second from the left, next to a visitor, Mr. Melville.
Marriage Date: 8 Mar 1922
Marriage Place: Chelmsford

Children:

1 Henry Dix Myers

Birth Date: 16 Oct 1922
Birth Place: Braintree
Death Date: 18 Sep 1943
Death Place: over Germany
Burial Date: 1945
Burial Place: Reichswald Forest War Cemetery
Occupation: RAF

Other information discovered: October 1942 at RAF training camp; 1943 at RAF Waterbeach; Died when shot down navigating a bomber over Germany in 1943. He was removed from his original burial place in 1945 and re-interred at Reichswald.

Spouse: Kathleen Farrow
Birth Date: 1923
Birth Place: Dover
Marriage Date: 22 May 1943
Marriage Place: Cambridge

2 Verity Dix Myers

Birth Date: 16 Oct 1922
Birth Place: Braintree

Apart from her birth record and the reference to her on the postcard to her parents, no other record has been found under Myers or Dix Myers or variants of these. She may have emigrated or she may yet still be alive and living in the UK.

Albert Pelham Joslin (your great uncle Albert's son, which makes him your 1st Cousin 'once removed') and his family

Birth Date: 6 Aug 1903
Birth Place: Braintree, Essex
Death Date: 1944
Death Place: Tooting, London
Occupation: Commodities Dealer

1942 Telephone directory gives address of Joslin A P as 16 Ansell Road SW17. He died as a result of a VI bomb, one of the first to land on London. This is the Albert who is sitting cross legged on the grass second from the right in the Longlands 1911 photograph.

Spouse: Hannah Brightside
Birth Date: 18 Sep 1902
Birth Place: St Marylebone
Death Date: Sep 1949
Death Place: London
Marriage Date: 19 Jun 1928
Marriage Place: Westminster

Children:

1 Ethel Beatrice Joslin

Birth Date: 10 Oct 1929
Birth Place: Tooting
Death Date: 7 Oct 1972
Death Place: Oxford

Ethel is the third woman in the picture from your kitchen drawer, together with your mother and Phoebe Marshall. Ethel is your 'second cousin', as are her sisters Violet and Rose. Ethel and her family are the once most often featured in the album with the seaside holiday pictures. When she added to the album Ethel wrote herself as 'self'.

Spouse:	Frederick Ingleby
Birth Date:	3 Jan 1924
Birth Place:	Hemel Hempstead
Death Date:	6 Feb 1975
Death Place:	Oxford
Occupation:	Electrical Engineer
Marriage Date:	3 Dec 1951
Marriage Place:	Chelsea
Children:	Susan Dorcas
	Paul Donald

2 Violet Hannah Joslin

Birth Date:	9 Jul 1934
Birth Place:	Tooting

No record of Violet has been found, other than her birth record.

1.3 Rose Elizabeth Joslin

Birth Date:	21 Apr 1936
Birth Place:	Tooting

Apart from her birth record, the only possible mention found of Rose is in a passenger list of arrivals in New Zealand in 1962. It appears that this Rose Joslin was killed in a motor accident a few months later.

Henry Myers (who married a distant cousin of yours) and their family

Birth Date:	1856
Birth Place:	Braintree
Death Date:	5 Nov 1928
Death Place:	Chelmsford
Occupation:	Shopkeeper

1891cen Braintree, age 34, shopkeeper's assistant, recorded as Dix-Myers, with his wife Martha (32) and son Henry aged 6 months born Coggeshall.

1901cen Braintree, age 44, shop manager, recorded as Dix-Myers, with his wife Martha(42) and sons Henry(10) and James(8) born Braintree.

Spouse: Martha Dix (your 1st cousin 'four times removed')
Birth Date: 1858
Birth Place: Coggeshall
Death Date: 3 Jun 1929
Death Place: Chelmsford
Spouse Father: James Dix (1815-)
Spouse Mother: Prudence Jolly (1817-1890)
Marriage Date: 2 Jun 1886
Marriage Place: Coggeshall

Children:

1 Henry Dix Myers

Birth Date: 22 Oct 1890
Birth Place: Coggeshall
Death Date: 1916
Death Place: Paschendale

Henry is standing on the far right at the back in the 1911 Longlands photo.

2 James Dix Myers

Birth Date: 4 Jul 1892
Birth Place: Braintree
Death Date: 2 May 1968
Death Place: Braintree

James is standing in the back row, second from the right next to his brother Henry in the Longlands 1911 photograph.

Spouse:	Barbara Vaughan
Birth Date:	1892
Birth Place:	Colchester
Death Date:	14 Jul 1920
Death Place:	Braintree
Marriage Date:	1919
Marriage Place:	Colchester
Children:	Bertram Albert Dix
Other Spouses	Alethia Joslin (your great aunt)
Birth Date:	2 Sep 1892
Birth Place:	Bocking
Death Date:	10 Jul 1970
Death Place:	Braintree
Spouse Father:	Albert Joslin (1851-1923)
Spouse Mother:	Pitternell White (1858-1931)
Marriage Date:	8 Mar 1922
Marriage Place:	Chelmsford
Children:	Henry Dix
	Verity Dix

Bertram Albert Dix Myers (a distant relation 'third cousin twice removed') and his family

Birth Date:	12 Jul 1920
Birth Place:	Braintree
Death Date:	1 Nov 1971
Death Place:	Chesham, Bucks

This is 'Bertie' from the 'RAF' album of photos. After the war he moved to southern Africa, possibly Rhodesia, where his son Andrew was probably born. Bertie was captured at an airfield in France in 1939 and spent almost the whole war in POW camps. He was in the well known 'Stalag Luft 3', which was the one that the film The Great Escape was based on.

Spouse:	Helen Fox
Birth Date:	15 Aug 1922
Death Date:	2 Nov 1975

Death Place:	Chesham, Bucks.
Marriage Date:	12 May 1947
Marriage Place:	Amersham
Children:	Andrew Stephen

1 Andrew Stephen Myers

Birth Date:	19 Dec 1949
Birth Place:	Rhodesia
Death Date:	4 Apr 1992
Death Place:	Oxford

Andrew died after a long illness in hospital in 1992. According to his death certificate he was born in the old Rhodesia (now Zimbabwe). He had an address in South Africa when his father died in 1971. By the time his mother died in 1975 he was living in Chesham, Bucks. Andrew possibly worked in Oxford as an advertising copywriter.

Spouse: Susan Dorcas Ingleby (who was also a cousin of yours, a '2nd cousin once removed' – her mother being Ethel Joslin)

Birth Date:	22 Sep 1952
Birth Place:	Aylesbury
Death Date:	3 Jul 2006
Death Place:	Oxford
Spouse Father:	Frederick Ingleby (1924-1975)
Spouse Mother:	Ethel Beatrice Joslin (1929-1972)
Marriage Date:	4 Apr 1976
Marriage Place:	Abingdon, Oxon
Children:	Simon (died in 1978 as an infant)

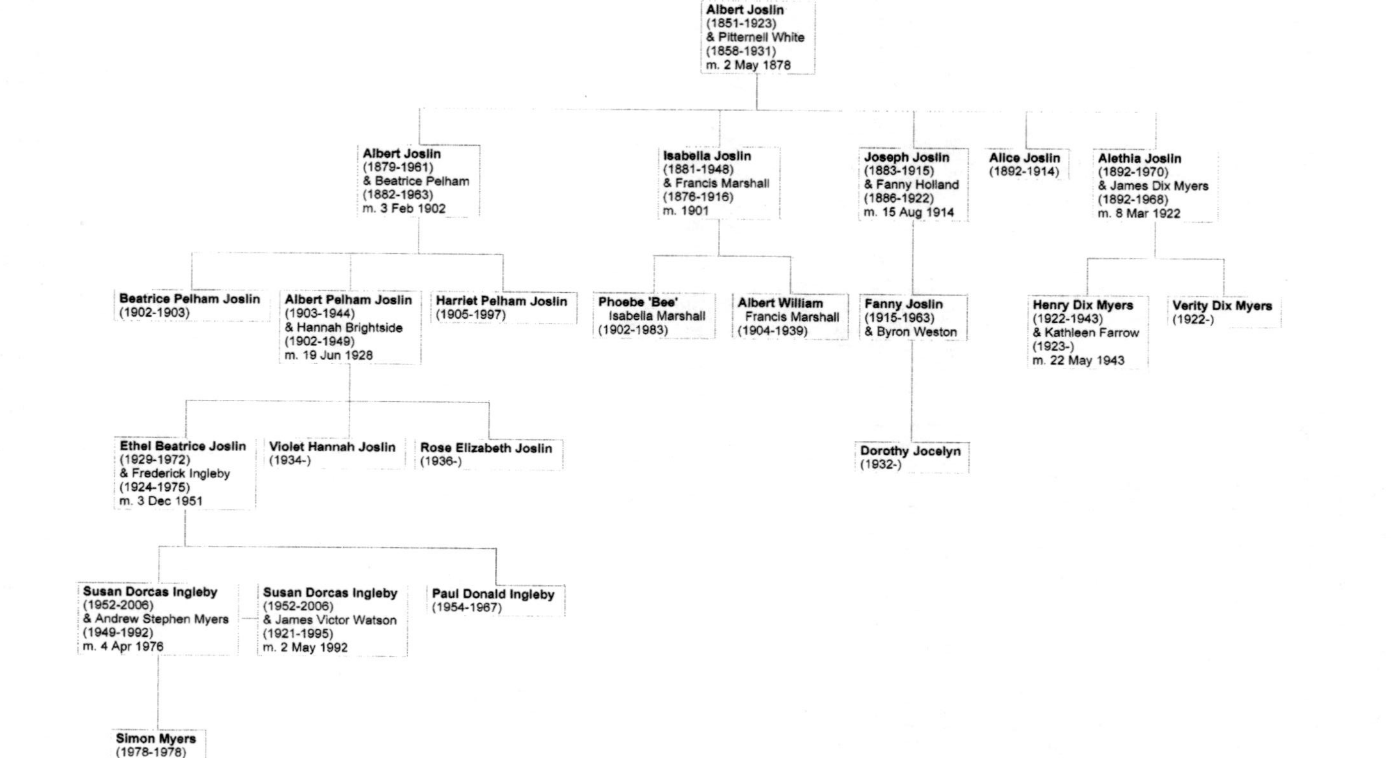

Albert Joslin
(1851-1923)
& Pitternell White
(1858-1931)
m. 2 May 1878
Albert Joslin
(1879-1961)
& Beatrice Pelham
(1882-1963)
m. 3 Feb 1902
Isabella Joslin
(1881-1948)
& Francis Marshall
(1876-1916)
m. 1901
Joseph Joslin
(1883-1915)
& Fanny Holland
(1886-1922)
m. 15 Aug 1914
Alice Joslin
(1892-1914)
Alethia Joslin
(1892-1970)
& James Dix Myers
(1892-1968)
m. 8 Mar 1922
Beatrice Pelham Joslin
(1902-1903)
Albert Pelham Joslin
(1903-1944)
& Hannah Brightside
(1902-1949)
m. 19 Jun 1928
Harriet Pelham Joslin
(1905-1997)
Phoebe 'Bee'
Isabella Marshall
(1902-1983)
Albert William
Francis Marshall
(1904-1939)
Fanny Joslin
(1915-1963)
& Byron Weston
Henry Dix Myers
(1922-1943)
& Kathleen Farrow
(1923-)
m. 22 May 1943
Verity Dix Myers
(1922-)
Ethel Beatrice Joslin
(1929-1972)
& Frederick Ingleby
(1924-1975)
m. 3 Dec 1951
Violet Hannah Joslin
(1934-)
Rose Elizabeth Joslin
(1936-)
Dorothy Jocelyn
(1932-)
Susan Dorcas Ingleby
(1952-2006)
& Andrew Stephen Myers
(1949-1992)
m. 4 Apr 1976
Susan Dorcas Ingleby
(1952-2006)
& James Victor Watson
(1921-1995)
m. 2 May 1992
Paul Donald Ingleby
(1954-1967)
Simon Myers
(1978-1978)

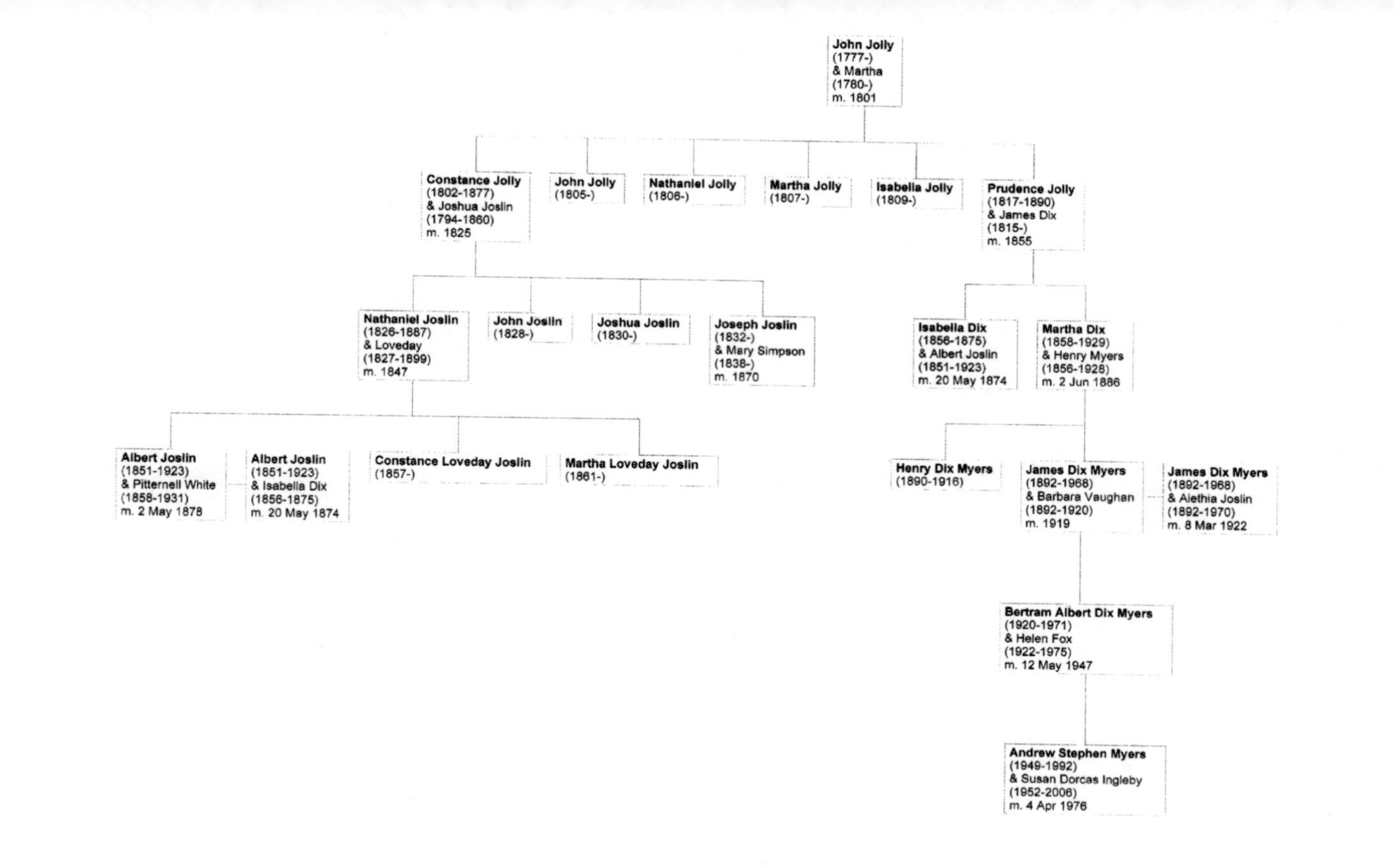
John Jolly
(1777-)
& Martha
(1780-)
m. 1801
Constance Jolly
(1802-1877)
& Joshua Joslin
(1794-1860)
m. 1825
John Jolly
(1805-)
Nathaniel Jolly
(1806-)
Martha Jolly
(1807-)
Isabella Jolly
(1809-)
Prudence Jolly
(1817-1890)
& James Dix
(1815-)
m. 1855
Nathaniel Joslin
(1826-1887)
& Loveday
(1827-1899)
m. 1847
John Joslin
(1828-)
Joshua Joslin
(1830-)
Joseph Joslin
(1832-)
& Mary Simpson
(1838-)
m. 1870
Isabella Dix
(1856-1875)
& Albert Joslin
(1851-1923)
m. 20 May 1874
Martha Dix
(1858-1929)
& Henry Myers
(1856-1928)
m. 2 Jun 1886
Albert Joslin
(1851-1923)
& Pitternell White
(1858-1931)
m. 2 May 1878
Albert Joslin
(1851-1923)
& Isabella Dix
(1856-1875)
m. 20 May 1874
Constance Loveday Joslin
(1857-)
Martha Loveday Joslin
(1861-)
Henry Dix Myers
(1890-1916)
James Dix Myers
(1892-1968)
& Barbara Vaughan
(1892-1920)
m. 1919
James Dix Myers
(1892-1968)
& Alethia Joslin
(1892-1970)
m. 8 Mar 1922
Bertram Albert Dix Myers
(1920-1971)
& Helen Fox
(1922-1975)
m. 12 May 1947
Andrew Stephen Myers
(1949-1992)
& Susan Dorcas Ingleby
(1952-2006)
m. 4 Apr 1976